WHITE
FEATHER

JENNIFER PICKTON

authorHOUSE·

AuthorHouse™ UK
1663 Liberty Drive
Bloomington, IN 47403 USA
www.authorhouse.co.uk
Phone: UK TFN: 0800 0148641 (Toll Free inside the UK)
         UK Local: 02036 956322 (+44 20 3695 6322 from outside the UK)

Published by AuthorHouse 03/26/2021

ISBN: 978-1-6655-8445-6 (sc)
ISBN: 978-1-6655-8446-3 (e)

CONTENTS

PART 1
The Old Life

PART 2
Transformations

PART 3
Another World

PART 4
The New Life

PART 1

THE OLD LIFE

CHAPTER 1

BEGINNINGS

White Feather was brought up as one of Black Buffalo's sons. His natural mother, Yellow Blossom, died shortly after his birth, and her sister became his mother. This information was revealed to White Feather when he reached manhood, when he had wondered why his colouring was different from that of his brother and sisters. His hair was deep chestnut-brown and not black, like theirs. His skin was tanned by the outdoor sun and wind so that he looked as dark as the others, but his unexposed skin was much lighter. His eyes were amber-coloured, the same colour as a big cat's, and his frame, now full-grown, was much taller and more muscular than that of his brother or father. He also showed more hair growth on his face, chest, arms, and legs.

It was the Indian way to be clean-shaven, so this task was a daily chore for him. His beard growth was fierce; it grew overnight to a length that other braves saw in a matter of days. In seeking an explanation for this, he had been told that his mother had been raped by a white man, a white soldier who had raided their camp. His uncle, Black Buffalo, had been asked to take news to his wife's parents and to bring his wife's sister and brother back to his home village to support his wife, who was due to birth their first child by the next moon. This child would be the first grandchild for Strong Arrow and Spring Blossom, his wife's father and mother.

The village housing Strong Arrow's tepee was south of the village where Black Buffalo and his family and tribe dwelled. It could not be reached directly through the hillside or highlands, as there were deep gorges separating the two villages. Black Buffalo would have to travel to the foothills and ride along the grasslands which ran parallel to the mountain range before ascending the mountain trail leading up to the higher pastures.

Throughout Black Buffalo's lifetime, there had never been any trouble with foreigners. The white man and the old trackers and traders rarely ventured into these high hills. This area held little attraction for them: The terrain very quickly lost its covering of vegetation, and the bare rock was exposed. In winter, it was an awesome sight, with the bleakness of the rocks casting long grey shadows over the immediate lowlands, making it seem a dark and eerie place.

Yellow Blossom had seen only fourteen summers when she left her father's tepee to visit with her eldest sister, who had married Black Buffalo the previous summer. The distance between villages was too great to reach in one day, so they made camp overnight. Black Buffalo and Yellow Blossom's brother, Grey Arrow, had gone hunting up the hillside for a rabbit or turkey to provide an evening meal, leaving Yellow Blossom and Black Buffalo's cousin, Black Elk, at camp to feed the horses and prepare the fire for cooking whatever animal was caught. The two were setting up the campsite when five white soldiers attacked. They had been tracking a renegade Indian scout called Red Foot, who had left the fort in disgrace. He had been drunk when he got into a fight with another Indian scout who had just arrived from another fort farther north.

Red Foot had stolen some travelling goods from the trading post storehouse before jumping on his horse and leaving the fort without permission. At first, he travelled west towards the great hills; this was the trail the soldiers followed which led them into the New Mexico Territory from their base in Fort Worth, Texas. Red Foot had left a deceiving trail for the blue coats to follow, to give him sufficient time to cross the Rio Grande, which was also the Mexican border lying due south. Once over the border, he would be free, as he would no longer be within American Army jurisdiction. It never ceased to amaze the Indian scouts how stupid the blue coats really were, for Red Foot was long gone by the time these five soldiers stumbled upon some new tracks, which had led them to the edge of the mountains.

It must have been just pure chance that these soldiers had found and followed Black Buffalo's trail, which led along the edge of the prairie to the campsite they had picked for their night's rest.

The soldiers did not stop to think or consider what they were doing; they just reacted at the sight of an Indian, whom they assumed was Red Foot. One Indian looked the same as another to them, and they had been trained to see all Indians as their enemies. The soldiers were all fired up at catching the Indian and shot Black Elk, thinking he was Red Foot. When they found an Indian female also, the soldier, a sergeant, took vengeance upon her, for he hated Indians with a passion.

Sergeant Wesley James Adams was twenty-three years old and had served in the army for five years. He had graduated from the academy with flying colours and gained distinction for his fearlessness against Comanche Indians, who had raised havoc on nearby wealthy ranchers, who were fencing off pasture areas as part of their land-holding claims.

Wesley had enlisted as an officer in the army corps that fought its way west to establish and secure Fort Worth and the surrounding area, as new lands were opened up for claiming. He enjoyed personal physical conquests and gained great satisfaction at inflicting pain and hurt upon native captives. Wesley's father had already put in one claim upon some land, although it was father south than they had originally intended.

Wesley was of Dutch and British stock, which explained his light skin and sandy hair colouring. His ancestors had come to the New World and proved to be the founders of many empires and landholdings in the eastern states. Wesley's father had spent some time in the army himself before he had caught the explorer's urge to conquer new lands in the south and south-west. He had seen the Gold Rush and vowed he would be part of the land rush to gain land suitable for farming or ranching as the south and south-west was opened up. Walter John Adams had encouraged his only son to join the army so it would make a man of him, and as a member of the American Southern Army corps, he would be in the front line to inform him of any new claims of conquered land as they became available.

Wesley's mother was Amy Van-der-Vault, who was of Dutch origin and of a gentle disposition and health. She did not survive the move south to a hotter climate and succumbed to one of many fevers when Wesley was twelve years old, after losing her fourth child, another boy, in a stillbirth.

The previous two pregnancies were girls born prematurely; neither child survived, as they were too small and undeveloped. Wesley had idolised his mother and was distraught at her passing, so it was understandable that his father indulged his only child and pressured him to succeed in every way possible.

The army was one way of achieving fast recognition and success, and Wesley had not disappointed. He had recently got himself engaged to the captain's daughter, Miss Samantha Prentice of Virginia, who was visiting her father at the fort. Wesley had seduced the eighteen-year-old virgin and then proposed to her, which she then felt she could not refuse. He chased after Red Foot to gain prestige, fame, and glory, so he could impress his prospective father-in-law. His brutal methods reflected his self-indulgent focus. The soldiers took the body of Black Elk with them when returning to the fort, as they believed it was Red Foot who had reverted back to his native ways.

When Yellow Blossom was attacked, she screamed and fought for her life, but she was beaten into submission and then raped. However, she managed to grab the soldier's identity dog tag in the struggle, and she still had it clenched in her hand when Black Buffalo found her. Grey Arrow, her brother, noticed that she was still clasping this metal tag in her closed fist. He prised it out of her hand and found it was engraved with a name and number. Black Buffalo asked Grey Arrow to keep this tag safe, for he felt strongly it would have some future value. He knew that the blue coats could not be identified without their tags, so if he killed this soldier, no one would ever know. It was like taking a person's soul.

This thought pleased Black Buffalo, as it would be a fitting revenge on the soldier who had violated Yellow Blossom and left her for dead. He also aimed to retrieve Black Elk's body, so he could deliver it to his relatives, who would bury him on sacred ground, as was the Indian custom. Black Buffalo spent the next two days tracking the soldiers on foot, as he followed their trail and the horses they had taken.

The fort was normally a ten-day ride, but the progress of the soldiers was slowed down, due to the extra horses and baggage they were carrying. All the soldiers had consumed the medicinal whiskey grog they carried in celebrating their good fortune. Each soldier was issued a bottle of whisky for medical emergencies, but on this occasion, they had broken into their stocks in jubilation. They had no reason to rush back to the fort quickly, as the more time they took, the more decomposed their captured body would become, which would mask any close identification. They could enjoy the freedom of the outdoors, by taking the journey in easy stages.

On the second night, Black Buffalo was able to silently creep up to their camp, while all but one was asleep, and set about systematically killing all five soldiers. Making no sound, he disabled the sentry, who had fallen asleep on the job. Black Buffalo then moved in silently to kill the remaining soldiers one by one, who were all bedded down. He showed no mercy or emotion for what he was doing. This was revenge, pure and simple, as it was justice in reciprocation for deeds done. By taking the identity tags of each soldier, he knew that the bodies would be exposed to the elements, and once picked clean by vultures, buzzards, and insects, only bones would remain, so nothing would be left as evidence of how these soldiers had died.

Black Buffalo had taken note of the one soldier without an identity tag around his neck; he took a long look at him so he would remember the face of his enemy. His white skin, sandy hair, and blue eyes were etched in his mind. He took his sword, a timepiece, a ring, and some trinkets from his pockets. All the saddlebags and equipment were attached to the spare horses which he roped together in a line, together with the horse carrying Black Elk's body.

Black Buffalo rescued his own horses and took the soldiers' horses, together with Army gear and personal clothing and items, being trophy payment for the suffering incurred. Rifles and knives were amongst the goods taken, so his village would be well armed for the future. Black Buffalo left the soldiers' bodies naked for the vultures to eat. It would be some time before a search party would come to find out what had happened to this patrol, and by the time they did, there would not be much left as evidence, to say what had occurred here. Black Buffalo had used his knife, so when the vultures and buzzards had eaten their fill, only bones would remain on the dry parched land, and the wind would blow them around far and wide. With no identity tags left upon the ground for anyone to find, there would be no way of knowing if the bones were animal or human. After Black Buffalo roped the horses together in a line, he used brush wood to erase hoofmarks from the sandy terrain.

Loose sand would blow over the tracks, but he wanted to make doubly sure and certain that nothing would lead searching soldiers in the direction he was taking. He went back to the temporary campsite using a roundabout route, where he met up again with Grey Arrow, who had been looking after Yellow Blossom. At first, she had been in a coma and had not made any response.

She was cleaned up and made more comfortable from her injuries, as she had a broken arm, cuts, and bruises, and every movement was painful for her. The slow journey back to the village was taken in silence, as both men were shocked and thoughtful after the recent events. Grey Arrow did not ask Black Buffalo what had happened or what he had done, as it was sufficient from his looks and nods that justice had been carried out. The evidence was there in Black Elk's body and the goods they carried back to the village, as proof of what had taken place.

Once back at the village, the women and healers took charge, and Black Elk's parents took his body. The village chief, Painted Feather, was greatly concerned over this event, as the Indians living in the hills were usually passive in their dealings with other Indians. They only became hostile when threatened in a life-and-death situation, or facing enemies, such as the white soldiers or cowboys turned Indian hunters. Sufficient violence could be found when hunting animals to keep the families fed and clothed. Killing each other was alien to this Indian tribe's culture; their spiritual understanding was based on living in harmony and peace.

Chief Painted Feather was now in his sixth decade and was father to a very large family. His story was well known by everyone who lived in the village, as he had ruled with honest and fair hands for over forty years. His first wife, his cousin, had given him two sons. She died shortly after giving birth to her second child, when she had been bitten by a poisonous snake, who was about to attack her new baby. Painted Feather's second wife was a girl he met at one of the Mexican festivals. She was a pretty dancer. He was taken by her looks, but she was always yearning to return to her former life and found village life dull in comparison to her former existence, filled with greater activity and excitement. She gave Painted Feather two daughters, who both inherited her good looks, but before they were very old, she too died unexpectedly, when on a visit to her relations. She was caught in a crossfire between two rival rancheros. It had been rumoured that she was the cause of the argument between these two men, but no one could confirm or deny this allegation.

Painted Feather's sister took over the raising of his children, as she did not have any of her own, and they came to love her as their mother. Mountain Fern was married to Silent Warrior, who was one of the village's chief hunters. Mountain Fern would have liked many children of her own, but it never happened, so she dedicated herself to raising her brother's children as best she could.

Painted Feather was reluctant to marry again, as he was quite happy with the arrangement of having his sister raise his children. They benefitted in having a mother and two fathers, but when he visited a northern village for a marriage ceremony, he was persuaded to take as wife a widow who had two young children of her own. White Moon was said to be a passive wife who was well versed in pleasing a man and running a household, as well as being a gifted cook and garment maker. Painted Feather enjoyed good food, and his village could do with someone who could instruct on making garments, as most of the village families were only moderately accomplished in practical household tasks. What he found in White Moon astonished them both.

White Moon was indeed an accomplished woman in more ways than Painted Feather could have possible imagined. She loved children and took over the running of a household of six children without any problems. White Moon and Mountain Fern became firm friends very quickly and were able to work together in accord. Furthermore, White Moon was a tall, imposing woman, full of energy. She set about to infuse pride in the other women about their cooking and households, and enlisted Mountain Fern's help at every occasion, to give credibility to her ideas and proposals. As the chief's wife, she had the authority to make changes within households containing women, which in turn affected all the men and their own domestic arrangements.

With Mountain Fern's agreement and help, White Moon showed the women ways to make new corn cakes, flat bread, and corn sticks. Using local plants and the minimum of meat from rabbits, turkey, and hare, she showed them the secrets of herbs and spices that were used in northern climes to keep bellies full and warm. As a bonus, a mutual attraction developed between White Moon and Painted Feather, and they soon added six more children to their family. They both worked and laughed and lived together, and while the men went hunting, White Moon would teach the wives and children. She told wonderful stories to the smaller children, while showing the women how to make clothes, weave tapestries, construct baskets, and make jewellery. Everyone lived in peaceful productiveness, and only when the tribal group was threatened, would they consider fighting a common enemy. Fighting skills were those of hunters, for every Indian needed to know how to catch his food from nature's store of wild animals, plants, and vegetation.

As Mountain Fern approached middle age, she found she was with child. This was a surprise to her and Silent Warrior, as they had given up any thoughts of having children of their own. In due course, she gave birth to a son, whom they named Bright Star, as he had arrived on a clear night when the stars were shining brightly in the sky. Bright Star grew up with the youngest children of Painted Feather and was part of an extended family, so he had plenty of friends and companions. However, he was a quiet child who spent much time observing others, and even as a small child, he often knew and said things befitting a wise adult. As he grew older, he took part in all the things other youngsters did, but when he reached manhood, he began to challenge the ways of Rainbow Man, who was the village shaman. He did not agree with some of the ceremonial rituals carried out by Rainbow Man and questioned why they were part of their customs.

Bright Star indulged in deep meditations and spent a great deal of time on the higher mountain slopes to commune with the spirits of Sky Ancestors. He believed he was a direct channel for the Sky Spirits and had little time for Rainbow Man, whose power he believed had become corrupted by the corn juice he drank and the hallucinatory herbs he smoked. Bright Star advocated purity and simplicity in all things, and no one could fault him. The dialogue he channelled from the Sky Ancestors was refreshing and informative, giving good guidance to individuals and the community alike. All spirit communication was conducted in the open, unlike Rainbow Man, who was secretive and moody, as he disliked losing his personal standing.

CHAPTER 2

KINSHIPS

Strong Arrow's village was located due south, and they normally visited two or three times a year. No threat by white men was ever expected, as the Army fort was too far away to be of any concern. Why the soldiers had attacked as they did was a mystery, for local mountain Indians had not given the Americans any cause to treat them ill. Red Foot's argument with a fellow scout had started a chain of events, which had resulted in six deaths. No one ever knew what the argument had been about, but it must have been sufficient provocation for the white soldiers to give chase; their captain ordered them to pursue and capture the renegade Red Foot.

Black Buffalo felt guilty for what had occurred, as Yellow Blossom was in his care, and he was responsible for her safety and welfare. Her injuries and also the death of his cousin Black Elk lay heavy on his heart. Although his uncles and aunts did not blame him, he felt the guilt for many years. Yellow Blossom was tended by the village people and began to heal. However, her mind was not functioning right, and she only knew and recognised her sister. She doted on her sister's new born son, Buffalo Horn, and spent hours rocking and singing to him, to quiet his cries. It was discovered after some months that Yellow Blossom was with child herself, but she did not understand how this had come about. She reverted to her childlike ways, and when it was time for her to give birth, she howled and hollered like a stuck pig, fighting her body's attempt to bring the child into the world.

The baby was large compared to Yellow Blossom, who was very small. She had small hips, and the baby inside of her was strong and violently pushed its way forward, in its attempt to acquire the first breaths of life. After a long and tiresome labour, her son was born. Somehow, she managed to become lucid at the birth of her child and named him White Feather. She was very weak from losing a great deal of blood, as she had torn her insides in the process of giving birth. She slowly began to mend and tended to her own child, as if nothing untoward had happened.

She became highly protective towards her son and treated him like her sister's child, always plying the baby with food and singing and cooing to it. White Feather grew very quickly. He was a demanding child, always hungry and never satisfied for long. Yellow Blossom grew thin and looked undernourished, and she started hallucinating in her sleep.

Her sister, Morning Flower, took over the caring of White Feather as soon as Yellow Blossom had finished breastfeeding him, which was the time when her breast milk dried up altogether. Yellow Blossom was too young and too small to be able to rear a demanding child, as she did not have the strength or knowledge of what to do. Morning Flower feared her sister was beginning to smother White Feather with her odd attention, and it looked like Yellow Blossom was reverting to her childlike ways again.

When White Feather was four months old, Yellow Blossom walked out of camp to go to the mountain stream and waterfall. This was used for bathing and washing clothes. While Morning Flower was looking after the two young boys, her neighbour rushed in to say there had been an accident. Yellow Blossom had gone to shower under the waterfall and had slipped on the rocks and fallen down the cliff face. Her broken body was found crushed in a bloody heap, where the waters ran clear and cold.

Had she taken her own life? This question could not be answered. Was it an accident, as it appeared? Who could tell? The truth would remain a mystery. The deed was done, and Yellow Blossom was at peace.

Morning Flower set about bringing White Feather up as her own, and Black Buffalo could not disagree, as he felt responsible. He felt it was partly his fault that this child had been brought into the world. He also blamed himself for Yellow Blossom dying but recognised that she had been taken into the great mystery, to set her spirit free.

As the days went by, Black Buffalo took a liking to White Feather. As a small child, White Feather followed his brother Buffalo Horn, who was only nine months his senior, everywhere he went. Black Buffalo could do nothing but treat the child as his own, as his love shone out to be accepted. He had a special place within his heart for White Feather, and as he grew, Black Buffalo could see that he would make a better warrior than his own son, Buffalo Horn, who was much slimmer and not as strong. White Feather was now an adult and a head taller than Buffalo Horn, with a much broader body frame. He was even slightly taller than Black Buffalo himself, who was considered a tall man. Black Buffalo and Morning Flower had three more children, all females.

White Feather's sisters were all good-looking maidens; unlike their brother Buffalo Horn, they were strong of body, adventurous, and hard-working. Buffalo Horn was not interested in competing, and Black Buffalo soon viewed his natural son with disappointment. When it came to hunting, fighting, and horse racing, Buffalo Horn was nowhere to be seen. He was not even interested in the marriageable females of the village, but hung about with the old shaman and healer, Rainbow Man. They spent their time together, looking for herbs and plants to grow and cultivate. Rainbow Man used certain herbs and plant extracts for making potions; his speciality was a corn brew. Some herbs were gathered and smoked, either by breathing in the smoke or by smoking a pipe containing the plant extract.

The effects were very relaxing and mind-bending; this freed the user to connect with the upper worlds of Ancestors and guides, or it could also lead to journeying to the underworld, meeting animals and unknown creatures such as demons, which fought battles with earthly elements. Rainbow Man was a master of magic, but Buffalo Horn began dabbling in things he didn't fully understand. Buffalo Horn was susceptible to the corn brew, which would render him senseless and often abusive. Buffalo Horn did manage to do some hunting, but only just enough to contribute to the household and hold his own, but he would not climb the mountains to lay traps, or visit other hillside groups or bother to find fresh mushrooms growing on the moist rock faces, to please the womenfolk.

All the women loved White Feather, for he would bring back from his hunting trips all sorts of interesting delights: rabbit, hare, goose, turkey, pigeon, partridge, blueberries, nuts, and edible plants and fungi. It had been Morning Flower who had been instrumental in getting White Feather to bring back these wonderful delicacies, as she loved such exotic things, and White Feather loved Morning Flower for being his mother. At times, he would bring back mountain flowers and other good-smelling plants; some were replanted within the village boundaries, and other plants left to dry out for their flavours or aromas.

White Feather was everything to Morning Flower that her own son was not. White Feather had grown into a very handsome man, and all the young women of the village were keen to see where his interest lay. Black Buffalo had taught both Buffalo Horn and White Feather all he knew about hunting the wild animals of the district. Morning Flower had taught them both about the natural plants, herbs, and lichen that could be gathered from the mountainsides.

Their village lay well hidden in the hills of the Rocky Mountains, away from the lowlands and prairies, where the white man had laid down his flag in the state of Texas. The buffalo rarely ventured into the hillsides, so it was quite an event when they were spotted on the grasslands along the eastern edge of the mountain range, which was only a short ride from the mountain foothills. This happened perhaps twice a year, so the braves from the village kept a lookout in the spring and autumn. National borders meant nothing to Indians, as there was only one country, and all land belonged to the Great Spirit, as everyone knew.

White Feather was now twenty-two summers; for the last seven years, he had assisted Black Buffalo in all the family's hunting activities. He was as knowledgeable as the other adult braves, having been on excursions to the north and west, visiting other tribal groups with Black Buffalo, Long Horn, and Lone Eagle, who formed one of the village hunting teams. Many of the highland villagers spoke both Indian and the Mexican dialect, and these languages soon became intertwined.

White Feather liked Lone Eagle, as he too was a product of mixed breeding. His father had been a pure Mexican whom his mother had met and married when attending a marriage ceremony of a close relative in El Paso, located on the Mexican border. His father, Miguel Cortez, had been called up into the Mexican Army and had been killed fighting for this country. Lone Eagle's mother had returned to her own people with her son, as she wanted to be back with her father and mother and six brothers and sisters in the high country. She married again, to Crooked Horse, who had bandy legs but by all accounts was a robust lover, for Lone Eagle was anything but lonely. He had eight brothers and sisters who were boisterous as he was quiet. Lone Eagle was a deep thinker, as was White Feather in his moments of introspection. Both had come to the reckoning that at some point in their lives, they would like to travel to see how the other nations lived. This included the Mexicans and the white man. Both came from so-called civilised nations, and yet they displayed violent natures.

Lone Eagle's Mexican grandparents were still alive, and there had been talk that Lone Eagle might inherit some land and cattle from his *abuelo*. It wasn't known if there were any Mexican cousins, as Lone Eagle's Mexican father had only one older sister, who had married late in life. The Mexican family name was Cortez, and his grandfather was named Emmanuel Cortez. Lone Eagle's Mexican name was Emile Cortez.

White Feather had visited other villages to the north where there were groups like his own village, nestled between mountain peaks. Each was very similar in construction and size, with a leader or elder ruling the group dynamics. To the west was even higher ground, and amongst these upper hills were sporadic groups of just a few households that occupied a mountain terrace, where a spring or waterfall could be found. These areas were very beautiful in spring and summer, but autumn and winter were difficult months, as snow covered the ground. Food was often in short supply, and families had to rely upon stored produce, or travel to lower ground not covered with snow in order to trap animals for food.

These family groups often lived in rock caves, and many inhabitants showed their artistic natures by carving and creating drawings and paintings on the cave walls. These pictures were viewed as history, showing the legend of the peoples over recent times and past centuries. Visitors could educate themselves by viewing these pictures and receive hundreds of years of historic knowledge. The elders relayed stories from these pictures, embellishing the details with fascinating tales of bravery and insight, together with successes of past tribal glories and the stories of battles lost and won. White Feather had not travelled farther south than the next village of his grandparents and had never travelled east. South and south-east was Mexico, and to the east were white settlements of one kind or another. Between the two areas was a river, which could be used as a gateway to lands in all directions.

The time was coming when White Feather would depart for a hunting trip; when this occurred, he would normally be away from camp a month or two at a time. He had decided that on his next trip, he would venture to new areas and find out what lay beyond his known boundaries. Lone Eagle would accompany him, and both friends would be able to see for themselves, what life was like elsewhere. Lone Eagle's mother had given him some directions and names of people he should contact. These were relatives or contacts of his natural grandfather, who lived in a Mexican village not far from the border. Lone Eagle did look more Mexican than Indian, as he had a rounder and flatter face than a true Indian. Wearing a Mexican sombrero and poncho, he could be taken for a native highland Mexican. The two friends had agreed that they would dress in Mexican clothes, so no one would know they were mountain Indians, which many disliked and feared, for many feared the unknown. White Feather could be taken for a gringo, a term used to cover all foreigners, including Americans, who often worked as cowhands.

Gringo was now a common word used in Texas to describe mixed-race cowhands and ranchers, who were used to dealing with prairie cattle and horses; many dressed in Mexican clothes, with ponchos and sombreros that suited the climate and way of life, which was spent mainly outdoors in the sun with little or no shade.

At the present time, White Feather could not speak American fluently; he knew some words but could not speak the language as you would expect a white man to speak, nor did he have rudimentary education that many American youths enjoyed. He could speak adequate Mexican, though, as the Spanish dialects were interchangeable with their own Indian one.

Lone Eagle could speak better Mexican than any other young village male, but even he was limited in what he could speak, as all he knew had come from his mother over the years. Both friends were the same age, and while Lone Eagle was not as tall as White Feather, he was taller and leaner than an average Mexican, who could be short in height and rounded in girth.

Before either of them could venture to foreign lands, they went to visit White Feather's grandparents in the hillside village located due south. Both Strong Arrow and Spring Blossom were elderly now and looked after by Grey Arrow and his family. There was another uncle named Grey Fox, who had been only five summers old at the time of White Feather's birth, so that made him just a little older than White Feather and Lone Eagle. Grey Fox was a good hunter and a fine-looking brave, as he was tall and slender with strength in his muscles and bones. White Feather was now a fraction taller than Grey Fox, and you could see the similarity between them when they moved, particularly in some of their actions and mannerisms.

Three summers ago, Grey Fox had married a wife who had always been of delicate health; one day, she decided to climb the rocks after some herbs. She slipped on the rocks and fell over the cliff onto a ledge. She had been found with badly broken bones, and there had been internal bleeding. The healers reset the bones in her arms and legs, but they could not save her from the damage done internally, as the great traumatic stress experienced proved too strong upon her life force. She died a few days later. This had occurred over six months ago, just before the last visit from White Feather. Grey Fox had not bothered to look for another wife, as he thought that the life in the mountain hillsides was risky, and he now sought a more peaceful existence elsewhere.

He too welcomed the opportunity to travel to new lands and wanted to explore other places to live; he had ideas of his own about starting a new family away from this place, which held so many sad memories for him. Grey Fox was ready for something new, so when Lone Eagle and White Feather visited the next time, his mind was made up to join them on their travels. He believed that life flowed in a pattern for each individual human being, and he felt strongly that now was the time to follow the life stream, to allow fate and fortune to take him to new places with new experiences. Grey Fox knew about Lone Eagle's heritage; he knew he was determined to seek out his relatives and find out if he had a place to fill within his Mexican family.

If it was true, Lone Eagle could claim whatever inheritance his grandfather left him. Lone Eagle also expected to be confronted with family duties which only he could fulfil, and he was committed to doing the best he could. It had been discussed between these three braves that a journey of this kind needed planning and preparation, and at the very least, if things did not work out well, then all three could work as cattle herders, cowhands, or horse trainers. Any farm or ranch work could be undertaken, as all three braves were good, strong workers and keen to prove their worth.

Horses would be their best bet, as each brave was used to dealing with the breaking-in and training of their own horse, having been caught from the wild herds located within the mountain valleys of their tribal area, and Grey Fox had specialised in training the horses in his village, an activity for which he was well known.

There was also knowledge held of locally grown produce gained from working in the fields of their Indian valley cousins, when more hands were needed at spring or harvest times to help with planting and harvesting. It was a way of combining family visits with working and assisting in community needs. In summertime, Indian and Mexican festivals were enjoyed by all. There was a great deal of merriment at these times, and many marriages were conducted at the same time as the festivals, so these celebrations could have many uses. At such events, there would be shamans and wise ones, offering healing and spiritual blessings for good fortune.

By giving special gifts to a shaman or a wise woman, you could receive a soul reading for your future.

Both White Feather and Lone Eagle had traded goods for such a reading, for they wanted to know what lay ahead in their lives, which might affect their proposed travel plans. Lone Eagle had been told of a visit to relatives that would change his life and an inheritance that would be his and his alone. He would marry a rich wife and have three children he would adore. One would become famous, while another would marry into royalty, and another would be a great musician.

Lone Eagle thought this was great and was full of praise for this wise woman's words. He insisted that White Feather have a prediction reading also, so this was how White Feather first learned something of what he might face in his new life away from his home village. White Feather was told a different story of intrigue and secrecy. He too would meet a mystery woman, but the path of true love would not be straightforward. He was told of sadness and happiness, and a struggle within himself to choose a life: one of familiar ease or a life of challenge to true love.

He wasn't told any specifics but was given a warning to keep his own counsel and to always honour the Great Spirit, for he would bestow upon him a great gift. White Feather was told to be wise and never judge others, for much mystery had to be unravelled before full understanding of his life's purpose was known.

CHAPTER 3

THE JOURNEY

White Feather had grown up with shamanic spirit understanding, and he knew that Black Buffalo had consulted Rainbow Man on many occasions in the past. The resident shaman had predicted events which had come true. This is why Black Buffalo tolerated his own son's behaviour and friendship with the medicine man, for he knew that Rainbow Man had once held great powers, although now in his senior years, his powers were lessening and were not so strong. Black Buffalo was not a particularly superstitious man, but because of the events surrounding White Feather's birth, he had come to the belief that the Great Spirit guided his life, and that of his family in all major events.

It had been Rainbow Man who had insisted on keeping the soldier's personal possessions many years ago; he had instructed Black Buffalo to give White Feather the personal items belonging to his dead soldier father, to take with him on his journey of discovery to the southlands. Rainbow Man believed that somewhere amongst the soldier's possessions there would be some information to unlock a heritage, which may prove beneficial to White Feather. Black Buffalo loved White Feather and was apprehensive about this proposed journey, as he felt that life was about to change and would never be the same again. It marked a significant rite of passage which would bring major changes to his household: Black Buffalo had fought against such change for as long as he could.

Black Buffalo remembered the face of his enemy from so many years ago and recalled the face of the white man with sandy hair and blue eyes. He could see that White Feather looked different from the other braves, but he could not see the face of his enemy in the face of White Feather. What he saw was a heritage from Strong Arrow, his grandfather, who had been a magnificent specimen of manhood in his younger days, with a solid body, strength, and wisdom running through his veins; he was a glorious sun-man whose destiny came from the source of sun-life, giving life strength to others, to bask in their own lighted presence. White Feather's auburn hair shone with golden highlights when the sun was upon him, and this gave him a magical and dynamic aspect to his looks and being. His skin was tanned by the sun to make him look golden.

Black Buffalo was wise enough to know it was time to let go and allow White Feather to find his destiny. He hoped that good would come from his personal discoveries and not disaster, as it had upon his mother. There had been no major hostilities or fighting for a long time now, as the Bluecoats had become dominant in the Texas state, and any Indians who did not wish to live under the white man's rule had migrated west to the hills. This is how a number of Plains Indian families had come to their camp and village, after being driven off their lands by white men.

Morning Flower was tearful, and her daughters all cried with her, as they too loved White Feather more than their own blood brother, Buffalo Horn. It was an emotional parting, with Lone Eagle's family saying their farewells and White Feather's family saying their goodbyes. The time came for White Feather and Lone Eagle to physically start their journey to the next village.

Bright Star, who was Painted Feather's nephew, was good friends with White Feather and Lone Eagle; he was around the same age, and a healthy respect existed between these young braves. Bright Star had made a point of coming to see Lone Eagle and White Feather before the start of their journey. This had been an honour for them, as they both respected Bright Star for his wise words and friendship. He had spoken to White Feather and told him to look out for a woman with golden hair and blue eyes, who smelt of flowers, for she was the one who would intertwine her life with his. As Bright Star spoke these unusual words, he looked straight at his friend; the meaning of these words became carved deep within White Feather's mind. As the two braves left the village, Bright Star could be seen on the edge of the gathering. He raised his hand in farewell, giving a blessing for the journey about to be taken.

White Feather wore the metal name tag of his white soldier father, which Black Buffalo had given to him as proof of past events after he explained his origins. He had also given him the Army sword, which on examination had some inscription upon it. The timepiece was also inscribed on its cover, and inside, it held a faded image of a white woman. Amongst the trinkets that Black Buffalo had secured from the dead soldier's pockets were a ring, a key, and a letter in an envelope. This had faded over the years, but the writing was still clear, even if no one could understand what words were written. The odd word could be deciphered, but the writings and inscriptions had never been explained in full. White Feather had been told by his mother, Morning Flower, to enlist the help of a Spanish missionary priest who could read English, as they were sworn to secrecy by their religion.

The monks would not disclose to anyone what was revealed. In fact, both Lone Eagle's and White Feather's mothers had insisted they contact the mission near El Paso, which they knew was friendly to Pueblo Indians, as they employed a number of native workers. Many workers were needed to tend the formal gardens of the mission and grow the vegetables and fruit which supplied the mission estate with its produce to make it self-sufficient. There were also corn fields to tend to, as this mission baked bread and had a small mill and cooking ovens to supply food to the many hands needed to run the complex.

It was a thriving farm, with many ethnic peoples coming and going with regularity. The work somehow continued around the mission, as if the same work force was in attendance. Native workers tended to live within the mission confines and rarely ventured to the nearby township, as their every need was provided for. Prayers and services were carried out twice daily, and visitors from the surrounding area attended service at the large chapel set in one corner of the mission land, which was nearest to the township. This setup had proved the test of time, and many a subterfuge had taken place when hostilities were raging around the local territory. Even in the present time, there was distrust amongst ethnic groups, and it was better that no one group knew what the others were up to.

Lone Eagle carried with him some private papers and a couple of his father's personal possessions. One was a silver cigarette case, which had been given to his father by his sister Anita; it was inscribed with a quotation of affection and signed "Anita, your loving sister." Another was a small Bible with Spanish writing on the inside cover, saying it was a gift to Miguel Cortez from his mother, Amelia de Silva Cortez. Lone Eagle's paternal grandmother gave this Bible to his father when he entered the Mexican military academy.

The leisurely journey to Strong Arrow's village proved uneventful. It gave Lone Eagle and White Feather time to talk and make contingency plans if their original blueprint of action did not work out. Once they had arrived at Strong Arrow's village, it was clear that all was not well. Strong Arrow was failing in health. He had been weakened by a fever last winter, and now he was struggling to keep food down. White Feather's grandmother, Spring Blossom, encouraged him to visit his grandfather, telling him it might be the last time they would meet. Grey Arrow and Grey Fox were with him, and aromatic smoke filled the air within the tepee, which made it easier to breathe. Strong Arrow was sweating in a fever, and cold water was being doused upon his forehead and arms to keep his temperature down and to lower his body heat.

It became obvious that White Feather and Grey Fox could not leave Strong Arrow at this time, so Lone Eagle resigned himself to a few days' rest to see how events worked out. On the third day, Strong Arrow breathed his last. This meant that Grey Arrow would become village chief and take his mother, Spring Blossom, into his household. With Grey Fox leaving the village shortly, this was the logical solution to a change in household dynamics. A spare tepee would allow a newly married couple to move into their own household. Grey Arrow's daughter was expecting another baby, and no sooner had Strong Arrow's body been laid to rest in the sacred earth than a new male life arrived. This was felt to be an omen from the Great Sky Spirit.

Spring Blossom took her new great-grandson and held him high, to be blessed by the Sky Spirit in a naming ceremony, which gave this new child the name of Strong Bow. The baby's mother, Morning Dew, was sad that her grandfather, Strong Arrow, had died but rejoiced in a healthy son, who would take his place in the grand cycle of life. She knew her grandmother would help with the new baby and looked forward to spending time with her, as she was a loving person. Involving her with this new baby would ease the grief of losing her husband and cement present relationships with stronger ties to the living.

After departing Strong Arrow's village, the first landmark to find was the mission, in particular, one Father Carlos Romero, if he was still alive and residing there. Lone Eagle's mother had told them that Father Carlos was a man they could trust; he was related somehow to two brothers who owned ranches on either side of the Mexican and American border. Father Carlos had acted in the past as an intermediary between opposing peoples, and he was respected as an impartial advisor to many in high office and position. He knew the main families and dignitaries within the state, as he had been at the mission for many years and had seen times change beyond recognition.

A niece of his named Consuela was married to a Mexican Indian mountain farmer, Fernando, who lived on the high hills overlooking El Paso. This hillside farm was a place where horses could rest and where information could be gathered about what was occurring in the nearby community. Consuela's husband was known to Grey Arrow. Grey Arrow had given Grey Fox, his younger brother, a token of recognition to give to Consuela and Fernando upon arrival, which would prove to them that he was Grey Arrow's kin.

This token was a knife with a carved handle showing a design made up of intricate symbols. These symbols could be read in a certain way to provide recognition. Coded designs ensured secrecy and security for ethnic peoples. This was necessary to safeguard native people from those who would seek to pillage their habitats and take their wealth. This method also helped to safeguard information and traditions, which was solely the province of native groups, particularly those living in the high country.

After several delightful days and nights on a mountain trail that took the three friends to high and low places, over many high points, the three braves emerged from a forested hillside to where they could see Fernando's farm and fields. It was around midday, and the sun was much warmer in the lower hillsides compared to higher climes. The three braves were dusty from their travels and decided to freshen up. They found a small pool inside the tree line just right for this purpose. Above it was a small waterfall that could be used as a refreshing shower if you stood underneath it. The pool also gave the horses a much-needed drink, and there was nice long grass nearby for them to feed upon.

The three braves settled around this pool, and while Lone Eagle and Grey Fox were refreshing themselves, White Feather saw to the needs of their horses, making sure they had all drunk some water, before nibbling the grasses under the tall trees. All of them had thought a great deal about their proposed journey and had purposely chosen horses that would be suitable for southern lands. Both White Feather and Lone Eagle had left their dappled ponies at Strong Arrow's village and swapped them for plain brown mares. Grey Fox had taken his dead father's horse, which showed a white blaze upon its face. It was a young horse which Grey Arrow had personally picked from a group of wild horses and trained for his own use.

Lone Eagle and Grey Fox elected to make contact with Consuela at the farm. A woman had been seen hanging out clothes to dry on a washing line, so they knew someone was at home. White Feather could take his shower and dip in the pool while the other two made arrangements with Consuela and learned how to get to the mission. A little while later, after White Feather had washed and showered under the waterfall, he began sorting out the Mexican clothes they had brought with them. There were white breeches and tunic tops, plus three colourful ponchos, but only one wide-brimmed sombrero. White Feather tried the breeches on, to find which one had the longest legs.

Because he was the tallest, he found the longest breeches only came to calf length on him, so he hoped this would be acceptable. He chose the plainest poncho as his choice of coat. Lone Eagle and Grey Fox returned with some bread and chili stew, which was spicier than what the three braves were used to, but with plenty of water around to quench their thirst, the pot was soon cleared. Lone Eagle and Grey Fox said they had found Consuela very helpful. She had told them to wait in the woods until after dark before coming into the farmhouse barn, where Fernando would meet them and answer all their questions. She did say that it would be best to dress in Mexican clothes if they had any, and that they had a supply of sombreros and sandals if these were needed, as well as an assortment of clothes to suit most occasions and sizes that would fit the tall and the short. There was plenty of serviceable cloth in store, and Consuela or her daughter could sew material into any style of garment, suitable for most workers, if this should prove necessary.

Consuela had also advised her visitors that they should groom any hair on their face to look like a Spaniard, as they looked upon a groomed beard as a sign of stature amongst men. Consuela had some scissors and a mirror and promised she would do her best with any unruly hair growth. As it happened, White Feather had allowed his beard to grow and had not yet removed it. The sight of this hair growth was a constant amusement to both Grey Fox and Lone Eagle. Lone Eagle had grown a moustache like many Mexicans, but Grey Fox insisted on staying clean-shaven. Grey Fox even refused to cut his hair but did make the concession to plait it and hide its length under his sombrero.

White Feather had not yet decided if he would cut his hair. He knew that most gringos had long hair but not as long as Indians, whose head hair could cover their complete back. White Feather would ask Consuela what she thought was best, as she would know what would fit in locally to blend in.

The few hours until dark were spent in rest. As the sun went down, the three braves made their way to the barn, where Fernando was waiting for them. The horses were placed in the penned area where Fernando kept other horses; there was grain and plenty of hay and water. Fernando was a man of Mexican and Indian heritage; he had lived on the outskirts of both cultures for as long as he could remember. He provided services for both races which seemed to have been lucrative for him over the years, as his farm was well managed and relatively tidy. It fitted well into the landscape of natural vegetation surrounding the farm, which was forest, then bush, and then cultivated fields, as the land descended down to lower levels towards the township.

Fernando informed them that twice a week, he took a wagon into town to bring his produce to the mission and the local market, and to pick up any items he needed for the farmstead. Fernando timed his visits with the chapel services held at the mission, so he could attend the services and talk in private to the monks without causing any suspicion. The monks gave him errands to do within the town, while he was delivering his produce to market traders. He also frequented the local inn for a refreshment of beer or wine, as this was another place to gain useful information. Local ranchers and farmers also frequented this inn, so it was a social meeting place to which many congregated. If a farm or ranch needed to hire new hands, the word would be left at this meeting house for willing responders. There was always some ranch or farm that needed extra help, particularly at harvest and planting times. Ranches needed cattle herders for general maintenance of cattle and horses, as well as for the droves to take cattle herds on the trail up to markets in the northern states of Kansas and Colorado.

As far as Fernando was concerned, these three braves had come to be mission workers. He dealt with many native peoples, both Mexican and Indian, who arrived unannounced to his farm, to gain work at the mission. Many tribes had fallen on hard times, and working on the mission was a way of feeding themselves, while earning a small wage to take back to their villages; they could also buy medicines and other goods.

Consuela had told her husband that there was an Indian, a Mexican, and a gringo waiting for him, and that the Indian had brought proof, by way of a coded knife, that he was kin to Grey Arrow. Fernando held great respect for Grey Arrow, who many years earlier had saved his life from pursuing soldiers, when both had been caught up in a skirmish when visiting a mutual relative.

This relative had been arrested as an informer during the times of trouble over twenty years ago. It was the Indian way to pay another for given services, and Fernando was intrigued to see who Grey Arrow had sent to him. When he met Grey Fox, he was suddenly taken back in time within his memories, for Grey Fox looked just like Grey Arrow as Fernando remembered him so many years ago. He asked if he was his son, but then Grey Fox explained he was his younger brother. Pleasantries were exchanged, and then Grey Fox told Fernando about his father's recent death and explained that Grey Arrow was now chief of his village; he was also now a grandfather.

He also explained that he had lost his own wife and had come on this journey to look at life elsewhere, and to help his friends, referring to Lone Eagle and White Feather, with finding their future. Fernando understood and said there would be no trouble if they wanted to spend time at the mission, as it was a perfect place to be, if you wanted to work and learn new things. The mission had an extensive library, and many of the monks undertook research on all sorts of things, besides the growing of food and the maintenance of the mission complex. The mission was a small village in its own right, as many activities took place behind its walls, and many secrets were kept from the town dwellers living only a short distance away.

Fernando smiled, as he recounted that he too was about to become a grandfather, with his daughter near her time. She was the other female in the farmhouse, helping her mother with household chores. His Mexican son-in-law, Pedro, worked on the large Cortez plantation over the border.

As Fernando was relating this piece of information, he looked at Lone Eagle as if he recognised him. He suddenly asked if Lone Eagle was related to the Cortez family, as he recognised a likeness to that family, having briefly known Miguel Cortez, who had been killed while in the Army.

To everyone's delight, Lone Eagle revealed that he was indeed related to that family and was the grandson of Emmanuel Cortez; he had come to pay him a visit, now that he had attained his adulthood. Fernando knew that the elderly Emmanuel had expressed a wish to meet his grandson from America before he died.

The group was conversing in Mexican dialect, interspersed with Indian phrases. They could all make themselves understood, but Fernando explained that Lone Eagle (Emile) needed 'polishing' if he was to be accepted in polite society, for his dialect was very much of a working-class peasant. Fernando suggested that a few weeks at the mission would allow Emile to brush up on the niceties of social interaction. Father Simeon would be of the greatest help, as he journeyed regularly to the Cortez plantation to provide Catholic services for the family members and estate workers. After a few weeks at the mission, Emile could make the journey with Father Simeon to the Cortez plantation; dressed in monks' robes, it would be unlikely that he would be stopped at the border. Fernando suggested that Emile wear the sombrero and poncho, as they suited him well. He then went to a wooden trunk and picked out some hats more suitable for Grey Fox and White Feather. He suggested that Grey Fox wear a wide-brim panama hat, the sort that many native workers wore in the fields to protect against the sun.

Grey Fox could also wear a poncho, as it was the sort of clothes suitable for outdoor field workers. When Fernando came to look at White Feather, he was somewhat puzzled. He had to look upwards to examine his face, as

White Feather was at least six feet tall, was broad of body, and had hair on his chin like an unkempt gringo. He could see that White Feather's hair was not as dark or black like a true Indian or Mexican, and he wondered if he had been an Indian captive. Grey Arrow had referred to White Feather as his friend but had not told him of the true relationship to him as his nephew, as this was private knowledge and personal information which should be kept from strangers.

White Feather's beard contained golden highlights, as did his hair, which sparkled in the setting sun's rays. Again, something niggled in Fernando's memory, but he could not recall who he reminded him of. He was certainly imposing, being tall and muscular, so an ordinary outfit of a peasant worker would not suffice. Fernando had to think how this man could be passed off in society. He would enlist the help of his wife to see to his beard and hair, to make him look like a Spanish dignitary or a gentleman farmer.

With his height and bearing, dressed in appropriate clothes, and hair cut short, White Feather could easily be an American cowboy, but not speaking American English was a handicap, so he would have to be of Spanish origins. Fernando had the very thing in his trunk for clothing: a grandee's travelling cloak and hat, as well as a long waistcoat. In addition, a pair of leather trousers was found, which Fernando was sure was long enough to reach his ankles.

CHAPTER 4

THE TRANSFORMATIONS

White Feather tried these new clothes on for size, and they fitted well. The trousers were not unlike his winter breeches, which were made of soft deer skin. These were a little coarser than what he was used to, but the white ruffle shirt and long waistcoat transformed him into someone else. A black grandee's hat completed the outfit to show he was someone of standing; a gentleman farmer of Spanish origin was the aim. With hair trimmed, Fernando was sure he would look the part.

It was at this time that the subject of names arose. Lone Eagle already knew his name was Emile Cortez, and White Feather had already decided to use the last two names of his white parent, as written on the name tag: James Adams. To this, he added his own name of White, so as to somehow keep his own identity. He would take the name of White James Adams. Grey Fox wanted something easy to remember, so it was decided he should be called, plain and simply, Joseph Fox.

Fernando explained that the mission monks could provide legal papers in the names agreed, so that any legal titles could be given to the person who showed an identity certificate, and this also acted as a pass for border control at the American and Mexican border. This was an important document necessary for safe travel in a civilised country. Large amounts of money could change hands for identity papers, particularly if one wanted to change one's identity for advantageous reasons. Such identity papers were recorded with the civil authorities and could be verified on a register for births, deaths, and marriages, as well as for legal ties to property and wealth as proof of family connections.

Shoes were the next items to be scrutinised, as moccasins were a dead giveaway of Indian heritage. Open leather sandals were found for Lone Eagle and Grey Fox and a nice pair of canvas loafers for White Feather. With the clothes sorted, it was now time to rest. Fernando suggested that the three travellers store their personal items for later use.

White Feather said he knew a place just inside the forest which was perfect to store their feathers, bows and arrows, blankets, and knives. White Feather had found this hiding place when he had showered under the waterfall and discovered a small cave behind it. This opening under some tree roots provided a clean, dry place to store their goods.

Fernando offered sleeping places in the barn, but the three braves preferred to sleep in the open and said they would find a place under the forest trees. Fernando invited White Feather to come to the farmhouse at daybreak so Consuela could cut his hair; he invited the other two braves to help him water and feed the horses in the penned area and then gather fruit from the orchards. The doctor was due to visit the next day to check on Lena, his daughter, who was expecting her first child shortly. He would take some fruit back to the mission on his return journey. Fernando offered food to eat for extra help around the farm. It was expected that the mission doctor would arrive around midday to check on Fernando's daughter, who had come home to her mother to have her first baby, as she was apprehensive about the birthing. Lena's husband, Pedro, was due to visit within the next few days, which was calculated to coincide with the birth time, scheduled in two weeks.

The three braves left their new clothes and footwear in the barn and put on their own clothes before going back into the forest to bed down for the night around the pool. They hid their personal goods under the tree roots in the small cave behind the waterfall and put what they needed in their personal canvas holding bag, which Fernando had given to each one. Most Mexicans and locals carried such bags with a shoulder strap. This bag would carry a change of clothes and their moccasins, as each brave had to get used to their new footwear. In personal and private times, away from prying eyes, moccasins could be worn to ease the comfort of the feet, if needed.

Since the doctor was arriving the next day, they decided to ride to the mission with him. The wagon would be filled with produce, so when they arrived at the mission, the braves would be regarded as mission helpers who had been picked up from the fields to help unload the produce. If they arrived in the morning, onlookers would suppose they were Fernando's hired hands helping him unload for the market.

When early morning arrived, White Feather presented himself at the farmhouse door, ready for Consuela's ministrations. He found that she had been up earlier, cooking stews for everyone to eat, and he could smell bread baking. This early in the morning, the light was bright and clear, so Consuela sat White Feather on a chair facing a window and put a cloth around his shoulders. She got to work with her scissors, cutting his long hair to his shoulders, which gave him enough length to tie it at the back of his head, away from his face, if required. She then began to trim his beard into a very smart colonial goatee.

After she finished, she gave White Feather a small mirror to look at himself. He was quite astonished at the face staring back at him, as he had never seen this view of himself before. He knew his father, Black Buffalo, and his mother, Morning Flower, would not recognise him now, as he looked very different from his normal self.

Consuela gave White Feather some bread, goat's cheese, and milk as breakfast; White Feather was thankful for this food, as he was rather hungry. The cooking stews were not ready yet, but the bread was fresh and warm and exceedingly tasteful, much better than the corn rounds he normally had to eat. White Feather had expected to have new experiences, and this included food. He had tried Mexican food before at the summer festivals and had always found it refreshing and tasty, although highly spiced. When White Feather finished his morning meal, Consuela asked him to bring water from the well out in the yard. As he brought a bucket of water back into the dwelling, he found Consuela with her daughter, who seemed to be in distress. She was clutching her belly and moaning in pain.

Consuela explained that Lena, her daughter, was having labour pains; she feared the baby might come before the doctor arrived on his scheduled visit. Her husband, Fernando, had gone to the fields with two of the regular hired hands. They had arrived at the farm just before daybreak that morning, and she feared that White Feather's friends were also with them in the fields, gathering fruit. She said she could picture them eating their morning meal, as Fernando had taken the first batch of bread with him when he had left earlier.

Lena was led to a bed in the next room, and Consuela told White Feather to stay with her while she looked outside to see if anyone was nearby. A few minutes later, she returned, shaking her head, and announced that the three of them were the only ones left at the farmstead. Consuela took one look at White Feather and told him he would have to assist her with the baby's birth, in the absence of any doctor or nurse.

First, Lena had to be made comfortable; White Feather could sit with her and talk to her so she could relax. Consuela said White Feather could hold Lena's hand if she needed to hang on to someone.

If Lena should become distressed, he was to call Consuela, who would be in the kitchen, but she reckoned it would be hours yet before the baby would arrive. Consuela went into the kitchen to boil water on the stove and make ready all the things needed for the coming birth. Although White Feather had never been present at a child's birth before, he did know what went on; also, he had spent his life with females and had heard the stories of many village births, as they were natural and normal events. He also knew of ways to help in pain relief, gained from Rainbow Man's influence. Bright Star had taught him some meditative techniques, which could help someone focus on other things and transport the mind-self elsewhere. He had seen this in action many times, only just recently when Grey Arrow's daughter gave birth to her new baby; the familiar techniques were used to alleviate discomfort, so that a normal pain-free birth could occur.

Soon enough, Lena started to become distressed; White Feather began to chant and speak to her in such a way that she became focused on his voice and the sounds he made. Soon, she was relaxing and breathing regularly again. He touched her forehead, and she responded by falling asleep for a while, giving her body time to adjust to the impending rigours of birth.

White Feather heard noises coming from outside and heard Consuela talking to someone. He presumed it was the doctor. He was surprised when a young woman entered the room with Consuela, who announced that the doctor could not come and had sent his daughter instead. Elaina Westwood, the doctor's daughter, would check on Lena's progress. She looked very young, not more than twenty years old, and spoke Spanish in a cultured voice.

Elaina said she was a nurse and would assist with Lena's birth. Consuela had told Elaina that she had a Mexican-speaking visitor with her, whose name was James Adams, explaining that while he had an American name, he had been brought up by a Mexican family. James hoped to learn the American language while staying at the mission, and Consuela also hoped that Elaina could help in this regard, as she knew that Elaina had taught the mission children in their rudimentary American classes. Elaina saw that Lena was in a relaxed and calm state and had her hand securely clasped in James's hand, while he was using the other to sponge cool water over her forehead. From what the nurse could see, everything was under control.

She examined Lena quickly and stated confidently that the baby was ready to come anytime now. In the next moment, Lena's waters broke; her body suddenly contracted, and she let out an almighty yell. White Feather instinctively reacted by touching her head again, and she fell back calmly in a relaxed state. He softly spoke to her in a firm manner, telling her that it was time for the baby to arrive and that all she had to do was push the baby out gently into the world, so it could take its first breath of fresh air. He instructed Lena by telling her that on the next of his signals, when he squeezed her hand tightly, she should push.

Elaina had never seen such a thing. But a few minutes later, James squeezed her hand, and Lena started to push when the next contraction came. Four more times, James squeezed her hand when the contractions came, and on the last push, a head appeared, and then with another little push, Lena's son came into the world. There had been no fuss, no distress as you would have expected at a birthing; all had happened smoothly and incredibly fast.

The baby was cleaned, wrapped up, and placed in Lena's arms. Lena was cleaned up and made comfortable too, and all the while, she still held James's hand tightly in hers. He was her saviour, for she had been extremely frightened, and not even being with her mother had lessened her fears. James had instinctively known how she felt and had taken the pain and distress away from her, so she could enjoy the birthing of her first child. She was overjoyed.

Consuela was crying with joy, Elaina was smiling, and White Feather wondered if he had done the right thing or revealed too much of himself. Consuela made some coffee, which the women drank, but White Feather declined and drank some lemon juice instead. He excused himself from the women, seeing that Lena was now sleepy and her new son already asleep. He went outside to sit on the veranda and finish his drink. His mind was now registering the doctor's daughter, who had blonde hair and blue eyes. Was this the women who would change his life?

It felt like time was suspended for a moment, and the Sky Spirits were checking to see if he had made the right connection. White Feather realised he was not dressed in his Mexican outfit yet, so he went to the barn and changed into his new clothes, putting his more leisurely ones into the canvas bag.

When he returned to the farmhouse, Elaina was waiting for him on the veranda. As he approached, he looked into her eyes in wonderment, to see her surprise at his formal appearance, as if he was now some unexpected person and not the one she had first met just a little while ago. She covered her surprise and fought a desire to ask questions, as she realised it was not her place to do so. She kept the conversation formal and politely thanked him for the assistance he had given to Lena, for it transpired that the two girls knew each other well, as Lena had helped out at the mission for a little while. Elaina had known that Lena had been particularly fearful about her pregnancy and baby's birth. Elaina said she would take James to the mission if he was ready to leave very soon, as she had to get back for other patients waiting for medical treatments.

White Feather went inside to say goodbye to Lena and Consuela, who already knew he would be leaving and travelling with Elaina to the mission. Consuela told him his two friends would travel with Fernando later on that day or early next morning, at the latest. More thanks were given from both women, who could not be more thrilled that the new baby was well and perfect, with mother and grandmother very happy indeed. White Feather, now with the new name of James Adams White (or White James Adams, as he couldn't make up his mind which way round the names should be), boarded the small wagon hitched up to two horses, which was termed a buggy.

In the back of the cart were bags of vegetables, including some peppers, which grew bountifully on the hill slopes that caught the daily sun. The cool winds at this altitude enabled the fruits to ripen without becoming overcooked and shrivelled, as would be the case on the lower land, where the mission was situated. The hillsides were ideal for plants and produce which required a gentler climate and personal handling. This was why Fernando cultivated these crops, which were suitable for his farm landscape. He had a ready market for his produce from the people living on the lower land.

When he went to market or the mission, he would exchange some of his produce for root crops, which needed flat ground and plenty of water. At the mission, the land had been cultivated and was supplied by irrigation channels that the mission workers kept open and operational. There was a small stream nearby, but most of the water was obtained from the wells sunk into the ground, from which water could be taken and distributed. Using a variety of pumps, water was distributed around the cultivated fields through human-made water channels, which fed the growing vegetation. Early morning and in the evening, you would see the field workers manning the water pumps, to send the water flowing around the crops. Water generally was conserved and distributed according to need.

Personal water supplies came from water barrels that could be seen at every roof corner. A water pipe from roof gullies and gutters directed the water into a waiting barrel, for the storage of any rain that occurred.

The journey to the mission was pleasant, with Elaina pointing out various crops growing, including tobacco, which the larger ranches or farms found lucrative as a side line to their main activities. When they reached the outskirts of town, Elaina turned the buggy north and followed a side road through a wooded area, which opened out onto a fertile valley, dominated by the mission buildings and its regal chapel. As Elaina rode through the mission's imposing gates, you could see that there were already a few people with children standing outside a main entrance to one of the larger buildings. There was a sign above the door showing a red cross on a white background, denoting the infirmary and doctor's office. They were all waiting to see the doctor or nurse for medical care and treatment.

Elaina stopped the buggy and informed James that she would leave him with Father Carlos Romero, who was now the mission's chief administrator.

He arranged for the field workers of the mission to be assigned quarters and given jobs. She led him through the entrance doors to a room which looked like an office, for it housed a desk and many books around the walls. Father Carlos was sitting at his desk and stood to welcome James and Elaina as they entered the room. He spoke in Mexican, as Elaina had indicated to him that it was the language to use. She also relayed to Father Carlos that Consuela had told her James was interested in learning American, so he could understand his relatives after he located them.

Elaina explained to Father Carlos that James had been extremely helpful while attending to Lena as she was giving birth, and all had gone very well, as Lena had produced a healthy baby boy, with both mother and child being fit and well. Father Carlos was to expect a visit from Fernando this evening or early morning at the latest, when he would bring another two more workers to the mission.

During the journey to the mission, when riding in the buggy with Elaina, James had been acutely aware of her presence. He had to hold himself in check to keep from continuingly looking at her, as she recounted the details of the landscape to him on their journey. Her presence made him short of breath, so he had kept quiet; he feared he may have presented himself as a loco, someone not too bright in the head, as he had not been very communicative. Elaina had not looked him in the eye since they had spoken on the veranda back at Fernando's ranch, when their eyes had locked in knowing, and she had not since made any reference to the incident.

Elaina seemed to be in a hurry to offload him to Father Carlos, but when all was considered, she had said there were other patients to see to. James would bide his time to see how events unfolded. He was not sure of what was going on. All these people were new to him, and he was finding it difficult to understand their relationships. He decided he would have to meditate to clear his head, so he could return to a more balanced, objective state of mind, which would be more conducive to his normal alertness.

Father Carlos asked James what he hoped to seek by coming to the mission. James, in his best Mexican accent, asked for work, in exchange for learning American and the ways of the American gentleman. He understood that the mission was a place of learning, and he wanted to know things that may be useful to him in furthering his life opportunities.

James then gave greetings from Lone Eagle's mother and explained that Lone Eagle, now known as Emile Cortez, was arriving at the mission shortly, as one of the two new workers.

James told Father Carlos that Emile Cortez and Joe Fox, another friend, were willing to work in the mission fields, in exchange for lessons to improve their language skills and understanding of American ways. Emile wanted to fit into his Mexican family and not seem out of place in any way. All three friends had lived in the hills away from civilisation, so each required some time to become acquainted with modern ways, knowledge, and traditions. Father Carlos was understanding and said that they would all meet again the next day, but first he would show James a place where he could sleep and eat. He took James outside to where there was a collection of smaller buildings and a barn situated at the end of the nearest field, near to a waterhole.

Father Carlos explained that the barn housed horses and was shared by the field workers to provide them with sleeping quarters in the soft hay lofts; there was also an open-air sleep area if preferred, under the arbour of climbing vines attached to the rear of the barn. Eating was carried out in the building attached to the main mission offices, where the kitchens and food storerooms could be found. A bell would sound to denote the time for ending work, and two bells were rung to denote eating times. Mealtimes were early mornings and early evenings. Midday eating consisted of cold food carried into the fields or eaten outside. It was expected of the field workers to feed and water the horses ready for early morning work and when they returned at the end of their working day. James was asked if he could make sure all the water pails were full for the returning horses that evening.

While James was carrying out this request Father Carlos went indoors to speak to Elaina with regard to the assistance she had implied was given by James when Lena had given birth. He returned again shortly, just as James was finishing his allotted task. Father Carlos asked if James knew anything about herbs that were used as medicines, and soon a common subject was being discussed using language that both men understood.

Father Carlos was keen to have James help in the infirmary after hearing what Elaina had imparted to him, but he knew that being indoors for any length of time, for someone who had spent most of his life outdoors, could pose a problem. He hoped that James would overcome any objections and obstacles, and spend at least some time helping the sick, injured, and infirm, where his personal abilities could be used for good purposes. Father Carlos was wise enough to take things slowly. Tomorrow was another day when arrangements could be made for all three friends.

In the morning, Father Carlos was available for consultations to talk over personal concerns. James had asked if he could translate some written words on paper that the friends carried, and he had indicated he would do his best. Father Carlos told James there were others in the mission with language skills, so if he could not help, one of them could help. James was left to rest in the sleeping quarters, where he found sleeping mats stacked in a corner. This was a very basic barn structure which was, however, clean, cool, and serviceable.

Two bells would be in about two hours, so James had time to rest and reflect. He could not settle, as his mind was busy with all the new things he had to assimilate, so he walked over to another building where two or three mission workers were making things. James became fascinated by one worker who was busy at a potter's wheel, his hands immersed in muddy soil, making an earth container. He had never seen a potter's wheel before, as the women in his village who made pottery used only their hands to mould the clay; they used sticks to shape and carve symbols on the surface. They also used wetted cloth to cover the item while it dried out, before it was baked by the sun. Sometimes, the women painted the outside of a container with coloured designs of their own making, using coloured earth. James noticed that the worker was making lots of drinking containers. All were newly made and had yet to dry out.

Milo, the mission worker, was finishing the last ones for the day. He found he had some skill as a potter, and as he looked up at James, he smiled. He gave a salute in greeting and spoke in a dialect that James at first did not understand, but he thought it must be American. When James responded using some Mexican words in greeting, Milo changed his greeting to Mexican, so he could be understood. Milo was an old man who wore eyeglasses to see. He was also rounded in his frame from all the years he had bent over the potter's wheel and from the many years he had spent bent over in the fields, digging and planting, weeding and harvesting. He now enjoyed his creative work with the potter's wheel, as well as his duties as kitchen helper, preparing meals for other mission workers. This gave him access to newly cooked food, which he fully enjoyed and never refused, for he remembered the lean years when food was in short supply, and there had been very few cooks of skill to make the flavoured stews and bread he and others so liked.

CHAPTER 5

ARRIVING AT THE MISSION

When Father Carlos visited the infirmary earlier, Elaina was recounting the events of the morning and was describing the way James had spoken to Lena and the beneficial effect he had achieved by his chanting and spoken manner. She asked her father if James could be used in the infirmary, as they needed someone who could pacify patients when they became anxious over treatments.

Father Carlos was not surprised to hear such things, as he had gathered much from talking with James about the use of herbs. He knew the young man was more knowledgeable than he was revealing. James came from the high hill country, and Father Carlos knew that shamans and spiritual leaders of a tribe who were the ones who carried out doctoring services. They also supplied potions for remedial upsets, which they procured and extracted from natural plants growing within their home locality. Father Carlos was always amazed at the extent of knowledge that was stored in native minds, when they had little exposure to civilised learning or academia.

He asked James if he would help in the infirmary, as Elaina and her doctor father would like him to assist in helping with patients. James had never considered being a medic before, as his own village had Rainbow Man and Bright Star to advise them. What he knew was common knowledge, for most minor injuries and ailments occurred within normal life activities. All family members were conversant with basic healing procedures, and his

38

mother, Morning Flower, had encouraged him to learn about herbs and medicinal plants. He watched his mother and other women mix certain plants to make medicinal potions and ointments.

From Rainbow Man, he had learned techniques to control pain, which had been furthered by Bright Star, with his knowledge of more gentle techniques in relaxation and mind focus, which attained the same effects more naturally. James was pleased that Elaina thought well of his abilities and felt his pulse quicken with the thought of being in closer proximity to her. He wondered what her father was like and looked forward to meeting him. Following Father Carlos as he led the way to the infirmary, he found the two people of his thoughts conversing over another pregnant woman who was lying on a hospital bed.

Father Carlos introduced James to Dr Jonathan Westwood, who was around fifty years old, with short grey hair and a pleasing, open face, which gave you the instant feeling of someone you could trust. He liked the look of Dr Westwood and was surprised when he spoke in Mexican with his greeting. Jonathan Westwood wanted to see for himself this young man who had impressed his daughter so greatly. Elaina was not a person to praise anyone without due consideration, but she hadn't been able to stop herself, telling her father all about the wonderful way James had pacified Lena and had controlled the events of the delivery in a most helpful and productive manner.

The patient lying in the bed was a young woman who was near her time, and her child was presented in the breech position. This was not an ideal state of affairs, as there were high risks to both the mother and child. Any help that was available would be welcomed, so the doctor wanted to appraise the capabilities of this young man, to see if he could indeed assist in this difficult birth situation. Father Carlos left James with the doctor and Elaina; he told them that a meal would be brought to the infirmary in about an hour's time. The doctor informed James that the patient was a young girl, an Indian who did not speak much Mexican or American; she was the daughter of a couple working at one of the nearby ranches.

They assumed that one of the ranch hands had sexually assaulted her, and as a result, this girl called Lois found she was expecting a child. Lois was only sixteen years old, simple and naive. She was also terrified of the birthing process, as the baby was large, and she was small, and someone had told her that because of her size, she could die when the baby came. Lois was afraid of hospitals but had come to the mission, as it was known that the doctor was a good medic, and the monks took care of people's personal problems and could arrange adoptions if needed. Lois's parents made it clear that they wanted the child to be adopted, as they were not in a position to feed another mouth. James said he would do what he could and would also follow the instructions from the doctor. The doctor and Elaina suggested that James should sit next to Lois to make himself known to her. Meanwhile, Elaina and her father would be getting things ready. James went to the bed and saw a very frightened young girl whose eyes were so large, they seemed to fill her face.

James remembered his sisters, one of which would be about the same age as this girl; without thinking, he greeted Lois in his native tongue. She responded in the same dialect, and soon they were conversing together.

James found out that Lois and her parents originally came from Strong Arrow's village and had left over ten years ago for a new American life, thinking it would be better than the life of a highland village. Her parents had worked hard but were treated badly and often unfairly by the American ranch owners, who regarded Indians as the lowest of creatures. Her two brothers were older and worked with her parents on this ranch located north of the mission. Lois admitted she had been raped by one of the young American stockmen, who had been drinking and wouldn't take no for an answer. She had been ashamed to tell her parents about the incident, so when they found out she was with child they decided to leave her at the mission, saying she was visiting relatives.

Lois had been living at the mission for the past four months, helping in the kitchens. Her labour pains had started that morning, but they stopped and then resumed again a couple of hours later. This had been going on all day; at the moment, they had stopped again. The doctor had said her baby was laying the wrong way round. Earlier, he had tried without success to turn it around. Lois was pleased that James would be with her, as she knew of Strong Arrow's family, and any friend or relation linked with that family was acceptable to her.

James did not tell her that Strong Arrow was his grandfather, but he did say that tomorrow, one of the new workers to the mission was the youngest son of Strong Arrow, who was a friend of his. James explained that when he lived in the hill country, a family adopted him, so he became friendly with the local shaman, who had taught him about pain control and other healing methods. James would help Lois through the birth and asked her to trust him, as he promised all would be well, as he had done this before. Well, he thought to himself, it was only this morning that he helped Lena to become a mother, and if he was able to do that, he should be able to do it all again. This time, he was more confident, as he had more knowledge about the procedures and requirements of a pregnant woman in her hours of painful struggle during nature's birthing process. The doctor returned to the infirmary with Elaina, carrying a tray of food. Once the doctor was satisfied that Lois was stable, he suggested James eat in his office. Elaina would sit with Lois for the time being.

There was chili and beans in a bowl and bread with milky cheese, which was very tasty. Dr Westwood asked James if he would like a drink, as he was making himself a cup of tea. He explained to James he was originally from the British Isles and still could not get used to the coffee drinking of the Americans. James did not know where the British Isles was located. He did know that it was overseas and that many Americans had come from the colonial British who had settled in the American lands. He declined tea and said water would be fine.

Dr Westwood studied James closely as he ate his meal and by way of conversation began to tell him something of his own heritage. He originally came from Scotland and relocated to the American continent after qualifying as a doctor, so he could help new settlers of the frontier towns in the Western states. He had met his wife, Maria, Elaina's mother, who was the daughter of a Spanish naval officer and an American socialite. This had been when he first worked in the Eastern states while earning some stake money, before travelling West.

Maria Silvano Westwood was half-Spanish; her mother, Catherine Silvano, was an American still living in Richmond, Virginia. Maria had been bilingual and had taught Elaina to speak Spanish, so that was why she was more conversant with the Hispanic and Mexican languages, as they were Spanish based. Jonathan Westwood had to learn the Spanish and Mexican languages by living and working with native peoples, but this had been over twelve years ago; he had been working in the West at the mission complex for all of that time. He had come here because the Mission de Corpus Christ de Ysleta del Sur at El Paso offered a great learning opportunity and because many who resided here were progressive intellectuals.

A large library had been established, and it housed many fascinating books of knowledge. The mission monks were progressive when dealing with subjects of a pioneering nature, and medicine and doctoring were such areas of interest that research was ongoing. Medicine was evolving as a science, and new techniques were always arriving to change some particular procedure, so working with the sick and suffering was a very challenging profession and a consuming interest.

Dr Westwood suddenly realised he was talking in American and surmised that James probably hadn't understood a word he was saying. Just then, Lois started moaning, as her labour pains began again. Everyone sprang to attention and took their places, with James sitting beside the mother-to-be, taking her hand in his. James began talking to Lois in her native language, taking her into a meditation to relax her body in order for the birthing process to proceed without resistance. James began stroking her forehead in a rhythmic manner, in time with his chanting voice. All was quiet and tranquil.

After a few minutes elapsed, the doctor examined Lois and nodded to James that she was coming to the time when she needed to start pushing, but not to push too hard. James then went through the procedure with Lois calmly and matter-of-factly, so that the fear he had previously seen in her eyes vanished and was replaced with trust. James kept his eyes on Lois all the time when he was chanting and holding her hand, and she soon drifted into a trance-like state. This allowed her to react physically without experiencing any conscious pain or discomfort.

James told Lois that when he squeezed her hand once, she was to push down on her abdominal muscles and that when he squeezed her hand twice, she should stop and breathe quickly to gather strength. James kept telling Lois that birthing was a natural process, so there was nothing to be afraid of, as the Great Sky Spirit welcomed all newcomers into the earth world with happiness and joy. Each new child was precious in the eyes of the Great Wise Spirit, as each child held a droplet of starlight within, as given by the Star Deity and administered by the Sky Ancestors.

About two hours passed, and then Lois was ready to start pushing; James began squeezing her hand as each contraction took hold. Lois kept pushing and panting, and soon there were two little legs protruding from her body. He squeezed her hand twice, to indicate that she should stop and wait for the next contraction. With a methodical and rhythmic tempo, this process was continued until first the torso and then the head of a baby girl gently emerged. James then touched Lois's forehead once more, and she relaxed into a light slumber to recoup her energy. This gave time for the doctor to cut the cord and give the baby to Elaina to clean up.

Shortly thereafter, Lois was awake again, with her baby tucked neatly in her arms. She had been weighed and was eight pounds, which was a good size for such a petite person to produce. Mother and daughter were well, but Lois was tired after the stress of the day, so the baby was put in a cot nearby so she could sleep. Before she did so, she told James that she would name her daughter Evening Moon, as it was what she had focused on when looking out of the window. Her American name would be Eve.

When the doctor was satisfied all was clean and tidy in his infirmary, he announced it was time for bed for all of them. He would sleep in his office, where there was a comfortable sofa, so he could be on hand during the night if Lois needed him. He said good night to Elaina and James, as they left the infirmary to go to their respective sleeping quarters.

Elaina had a room upstairs above the infirmary but walked James outside to the courtyard. She again thanked him for his help and assistance, asking him how he had come by his gift of being able to pacify those who were in pain or distress. She had heard him speak the native Indian dialect, and this explained much of the mystery about him. At first glance, James did not look like a native; it was only in some of his ways and understanding that the heritage showed through.

James briefly said he had been friends with a native shaman, who had taught him many things. It was late, and so Elaina said good night to James, who walked towards the barn, where he would spend the night. James elected to sleep under the stars, outside at the rear of the barn. He retrieved his sleeping blanket and mat from the hayloft while the other mission workers were asleep.

At daybreak, he awoke as workers were stirring and found a bathing pool behind a cluster of trees, which he used to freshen up. The bell rang for the early mealtime, so he made his way to the kitchens and eating area, which was a large cantina housing a number of trestle tables. There was bread, cheese and milk, fruit, a cereal mixture made with grains, nuts, and plenty of coffee. James was not used to coffee, so he chose some bread and cheese with a slice of melon. Milo beckoned to him to sit with him at a trestle table, so he went over and sat with him while eating this first meal of the day.

Milo told James he was on kitchen duty this morning, washing up and preparing vegetables for cooking. He also had some storekeeping to attend to, as Fernando had promised to supply some fresh chili and peppers for their supper meals. Milo hoped he would also bring some melons, as stocks were running low. Melons grown by the mission had already been harvested and eaten. Because Fernando lived at a higher altitude, the climate was milder, and the same crops would mature a little later than at the mission, because of the differences in altitudes. This arrangement extended the harvest season of certain crops, giving greater variety of produce for longer periods. Milo asked James what he was going to do today, and James replied he had a meeting with Father Carlos when his two friends arrived, but he would first go and visit Lois, who was in the infirmary.

Milo said that was a good idea, as he had already taken food to Lois and seen her sitting up and nursing her new baby daughter. She had asked after James and said she would like to see him.

James made his way to the infirmary to find Lois and her child alone. He sat down on the chair beside the bed and looked intently at the new born child. It struck him that his own natural mother, Yellow Blossom, who was only fifteen summers when he had been born, would have been much like Lois, and the similarities of circumstances surrounding this birth did not go unnoticed, either. James wondered what the future held for Lois, as she was far from simple. Others had labelled her simple because she did not speak Mexican or American fluently, and she had not made herself understood properly, because she did not fully trust anyone. Lois told James that both the doctor and Elaina had gone to the morning church service, which was held in the chapel, and they would be about half an hour. James asked Lois what she was going to do with her baby. She told James she did not want to give her daughter up for adoption, like her parents had wanted her to do, so she couldn't go back to the ranch, as it would bring shame upon her family.

Lois confided to James that she would ask the mission monks if she could continue working there as she had been doing these past months; if allowed, she would bring up her daughter herself. When her daughter was a few years old, she could then get a position in someone's household, who would employ her as a house servant. She had to find a place where she was safe and secure and not be at risk of being attacked by unruly young men. Lois was a pretty young girl who would mature into a great beauty in the next few years. Her eyes dominated her face; her expressions moved like dancing lights upon her features, and at present, she was glowing in the light of motherhood, which was so joyous to witness. James assured her that everything would work out alright, as he had seen the early morning sunrise and been told by the Sky Spirits that all was well, and she should blend with the wind and flow with the events of the life stream.

Jonathan Westwood and his daughter return to the infirmary and signalled in greeting to James and Lois. Elaina came over to tell the two that she would be starting language lessons the next day, outside in the courtyard, where there was shade. The afternoon was the traditional time of the siesta when the field workers would rest, and work would stop to allow the midday's heat to dissipate. Smiling, Elaina then informed James that Father Carlos would be in his office and was ready to speak with him and his friends. They had just arrived and were presently unloading produce from Fernando's wagon. Lone Eagle and Grey Fox had brought a full load of produce from the farm. Lena and Consuela sent their good wishes to James and also sent news that all was well with them.

James then thanked everyone in his best Mexican, which amused Elaina and Lois. Dr Westwood was impressed with this civil display, as it showed how talented James was with adopting a persona to fit any occasion. By the time James had reached the front lobby, Grey Fox and Lone Eagle were entering the front door with Fernando. Greetings were given to all; Fernando couldn't stop shaking James's hand in gratitude for bringing his first grandchild into the world.

Grey Fox looked at James as if to say "What on earth have you been up to in our absence?" James could only shrug his shoulders, as if to say the Great Spirit had sent him to do unusual things. Grey Fox was looking at

James rather peculiarly, as he had not seen him transformed into a Mexican gentleman and wondered for a moment if this really was his nephew. Lone Eagle grinned, as he knew his friend was just itching to take on the role of another persona, just as he was going to take on his Mexican role. Both Lone Eagle and Grey Fox had come dressed in their respective roles, so one looked an authentic Mexican, and the other a native worker with regal bearing, who did not look like a subservient field worker, but a high official with his straw hat acting as a crown upon his head. James would have to have words with Grey Fox later, to tell him not to look directly into other people's eyes, and to bow his head, subservient like, when speaking to others; otherwise, no one would believe he was an impoverished native. Fernando excused himself from the group and said he had to see Milo in the kitchens about the produce he had brought. This left the three friends to find Father Carlos in his office.

Lone Eagle, now Emile, took the lead, as he had his official papers with him to show to Father Carlos and wanted to know how he stood regarding his claim of being his grandfather's heir. Father Carlos was delighted to make the acquaintance of Emile Cortez and commented that visually, he would have no trouble in proving he was the grandson of Emmanuel Cortez, as the likeness to his grandfather was uncanny. Father Carlos could remember his father only briefly, as they had met just a few times, the last being at the marriage ceremony when he had officiated at the wedding between Miguel Cortez and Emile's mother over twenty years previously.

PART 2

TRANSFORMATIONS

CHAPTER 6

WORK AND PLAY AT THE MISSION

When Emile heard it had been Father Carlos who had married his parents, he knew that his mother was correct when she had told him Father Carlos could be trusted. He then felt it was appropriate to tell Father Carlos that all of them had grown up in the high hill villages and that he and James were from the same village, with Joe Fox being an uncle of James, who came from Strong Arrow's village, the home of his grandparents.

This explained a lot to Father Carlos, who loved nothing better than an intrigue. He suggested that the three of them stay at the mission while they learned the American language and improved their Mexican, which would enable them to move in different circles. In addition, they could earn their keep by joining the field workers, as there was plenty of harvesting and planting to do at this time of year, for as one crop was harvested the ground was cleared to replant for the next crop, as the climate allowed two crops to be grown each year.

Father Carlos estimated that in three months, Emile would be sufficiently schooled to be able to journey to his grandfather's estate to find his personal destiny within his father's family, as it was generally known that Emmanuel was waiting for his arrival, which he knew would happen some day when Emile was full grown. He also suggested that Joe Fox might like to travel along with Emile as his friend or servant, so he had someone he knew near to hand. He suggested that the new experience for Joe Fox was in response to his statement he wished to see life elsewhere and was particularly keen on working with horses on a large ranch.

Father Carlos knew that with his recommendation, Emmanuel Cortez would take Joe Fox as one of his workers and jump at the chance, once he knew he was a horse trainer, as horses were his passion. Father Carlos examined the paperwork Emile had brought with him and was able to confirm their authenticity; he told Emile that he would have his monks write out an identity certificate for each one of them, so that their names could be logged with the authorities. This would add weight to any formal enquiry or future hereditary claim.

Once Father Carlos had dealt with the immediate affairs of Emile and mapped out a plan for Joe to follow him and work on the Cortez plantation, his attention then swung to James. He suggested that Emile and Joe should find Milo in the kitchens and ask him to show them around and in particular the barn used for the workers' sleeping quarters, the well, and other essential landmarks. Milo would explain the regime that the mission followed, and they could all meet back at the cantina, attached to the kitchens. He asked if James would stay and discuss his circumstances more fully, as he had some suggestions to make.

When the two had left the office, Father Carlos turned to James and began looking at the letter he had given to him to read, as it was written in the American language. The paper was very old and thin, so it had to be handled with care, as it was very delicate. The written words were fading but were still readable, which was remarkable considering how old this letter was, not to mention the circumstances in which it had been obtained and since kept. The letter was addressed to Wesley James Adams and was from his fiancée, Samantha Prentice, telling him she had left the fort to travel to his father's ranch, where he should meet her. The wedding would be arranged for when Wesley began his leave in two weeks' time, straight after he returned from carrying out his latest duties, which were to catch the renegade scout Red Foot.

He could travel with her father Captain Prentice, who would be taking his leave in order to attend his daughter's wedding. The letter was dated not long before Wesley had been called to lead the squad hoping to capture the renegade Indian scout, which meant he had received this letter just before he left the fort to go on the raid. Miss Samantha Prentice also informed him that she was two months' pregnant and asked him not to delay, as it was now a matter of urgency that they marry. There was other small talk of little consequence which Father Carlos did not bother to translate.

There was quiet, while the two men sat thinking about what had been relayed. Father Carlos said he had heard of this family who he believed ran a large ranch some distance south-east of Austin, which was another town east of the mission, but he did not know them well, so he would have to make enquiries. What he did not tell James was that he had known Walter John Adams quite well at one time, when he had first come to the area twenty-five years before.

He knew there had been some tragedy, but also that Walter had married an heiress who had invested a great deal of money in his ranch and assured its success by gaining contracts to supply horses to the Army, as well as the breeding of cattle to feed the ranks. He also knew there had been a daughter born to Walter and that his wife was a much younger woman, there being a twenty-five-year age gap. He had heard stories about the wife who incited younger men around her, but for some reason, Walter turned a blind eye to her actions and concentrated on the ranch and the daughter he adored.

The family was well connected with Eastern politicians and high-profile businesses, and several family members were political figures. He tried to rack his brain about the wife, whose new husband was a senator and financier from Boston. Unfortunately, he could not remember the details, so he would have to delve deep and investigate further. In the meantime, James could work in the mornings with his friends in the mission fields and join the class for language skills in the afternoons.

In addition, any help he could give to the infirmary or to the Westwoods with their healing and medical work would be very welcomed. Father Carlos was intrigued and very impressed with James; he wanted to find out all he could, so he could help this young man find his rightful status in life. The mission had to run like clockwork, so he dismissed James for the time being and told him to find his friends. When James went outside, he did not see Emile or Joe; he retraced his steps towards the infirmary. There he found Lois up and about, packing her things.

She told James she had spoken to Father Carlos earlier, and he had given her permission to stay at the mission, as long as she worked in the cantina and helped Milo in the kitchens. Father Carlos had told Lois that Milo was getting old and could do with extra help preparing and serving the daily meals. While the baby was young and breastfeeding, she could work while the child was asleep. In the afternoons, she was to attend the language lessons given by Elaina to improve her communication skills. Lois was moving her things out of the infirmary, as she had been given the room upstairs next to Elaina's, who would help her care for the baby.

James was now impressed as Elaina was becoming all things to all people; her knowledge and abilities were endless. He looked around for her and saw that a long line of people had queued outside Dr Westwood's door. James looked in the office and asked if he could help in anyway.

Dr Westwood looked up and asked him if he knew how to make a poultice. James did not understand what he meant, but after he explained it was a potion pad to extract poison from a boil or infected area, the young man said he did know how to treat such ailments. He offered to go and get some leaves that would do the job. He had seen some river weed growing beside the pond when he had bathed that morning. He was always looking for special plants and had an eye for locating those used for medical treatments. Jonathan didn't know what leaves James was talking about, as he had been referring to crushed herbs held in storage, which they bundled into a small pad and placed over infected areas.

Juan, the boy with the boils, was asked to sit and wait for a moment, while the doctor's assistant fetched some ointment for treatment. James rushed to the bathing pool and pulled up a clump of river weed, which was thick and green with large fleshy leaves. He tore a number of leaves off the stalks and began layering them to make a pad. After he returned, he asked Juan to show the location of his boils, which were on his upper arm. They were a nasty mess, and the arm was swollen. The boy was not very clean; his clothes were dirty, and his face and hands were covered in grime. This did not bother James, as good dirt could aid in treatments, but when it entered a cut on the skin, it could become inflamed, and this is what happened to Juan. James did not judge the boy; he just placed the leaves over the infected area and tied them in place with a reed string.

He told Juan on no account must he take this pad off, even if his arm began to itch. Tomorrow, he was to return to have more leaves put on the infected site, and he would be asked to take a wash in the bathing pool, to clean off the dirt which had caused the infection. He was not to be surprised when they removed the first leaves, as they might smell because the poison had soaked into the leaves; this was to be expected. If the boy did what he was told to do, then in three days, the infection would be cleared, and the boils would start to heal. James's manner to Juan was calm, kind, and yet authoritative. The boy nodded and said he would follow the doctor's orders to the letter. Sure enough, three days later, it was found that the poisons were gone, and the boils had already begun to heal; Juan's skin was clean and fresh. Hence Dr James was born, as word spread that there was a natural healer working with Dr Westward.

From that moment on, every afternoon at four o'clock, a dozen or so people would line up for natural treatments, ranging from infected toes and feet to boils, rashes, cuts, and grazes. The bathing pool soon ran out of river weed, so Dr Westwood showed James another place farther downstream where it was plentiful. Dr Westwood also showed James how to harvest the weed and crush it into a paste so it could be made into ointment to spread over a wound. This way, just a little ointment was used for an infection and that would allow supplies to last much longer.

Early morning until midday was spent working in the fields; the three friends would ride out to their working area, ready to enjoy working together in the outdoors. All were used to physical labour and relished the exercise of ploughing ground, planting seeds, and picking crops, as the Mexican ways of mañana and siesta times seemed somehow wasteful and unproductive. It was hotter here than in the high hill country, so much of the heavy work was saved for early morning, before the sun was high. Fields workers started their day at sunup and returned at midday for their afternoon siesta or stayed in the fields to eat their lunch and lay under a tree or other shelter before resuming their work if needed.

Each afternoon, the lessons for language skills continued with Elaina. Lois joined the lessons at first with apathy, but as soon as she met Joe Fox, she seemed to brighten up enormously. It was discovered that Lois's family originated from the hill country and at one time lived in Strong Arrow's village. Joe Fox seemed to remember the family vaguely, as they had left the high hills to find better living conditions elsewhere. He remembered the eldest brother of the family, who he had once played with many years ago, and who had been called Wild Wolf. He remembered a baby sister named Little Fawn who was very small and fragile who everyone thought would not live to adulthood. Lois, it transpired, was Little Fawn.

Elaina made it a rule that the only language's spoken in class was American or Mexican. It was necessary to eradicate the peasant dialect of Emile's communications, so they acted at being important dignitaries from church and royalty. Emile took to these roles as if they had been made for him and relished the day he would be leaving the mission to meet his grandfather, Emmanuel Cortez. Already he felt comfortable in a royal role, playing the grand king of the land. What Elaina did not know was that the three Indian friends were all able to change roles, as their culture of shamanism enabled them to shift into the personalities of animals and natural elements.

This is how all Indians are taught when young and is something like what the Western races use when role-playing or fantasy to teach new skills. Indian culture taught the values of earth, fire, water, and air, as well as the manipulations of such elements. Animals were also highly influential in human characteristics, as the names adopted from animals were bestowed upon young humans. All three braves had undergone a vision quest to find their totem animal. As expected, Lone Eagle had found his Eagle Guide, who flies high to reach the Great Spirit and yet is able to live in connected harmony with the earth world. Lone Eagle's present journey to fulfil his destiny was partly energised by his Eagle Guide.

Emile aspired to reach a state of peace through hard work, understanding, and the completion of tasks set by his grandfather, to show he was worthy of receiving his personal power and status. Lone Eagle knew that he had to fulfil this journey of destiny, before he could use the essence of Eagle medicine, as he knew it had to be earned. He also knew he had to have courage for this journey and recognised that staying at the mission was indeed opportune, as it would provide many of the skills he would need in the future. Lone Eagle was ready to absorb all and everything, to overcome personal fears of the unknown. It had been fear of leaving his Indian family that had prevented him from taking this trip sooner.

Grey Fox remembered when he took his first vision quest and met his Fox Guide. He knew he was a good hunter and could merge with undergrowth to become hidden. The forest was a fox's best camouflage when observing the activities of others. Joe Fox had inherited the qualities of adaptability, cunningness, observation, integration, and quickness of thought and actions. He was cunning when he wanted to be, and he was now biding his time before he acted. And when he did act, he was usually fast and accurate. He summed up the opportunities that were presented around him at this time and found he was enjoying the new experiences life was offering him. In particular, little Lois was gaining importance in his heart, as he could see her beauty developing as a young mother, and this appealed to him, as he missed his late wife and the family he never had. Lois was young and could have other children. He had decided to go with Lone Eagle and accompany him on his travels to his grandfather's plantation. Over the years, Grey Fox had become more confident in his abilities; he had learned that by observing carefully, you could be fairly sure about possible outcomes.

Grey Fox still had difficulty thinking Lone Eagle was Emile, but this role playing was pretty good, and his Mexican and American languages were improving in leaps and bounds. He was beginning to think of himself now as Joe Fox, the Indi-American. Lois was helping him understand American ways, which she had learned while living on the ranch, and as he had ideas about running his own horse farm, all the knowledge he could gather would make his dreams more accessible. If Lois were to accompany him to Mexico, and Emile's grandfather gave Joe Fox a job, then they could have a good life, working towards building their own family and farm. The more Joe Fox thought about this idea, the more he liked it. He sent up a silent prayer to the Sky Spirits to aid his quest. If it was meant to be, it would happen, he felt sure.

James had taken his vision quest only three summers ago, as he had never been particularly curious about any one animal, but seemed to get on with all of them. By being named White Feather, there were a number of white-feathered birds that could be his totem animal. The one that he thought would be his choice was a white owl, as it symbolised the wisdom and illumination he sought. From the time he had taken his vision quest, he had developed inner-seeing, which was an extension of his gift of contemplation, from when he had journeyed into the mountains to commune with the Sky People. An owl feather is silent, and he had always been able to walk silently, coming upon people who had not been aware of his presence. He had cultivated being silent in his movements, so as not to draw attention to himself, and this allowed him to move at will and be aware of things others would not.

James knew that he could judge a person's character and know if he was true, no matter how he was disguised. Rainbow Man was such a fellow, as he had changed a great deal and lost the magic he once had, all through overindulging in pleasurable pursuits. He had forgotten that hard work brings its own rewards, and physical endeavours sharpen the mind's focus. James knew he could access the soul's qualities, and he knew Elaina was a good and loving person, as was her father, Dr Westwood. He had observed some of the monks who worked around the mission, and while many of them meant well, others had self-interest in their hearts, and they were not so discriminating when dealing with local suppliers who were devious. He could understand this, though, as the mission monks were trained to be kind to everyone, regardless of origins, and so treated everyone with respect and dignity, even if this was not always warranted. They were often short-changed when dealing with outsiders who saw their kindness as a weakness.

At other times, James had seen the generosity of people from the poor and suffering who came to the mission for help. The afternoon lessons were beginning to become a trial to James, as they put him constantly in Elaina's company. He had to sit near her and converse on all sorts of subjects in American and Mexican; he wondered how long it would take for her to drop her guard, for she had consistently kept their relationship on a professional basis. He could feel himself react to her nearness and sometimes caught her eyes looking at him. Dr Westwood had encouraged him to shave his beard and adopt a more American style of clothes from the Mexican ones he had first worn. This gave him the look of a suntanned American, like many others who were seen around the town.

Father Carlos had asked Dr Westwood to encourage James to become more like an American. As a consequence, his hair had been cut again to collar length by a Mexican woman called Juanita, who had offered her services in return for her son's treatment and cure from an infected leg.

She had also brought James a fruit pie, which he shared one evening with Emile and Joe. Juanita was the same woman who had brought some baby clothes and blankets for baby Eve. It transpired that Juanita had six sons, and James had helped three of them from various infections and hurts, using his natural cures and remedies.

CHAPTER 7

DEVELOPMENTS

Father Sebastian and Father Ricardo were the two main monks who organised the twice-daily mission services and encouraged attendance by everyone, whether they liked it or not. The three friends were not religious in any way but understood it was the religion of Emile's family, so they should at least try to understand Catholicism's practices, for all things that provided knowledge could somehow prove beneficial in unlikely circumstances.

After language class one afternoon, Father Carlos visited them and began to explain the fundamentals of the Catholic religion. In particular, he talked of the holy sacrament, Communion, and the forgiving of sins. He explained it was necessary for Emile to know about such ceremonies, as he would be a part of a highly significant family who were staunch Catholics, and they had to set an example to their employees by showing a high regard for God and demonstrating in their lives godly qualities of leadership and compassion to establish good relationships with those who held the faith. Joe Fox and James looked at each other in silent resignation, knowing they would have to go through this ordeal for the sake of their friend Emile. Following this talk, the three of them attended the evening chapel services.

One of the leading monks would take the evening service in the American language and give a sermon. At first, the three friends could not understand all the words, but after a few weeks, understanding dawned, as some words began to make sense, and it was realised that the sermon was about a man called Jesus, who told stories for ordinary people to understand.

As these stories were repeated each week, the audience of three began to soak up additional words, and their understanding broadened considerably. It was nice to sit and relax for an hour, if nothing else. The statue of Mother Mary with baby Jesus was situated at the centre of the altar. James found that his concentration was always directed to focus on this statue; Mary and Jesus kept catching his attention, and suddenly he found he was dreaming of a ranch where he and Elaina were living, and it was she who was holding a young child in her arms.

He knew instinctively it was his child, with his eyes and hair the colour of the sun. He was shaken by this revelation, as he knew that since the vision was so clear, it had to be a premonition. James had often received visions of living on a ranch surrounded with horses, and in the distance some mechanical structure was working, which he could not identify. There was also another young woman nearby with hair much like his own, but he had put this down to his fruitful imagination and his desire to find what American life was like. He had never been able to see as clearly as the vision he had just received. He felt cold tingles down his spine.

James decided that this Catholic God must be as powerful as the Great Sky Spirit, and perhaps it was so that the son of the Great Spirit was this Jesus, who had come to other peoples as their God, for he dominated the lives of those who worshiped him and followed this religion. James observed these ceremonial services and recognised that powerful energies were generated by the many prayers sent as healing thoughts, to help people and bring peace between all. James could not fault the sentiments generated by the prayers from the mission monks, but preferred his own personal communication experience at dawn, when he would commune with the Sky Spirits, who would answer his questions directly. Native people would congregate in groups at opportune times to align with nature's monthly moon and solstice events. James did understand that the evening services of hymns and sermons were the Catholic way of raising the energies to the higher vibrations, where communion to spirit sources could be made. What he couldn't understand was why they needed to have twice daily services, unless there were so many people who required spiritual aid, for which two services a day were warranted.

Fernando visited the mission twice a week, and each time he came, he brought greetings from Consuela and Lena. Lena's husband had arrived two days after the baby was born and was surprised at the happiness of his wife, who had been so worried and depressed before the arrival of their son. Pedro had come with Fernando on this visit, just to thank James and Elaina for their assistance at the birth. He was surprised to find James more of an Americano than a Mexican and thought his wife and her mother had mixed things up when they had described him. Pedro was introduced to Emile and was sworn to secrecy about his relationship to Emmanuel Cortez. Pedro was able to confirm that the Cortez ranch required more horse trainers, particularly good ones, and in fact required a senior horseman, as Sanchez Cordello had left recently on receiving a call from the palace in Mexico City.

Pedro volunteered to take a missive to the Cortez family, informing Emmanuel Cortez that his grandson would be visiting shortly, as after his visit to the mission, he would be travelling with Father Simeon, who was scheduled to visit the plantation within the next month to take the monthly church services. He could also inform the Cortez family that Joe Fox would be accompanying them and was recommended by Father Carlos to fill the role of the senior horse trainer. As a result of this information, all was set in motion for Emile and Joe to travel to Mexico with Father Simeon, when he next left for the Cortez estate.

That evening, Joe took James to one side and told him how he felt about Lois and the plans he had in mind. He wanted to take Lois and her baby with him to the Cortez plantation, so they could make a new life together. He knew Lois was young, but she liked him and admired him, and Joe was sure she would eventually come to love him. He would treat her well, so she felt loved and secure. He wanted children of his own and knew that Lois would make a fine mother, as she was displaying strong instincts towards the child who was born from her violation.

Joe said he would have to ask Lois if she would marry him and rushed off to do just that. Lois had just put Eve to sleep and was descending the stairs to where Joe was waiting for her. Her tummy always fluttered when she was in his presence, as he had a powerful effect upon her. She thought it must be her hormones, but she did like him so much, as he represented strength and safety, and made her feel special and wanted.

Joe held out his hand to Lois and asked her to come outside with him, as he had something he needed to ask her. He had already told Lois about his dead wife and had indicated he wanted a family of his own once he had found a new life opportunity. Outside, he explained to Lois that a life on the Cortez plantation would be a good experience and asked her to come with him to share this new life. Of course, she would have to be his wife, and that way he could be father to little Eve.

Lois was momentarily taken aback, as Joe was offering her all she desired, and she was overcome. She flung her arms about him, and they embraced in a passionate kiss which gave him her answer and sealed her future. By the time James and Emile had reached them, the two were laughing and smiling at each other. Congratulations were given, and plans discussed for a quick wedding before their departure. Father Carlos was consulted, and the wedding arrangements were made for the following week. Father Carlos was pleased with this development, as he knew that Lois would be well cared for by someone who understood her and had sufficient experience of life to know what was most important: family living and relationships.

For once, Father Carlos would be pleased to inform her parents of a happy outcome. Father Carlos was always happiest when his plans and schemes came to fruition, as he held great store in the power of prayer and God's benevolence, when he saw the workings of life reveal the hand of divine providence.

The question now remained, what was he to do about James? He had made further enquiries and ascertained that Walter Adams had married Samantha Prentice, twenty-five years his junior, who had produced a daughter only a few months into the marriage, and this daughter would now be twenty-two years old. The wife had gone back East, taking her daughter with her after five years living on the ranch. The daughter had spent school holidays each year visiting her father, until she had finished school at the age of eighteen. She had decided to stay with her father on her last visit, as her mother had remarried and was helping her new husband with his political campaign to be a senator. She had lived at the ranch ever since. Her mother, Samantha, had met and married her second husband after divorcing Walter. The daughter either did not get on with her new stepfather or preferred the freedom and climate of Texas life over the stuffy rounds of political gatherings, where everyone's private affairs were under scrutiny.

Father Carlos was waiting for current information relating to the family, as Walter must now be about sixty-eight years old. He knew Walter's in-laws had invested in his ranch in the early days and presumed that the daughter was looking after her inheritance, as she was his only child and heir. He knew also that Jonathan Westwood's late wife had been a relation to the Adams family, and he believed that Elaina was a distant cousin to the Adams girl. He should receive a letter shortly which would tell him what he wanted to know, so he could put in motion some more plans, which should offer life opportunities to Elaina and James. Father Carlos had persuaded James to remain at the mission on the pretext he was fixing him up with a job on an American ranch, so that he could improve his language skills further and learn the culture first-hand.

During the next week, Fernando brought extra supplies to the mission, so they could have a wedding feast Mexican style, as this was all that was needed for everyone to get excited. The Mexican culture loves celebrations, and the mission monks were pleased to conduct a marriage service, particularly a Christian service for a couple who were ethnically non-Christian. Juanita with her family called all her women friends together to enlist their help. They found a wedding dress and veil, suitable for Lois to wear.

Milo magically produced a white suit for Joe but would not tell anyone where he had obtained it. The afternoon language lessons were conducted in American, the topic being marriage and married life. The tension James was feeling each time he faced Elaina was building to breaking point, and he wondered how long it would be before either of them acknowledged what was growing between them. It was during this week of arrangements that Father Carlos received the information he was waiting for.

More information revealed that the daughter of Walter Adams, named Julianne, was in fact his granddaughter. He had married a pregnant wife and taken her expected child as his own. Samantha Prentice had been engaged to Walter's son Wesley, who had been killed by unknown assailants, and Walter had married this young lady to save face and protect his family name. Now Father Carlos knew that James had a grandfather and half-sister as American kin. Whether either one would welcome James as a relation would be another matter, but Father Carlos had already got James an identity certificate and lodged it with the Records Bureau.

The records now showed the name of James Adams, son of Wesley James Adams. The record clerk had interpreted the word "white" as descriptive, being a white American as distinct from a Negro, Mexican, or Indian. He had recorded the relevant dates of birth, provided by the details engraved upon the identity tag James had provided, and James's own statement of his birth date, which was exactly nine months after Wesley Adams went missing. Father Carlos intended to get James to visit his grandfather's ranch, either by working as a hired hand or by some other method he had yet to work out. Providence would provide, he would say, as his request to the Lord above had been sent out, and he was certain that something would turn up in answer to his call.

Meanwhile, James must be kept active and he had an idea that helping Dr Westwood would be just the ticket. Elaina was due to visit her grandmother soon, as she did each year, and would have to journey back East. She might need a travelling companion, as Dr Westwood had indicated he had too much work to do at the mission and couldn't take three months off for an annual holiday.

The journey to Richmond could take from two to four weeks overland. This all depended on the regularity of stagecoaches and trains. Father Carlos would have to have a chat with Dr Westwood to sound out his plans for Elaina, so they could both put their heads together regarding the young people. The wedding celebrations were set for the end of the week, when there would be a lull in harvesting and replanting.

The stables needed cleaning out and the courtyard tidied and decorated for the celebratory event. Emile, Joe, and James volunteered to clear the stables, as they were used to doing this sort of work, and it made a change from working in the fields. They would make a space for storing bales of hay and straw, which could be brought in from the fields after harvesting, so a lot of coming and going would be eliminated by having many people fetch the bales of hay. A large stock could be stored adjacent to the stables, and some of these bales of hay could be used for seating during the wedding feast.

Everyone was busy doing something, and James seemed to be even busier at the clinic than ever before. Sometimes, a person would arrive with an ache or a pain, and James would prescribe a hot or cold compress to ease muscle cramps. Then he would be given a present for the marrying couple or even something for himself, which he found touching. By the evening of the wedding, there was a small pile of wedding presents stacked in one corner of the infirmary. All of the presents had been donated by the local families, whose family members had received recent medical treatments. This was the ethnic community at their best, ensuring that they would all receive an invitation to the celebrations, as the mission would not deprive them from such a joyous occasion.

The stables had not been so spick and span for years and now held three more horses, being those the three friends had left behind at Fernando's farm when they first arrived at the mission. Emile and Joe would need their horses when they travelled next week to the Cortez plantation. James was pleased to have his horse available, so he could get back to doing some proper riding. Fernando had brought an old saddle from his barn and told James he would have to put this on his horse if he was to pass for an Americano. An Indian horse blanket would not do at all. There remained only one thing outstanding, and that was to retrieve the goods hidden in the cave behind the waterfall. Horse feathers and decorations, blankets, knives, and their Indian clothes were not essential, but the one thing James wanted to retrieve was the Army sword of his white father, and the small pouch which housed his crystal stones, medicine leaves, and the ring, key, and timepiece originating from his birth heritage. The timepiece was particularly important, as it was fashioned as a locket which opened to show an old picture of a white woman. While this had faded a little, it had kept its clarity, as it had been closed and kept in the dark for the past twenty or more years.

James had only seen this picture once, when Rainbow Man had handed over these items, which he had kept secure throughout the years. A thought came to him when he could accomplish the task to retrieving these items. He would have to visit Fernando's farm on the pretext of seeing how Lena's new baby was growing and say goodbye to Lena and Pedro before they departed for Mexico. If he could persuade Elaina to accompany him, it would be a nice afternoon's ride with a meeting to enjoy with friends as well.

It was a Saturday and the day of the wedding between Joseph Fox and Lois Reno (or Grey Fox and Little Fawn). The chapel service was held at midday, with Lois looking like a beautiful blushing bride, all dressed in white, with a beautiful white lace Mantilla headdress. Little Eve was also dressed in a white flowing gown, as her christening would follow the wedding ceremony. Eve was held in Juanita's arms, as she was acting as maid of honour, and her six sons followed behind her, all cleaned up and wearing a colourful collection of shirts. Following behind them was her husband wearing his Sunday best, which could have been the same suit he had worn for his marriage to Juanita twelve years earlier.

All the men who entered the chapel wore hats of either black or brown leather, panama straw hats, or wide-brimmed sombreros. Women wore straw hats or scarves, and those who wore scarves were most colourful. Joe Fox wore the white suit given to him by Milo, which consisted of white cotton trousers and white shirt, with a long cream embroidered waistcoat, which was obviously a treasured article which someone had loaned for this occasion. The long waistcoat was embroidered with a design stitched with pearl beads and was a most splendid ceremonial garment. Joe wore his hair as one plait down the back under a fine panama hat, with a cream ribbon around it, to match the waistcoat. The two made a remarkably good-looking couple. James and Emile had dressed in their white outfits, which were newly starched, with cotton trousers and white shirts.

Emile was wearing a colourful Mexican waistcoat, while James wore the dark plain hat and a long coat of the Mexican gentry, with a red and orange cravat, which livened up an otherwise plain outfit and matched the ribbon around his dark hat. It had been Lois and Elaina who had authorised their outfits as being acceptable for such an occasion.

The chapel was packed with many of the mission workers who had been given a day's holiday, together with locals who were either merchants or clients who had received medical treatments from the Drs Westwood and Adams.

Elaina was Lois's bridesmaid and was dressed in a simple but lovely blue cotton sundress, which made her look cool and collected. She was smiling as she took her place in the front row of pews, set aside for near family relatives. Since Lois did not have her family around her at this time, the Westwoods had stepped in to be her surrogate family. James had been commandeered to be best man, seeing he was Joe's nearest relative, and Emile was second attendant to the marrying couple.

James found himself standing next to Joe, his uncle; he held in his hand two plain gold rings, which had been given to him by Father Carlos to give to Joe at the ceremony. The small one was to be given to Lois as her wedding band, and the larger one was for Lois to give to Joe, as his wedding band, symbolising their joining. These two gold rings were the wedding presents from the mission monks, who were all for regularising their practitioners. Following the wedding ceremony was the christening of baby Eve and her formal adoption by Joe and Lois. After the ceremony, people found their way out into the large courtyard for refreshments and toasts.

During the exodus of a hundred people from the chapel, Father Carlos arranged for Joe and Lois to sign their names on the legally binding paperwork, which sealed their fates together and legitimised baby Eve. These documents were to form the basis of their new lives and that of their children. Their joining was now documented in official records, and any property or wealth that either party generated in their lifetime and wanted to leave to their children would be governed by this documentation. It would prove legal ownership to those who were legitimately related.

CHAPTER 8

MOVING ON

The wedding guests had congregated outside in the courtyard, which was shielded by the buildings and chapel where food and refreshments were being served. Music was played on guitars and tambourines, and people were mingling or sitting on the bales of hay, chatting to each other. An Indian worker came up to James to ask if he could attend his father, who had been bitten by a snake and whose leg was swollen so bad, he could not walk.

Dr Westwood was busy socialising, so James asked Father Carlos if he wouldn't mind if he left the wedding party to attend to this emergency. At that moment, Elaina was joining them with two drinks in her hands. She enquired where the incident had taken place and where the patient resided. It was in the far fields where James had not ventured to before, so they were told. Elaina offered to go with James to show him the way and to be on hand if he needed any help, but first they would have to change into work clothes and more sensible footwear. The part of the estate where the Indian worker had indicated his father was located was out of sight when viewed from the main mission buildings, as it was too far away to be seen directly.

A group of Indian workers had set up camp there, preferring to keep to themselves. Elaina knew of their location but had never visited their base, as they were Indians from the Shoshone and Comanche tribes, originating from the interior plains and desert. One or two were involved with the cattle drives, which took them homeward for a visit, but at other times, they preferred to live as farmers, working the land and growing food for themselves and the mission.

Elaina had never had anything to do with this group before and was glad that she had James for company. After finishing their drinks, they both changed into trousers and boots. James had asked the Indian messenger to gather some river weed and had explained where it could be found. He would meet him there shortly with his horse. The messenger had come on foot, so he rushed off to do James's bidding. Instinctively, James went to his own horse to ride, but it had not yet got used to a saddle, so he had to ride it using a horse blanket.

Everyone was involved in the wedding celebrations, so it was unlikely that anyone would take much notice of what James was doing. Elaina had picked up a medical bag and was saddling her horse, Silver, a grey mare. They began riding towards the river, where they would meet up with the Indian messenger. It occurred to Elaina that the messenger had spoken in a Mexican dialect, although she had overheard words spoken in another language, which must have been Indian. Elaina knew that this group of Indians belonged to a different group from James, so she wondered how he would react and how they would respond to him.

Word had spread throughout the mission that he was a natural healer, and that appealed to the ethnic population, as they revered shamanic practices and looked on white man's medicines with some suspicion. The messenger, who had introduced himself as Fast Walker, was waiting for them with two large clumps of river weed in his hands. James jumped down from his horse and gathered up some different water vegetation, saying it might also come in useful.

The Indian doubled up with James on his horse, and the three rode off at a good speed. As they turned a bend, they could make out the Indian camp in the distance. On arrival, it was found there were six dwellings made of earth bricks and twigs, and a lattice framework provided shade covering between the structures. Under the first of these lattice coverings was an elderly man with a swollen leg. He was lying on a sleeping mat, with his head resting on a cushion. His eyes were glazed over as he was beginning to suffer from a fever brought on by the poisons in his bloodstream. A much younger Indian youth who could have been his grandson was bathing his forehead with cool water.

The sun was still strong overhead and had yet to subside into its afternoon setting mode, so the shade from the lattice framework overhead was a blessing. James spoke Indian to the attending youth and then Mexican, so that he could understand. He repeated his instructions in both languages, while Elaina listened quietly. First, the man needed to be bathed in cold or cool water to reduce his temperature; this could be accomplished by using cool stones from the river. Elaina volunteered to fetch these as she knew where the river curved and where smooth flat stones could be found. James also asked her to bring back some river mud, so she took two leather water-carrying bags with her.

They put the river weed into a bucket to keep it moist, and the other weed James had picked from the river was put in another pot, which he asked the youth to boil.

James explained that the goodness in the plant would mix with the water, making it a medicine drink, which was a blood purifier and ideal to bring down fevers and attack the poisons in the bloodstream. It contained absorbing compounds from mountain salts, which acted as a strong blood cleanser. This meant that the patient had to drink as much as he could of this green liquid, as it was vital to eliminate the poisons from the body as quickly as possible. The patient may become delirious first, but once the fever had broken, the healing could begin. James stated that the leg would need cutting, so that the river weed dressing could be packed inside the wound where the snake had bitten; this would allow the healing properties to draw out the poisons gathered locally in the leg. These dressings needed to be repeated every two hours until the fever broke.

In addition, James was going to try something he hadn't done before at the mission. If he had been back at his mountain village, the healers would have used blue earth to cover the patient, so it could also draw out the bad demons raging within the body contours. In the mission grounds, he had not seen any blue earth, so he would have to use the river mud as the next best thing. He logically deduced that the river mud must be full of nutrients brought down from the mountains, so the ingredients would serve just as well.

When Elaina had returned from the river with the stones and the river mud, James instructed that two large flat stones were to be placed under each foot, one in each hand and two more on the belly. While Elaina had been away, James had cut the leg and allowed the pus and poisons to seep out. He had then packed the river weed in and around the wound and tied it up with twine. During this process, the patient moaned in delirium. Once Elaina had returned with the river mud, this was systematically painted on the patient's face, torso, and legs. The mud even covered the wound dressing; the old man looked like a brown-encased mummy.

It had taken approximately an hour to carry out this treatment, and preparations were needed to repeat this all again one or two more times, before the fever broke. The heat of the day was beginning to drop, but it was still warm; Elaina and James decided to take their horses to the river for a drink and to gather more supplies of mud and stones. There was a small well nearby, supplying drinking water, but this was warm water coming from underground.

While the patient was sleeping, James and Elaina went to the river and left Fast Walker and the Indian youth watching over their patient with instructions to get him to drink the green liquid if he should wake. Elaina was anxious to ask James what he thought about the success of his treatment, as she had not seen a mud wrap used before. James was in deep thought, and because he was so used to being with Elaina, he did not register her words at first. He didn't feel like being examined and resented the momentary intrusion into his thoughts. He recovered to find he was more anxious to bathe in the river water, as he was hot and needed to cool down.

He suggested that Elaina do the same, as it could be a long time before their patient was in the clear. He started to disrobe down to the short pants he wore under his riding trousers; Elaina stared open-mouthed at his strange behaviour. But since no one was about, she did as was suggested and disrobed herself to her shift, wading into the shallows at the river's edge. She piled a number of flat stones at the water's edge and then moved to where the water was cool and flowing.

It wasn't a deep or very wide river, so it was quite safe to use for bathing. Elaina rested on a boulder, allowing the stream to wash and cool her. She didn't know where James had got to, as he seemed to have disappeared, but he did this sometimes, so she just allowed the elements around her to cool her down and the sun to keep her warm.

James had found a quiet spot, as he needed a few moments to himself. He realised when he was attending this Comanche elder that he was reverting to his Indian instincts and feeling things with a greater intensity than he ever thought possible. He could feel the concern emanating from the youth and the fear of losing his father coming from Fast Walker.

The weight of responsibility upon him was almost unbearable, so he had to make contact with the Sky Ancestors to relieve this burden from his spirit, which only seemed at peace around Elaina, where he felt he belonged. He didn't understand this feeling building inside of him, where he was not in control. He looked around him and saw Elaina basking in the sun while her body was immersed in the cool water of the river. He crept up to her silently and began trailing his fingers along her body form; he just couldn't stop himself. His nostrils were alive with her feminine scent, and he felt his body reacting in desire. Elaina's eyes sprang open in alarm and then she smiled in recognition, as James held her waist while she found her foothold.

Their bodies were close and fitted together snugly; they could feel each other's heat and interest. James looked in Elaina's eyes and said very quietly, "Now is not the time or place for you to become my woman, but soon you will be, so make up your mind to join with me, or I shall have to make your mind up for you."

Elaina was dazed for a moment and opened her mouth to say something, but before she could speak, James covered her mouth with his. Passion flared instantly between them, and Elaina's hands began entwining James's hair. Just as Elaina was about to succumb to what fate had decided for her, James wrenched her arms from behind his head and stated loudly that they had work to do; they needed to dry off, dress, and take the river supplies back to their patient.

He was right, of course; someone had to be sensible, and on this occasion, it was James. The sun must have got to her head, she told herself, but then did not believe a word of her thoughts. Elaina had to acknowledge she loved James but could not always understand him, for just as she had got to grips with what she thought was his character and personality, he then surprised her again, and again, with his inherent knowledge and abilities. In a civilised world, he would not be her equal, for he did not possess a formal education, but he knew things others did not.

She knew they were both attracted to each other, for she could not dismiss the feelings arising during class time, when they had spent the entire afternoon in intimate conversations under the pretext of language tuition. Elaina scrambled up the riverbank and went behind a boulder; she discarded her shift before dressing in her shirt and trousers. She was much cooler now, and her rational thinking had returned. She gathered the stones, filled another bucket with mud, and met James where the horses were tethered. He nodded in acknowledgement, and they rode back to their patient, resuming their professional relationship of knowing looks and curt instructions. The patient was bathed and rewrapped with dressings, cool stones, and river mud while encouraged to consume the green liquid.

Three more Indian field workers had arrived at this campsite and were taking turns attending and washing the patient. By six in the evening, the sun began to set, and the patient's fever broke. Another wound dressing was placed on the rapidly healing site, which was beginning to show some normal colour. Some of the swelling had subsided, and James said it should be near normal in a few days. He said he would come back the following day to check on the patient.

James explained that the green liquid was to be consumed throughout the night, followed by fresh clean water the next day. No food should be taken until after he had next visited. Fast Walker thanked James and Elaina for their help and marvelled at how well the two of them worked together in accord. He relayed in the Indian language, which Elaina could not understand, that he wished James a long and prosperous life with his yellow-headed wife, and may they have many yellowed-haired children. James smiled and thanked him for his well-meant words.

James and Elaina took their leave from the Indian quarters, feeling that they had both experienced a trial and had triumphed. It was now twilight, and in the distance, you could still see lights in the mission courtyard and hear faint music. James didn't feel like celebrating anymore and stopped the horses beside the river, where they had bathed earlier. He tethered the horses to a bush and then went around to Elaina and lifted her out of the saddle to stand before him.

"Come," he said. "Let's look at the setting sun."

They sat on a grassy spot beside the river and watched the sun sink deeper into the horizon. It was deep orange with reds and pinks, producing a beautiful sunset. James nuzzled his face in Elaina's neck and blew kisses into her ear, arousing her senses, and as expected, she turned her face so their lips could meet.

This time, passion simmered, as James began a slow but determined assault upon her senses; they lay together under the setting sun making slow, passionate love. How they became naked, Elaina was never sure, but she relished the sensual onslaught from James, who was able to achieve erotic delights, inflaming her senses again and again, as he made very sure she became his woman. She had never felt so greatly loved as at that moment, when the stars and sky exploded around her. Afterwards, James took her hand and pricked her finger with his knife until blood trickled. He did the same to his finger and laid both together so their blood joined. He performed this ritual as a small ceremony.

James held her face in front of him and told her, in exemplary American, that from this point onwards, he would follow her wherever she went, until she was ready to follow him. They would always be tied together, for the Great Spirit had decreed as such. James then pointed up to the large star overhead in the sky, which sparkled most brightly. At this precise moment in time, Elaina was certain that James commanded the star movements in the heavens. James suggested they should follow Joe and Lois's example and get married at the mission.

James told Elaina he had contacted the Sky Ancestors, who had encouraged him to make his move now, because events were about to change and it was imperative that they were both joined in their life journey. This was so they could travel together, and James could protect her. Elaina had never been one to take predictions seriously, but when James said something with conviction, she was inclined to believe him, as he was not a person to make things up. She had not told him about the proposed trip back East to visit her grandmother and her other relations. This was part of the conditions she had agreed to, when she had requested to follow her father in his healing ministry at the mission. There were a lot of things James did not know about Elaina.

Somehow, James acted as if he knew that these things did not matter. Elaina was sure a solution would present itself when she spoke to her father, as he was a very level-headed man. It was dark by the time James and Elaina returned to the mission complex. Tomorrow was Sunday, and Joe, Lois, and Father Simeon were to leave the mission and journey to the Cortez plantation in Mexico. It was nearly midnight by the time they both bedded down their respective horses and met again in the infirmary.

James and Elaina had brought back some river weed with them, which would be used in making some more ointment. They also had to replace the medical bag that Elaina had brought with her. James kissed Elaina good night, and both departed for their respective beds. Unbeknown to either of them, Jonathan Westwood had waited up for their return and had dozed off in his office. He had woken when he had heard sounds and witnessed the kiss between Elaina and James and the easy way between them.

He wasn't sure how he felt about a liaison between his daughter and this half-American, even though he liked and admired James, as he just didn't know enough about his background. He would sort it out tomorrow, when all would be back to normal again. It had been a hell of a day, this day of celebration, with many people doing and saying things they would not normally have said or done in ordinary circumstances.

Allowances must be made, as even he had been affected by a visiting American widow, who had approached him with regard to training as a nurse. Camille Stewart was in her late thirties and was a beautiful-looking woman with unlined, perfect skin and complexion. She had lost her husband two years ago when he had fallen from his horse and broke his neck. They had no children, so Camille had stayed at the ranch as cook and general helper to Old Man Thomas, who had recently retired. He had recently sold out his remaining interest to his neighbour, who had bought into the ranch some years before.

Old Man Thomas was a hard task master, but he did have a soft spot for a pretty woman. Looking upon Camille's face and peaceful countenance had served to soften his gruff manner and bring out his human side. Her cooking helped as well, as beef and beans got very boring, so having proper home cooking with a woman's style and touch was a real treat. Old Man Thomas was now going to move in with his daughter up north and had resigned himself to live out his retirement in a more peaceful manner, which did not involve roping horses and branding cattle. He had enough money to last him his lifetime and leave sufficient for his daughter and grandkids thereafter.

Camille was looking for another position which would provide accommodation and give her something to work towards. She liked helping the poor and sick, and was a faithful supporter of the mission, as she had been helped by the monks when she and her husband had first come to this region some six years earlier. Dr Westwood was thinking that he would need another assistant if Elaina went to visit her grandmother. If James went with her, it would leave him on his own to cope with the expanded practise that had developed as a result of James's role as a natural healer. Jonathan had learned a lot from James's natural therapies, but he had also passed on some conventional medical knowledge to the younger man, which would be useful in differing environments.

James should now be able to operate in two different worlds, which would prove useful to him in his life's changing circumstances. Tomorrow was another day, when the wedding party was departing to Mexico and Fernando's daughter Lena needed to be checked to make sure all was okay before their departure back to the Cortez estate. Pedro and Lena would travel across country through the back trail over the high hills, where there were no border guards. The monks with their entourage would take longer on their journey, as they were carrying supplies of religious Bibles written in the Mexican language. They distributed these wherever they went, and this meant stopping at every village on the way. It was their way of spreading the word of God.

CHAPTER 9

BREAKING AWAY

As always, the mission awoke early at daybreak, so there was some movement when Lois and Joe emerged from what had been Lois's bedroom. It was the first time Joe had slept indoors, but it had not registered in any great way, as his mind was on other things. He did so love the big soft bed, for that was where he had initiated Lois into the beauty of erotic lovemaking, as she was innocent, even though she had birthed a child. Little Eve had slept throughout the night while the two adults had enjoyed each other. Lois was still full with breast milk, and this became a sensory delight when Joe caressed, cuddled, kissed, or licked virtually every inch of her body. Lois had never been made love to before, so it was an initiation which she found exceedingly pleasing. Joe was delighted at her responses, as he knew instinctively where to touch for arousals of the best kind. Lois was so small, but so exquisitely formed. It was lovely to have such a responsive wife, who enjoyed all the things that went on between a man and woman, that they both favoured and received pleasure from. The two newlyweds, with little Eve duly fed and cleaned, came down for breakfast with wide grins on their faces.

Most of their belongings, which were not that much to speak of, had been packed and were already loaded on the travelling wagon, which was transporting some basic furniture and the mission Bibles. There were more personal items yet to be packed, if you counted the wedding presents, many of which were still unopened. Joe and Lois had sufficient for the journey, so the wedding presents were packed in a sack, to be unwrapped when they reached their destination. The assembled travelling party was ready to leave by late morning.

James and Elaina had met in the infirmary with the express wish of talking to Jonathan, but he was busy with two patients and suggested that the two of them go to visit Lena and her baby before they departed for Mexico. This request fell in with James's wish to retrieve his personal belongings from the cave behind the waterfall, behind Fernando's farmhouse. James nodded in agreement to Jonathan and said they would see him again tonight on their return and give him all the details of what they encountered at the Indian camp last evening. They would visit Fast Walker's father on their way to Fernando's farm, to make sure he was recovering.

It was decided that James would saddle his horse to see if it would take the saddle with ease or require some coaxing. Elaina would take the buggy so if there were any fruits or vegetables ready to bring back, they could be loaded in the back. They both went to the barn to saddle up. As soon as they entered the shadows of the barn, James pulled Elaina to him, catching her unawares. He kissed her fiercely and then deepened the kiss when he felt she was responding to him. Some noise disturbed their brief interlude, but both felt the electricity still hanging in the air.

It was James who spoke first, saying, "Come, we had better hurry, or we will never get to Fernando's farm to say goodbye to Lena and her family."

James followed the buggy around the dirt track at the edge of the mission's fields and followed it around the bend to the Indian camp. James told Elaina to stay in the buggy while he attended to Fast Walker and his father. He found Fast Walker's father sitting up and being attended to by the youth he saw yesterday, which he confirmed was his grandson. They were pleased to see James and introduced themselves formally as White Water and his grandson, Long Walker, son of Fast Walker. Fast Walker was working in the field today and had left the two looking after each other. Long Walker was about fifteen summers, and his grandfather was elderly and weather-beaten from living in the sun. James inspected the wound, which was still swollen, but the swelling had stopped spreading, and the fever was now gone.

White Water had been washed free of the river mud and complained that the green liquid made him want to pass water every hour, so he had to keep relieving himself. James smiled and explained that the green liquid was supposed to flush away all the poisons in the body, to leave the blood pure and free, to effect the healing of the wound area. The wound still needed to be dressed using the leaves of the river weed, as this kept the area clean and free from further infection. James suggested that if White Water could manage to get to the stream, he could bath in the cool waters and dress the leg afterwards. If he could manage to walk a little, it would restore the blood circulation to the body and make him feel stronger, as he bet he felt pretty weak right now.

James thought it would give the two of them something to do, even if they both felt as flat as a burst balloon. James then suggested that while they were at the river, they should contact the Sky Ancestors to ask for spiritual healing.

James told them he was a great believer in seeking help from the Sky Spirits, as that is where he got his strength and knowledge from. White Water was impressed and caught his arm in a gesture for James to listen to his words. He told James he had already been visited by the Great Sky Spirit, who had helped him overcome the fever and was responsible for sending James to him. James ought to know that his life was being directed from the Sky Spirits, who had told White Water that James would soon be leaving the mission and journeying to new lands with his new wife. James was to make sure he was formally and legally joined before they set off on their journey, for if they were not, forces would arise to separate them.

White Water told James to watch for his first-born, who would be blond and golden eyed: a golden boy of talent who would command the earth and sky. This child would be greatly blessed as much as James was by his gift of healing bestowed upon him from the Great Sky Spirit. He also told the young healer he would never want for money, as he would be offered more than he could ever possibly need, but he would have to decide where he would live to appease those he loved around him. He must never forget to honour the Sky Spirits, for they were ever present, wherever the sun rose and set. The Great Sky Spirit could take many forms and would show himself in different guises where truth was paramount.

James took his leave and returned to Elaina, who had watched the proceedings. She had not understood the words spoken, as they were in an Indian dialect, but she had got the gist of praying to the Sky Spirits, which to her was the ethnic way of saying thanks to God and the Christian Lord. James just told her that things were alright and progressing well, so there was nothing to worry about. He motioned to turn around and retrace their steps to pick up the road out of the valley toward El Paso, where they would be turning right to follow the hill track to Fernando's farm. It was now high noon, and the sun overhead was at its peak. James was wearing a leather cowboy hat, and Elaina was wearing a wide-brimmed straw hat with a string tied under her chin. The pony seemed to be comfortable bearing a saddle. This one was very old and supple, being made of very soft leather.

Elaina looked at James, who looked just like an American cowboy with soft leather jeans, cotton shirt, and a Stetson hat. She wondered at the change at him in so short a time and remembered the first time she had really looked at him, when dressed as a Mexican grandee.

He had seemed so aloof and grand; she had wondered if he was a Mexican royal, as he had that certain standing which commanded your attention. She had fallen in love with the healer, the dreamer, the eager student who loved everything about her and took what she said to heart. She loved his sense of humour, as it was subtle and deep.

Elaina loved James's great human understanding that cut across religion and culture, as he treated people the same regardless of race, colour, or creed. To Elaina, he demonstrated all the good virtues that were preached in the Christian religion, even though he didn't fully understand the doctrine. He knew the spirit of the deity, whatever name was used to describe it. James knew how to love and demonstrated it in a hundred ways, by the little niceties of giving, which was love in action. She was still glowing from last evening's lovemaking, and the quick kiss and caress in the stables confirmed he was still consumed with passion for her, as she was for him.

By the time they reached Fernando's farm, they were both hot and dusty. It was the traditional time for a siesta, and Elaina wondered if they could have a nap to restore their strength. The horses were tired, having been ridden uphill all the way. On the farm door was a note to say everyone was out and would be back by six in the evening. There was an invitation for anyone to help themselves to water and food in the kitchen. James unhitched the horse from the buggy and put him in the corral, where there was shelter in the barn, plenty of hay, oats, and a water trough. He told Elaina to mount his horse, as he knew a nice place to cool off. She did this, and James walked the horse towards the forest tree line. Once in the shade of the tall trees, it was much cooler, and if you listened carefully, you could hear water running in the distance. James followed this sound and stopped beside the pool with the waterfall which looked inviting.

"Thought you might like a swim," he said to Elaina, and her eyes lit up at the thought of all that cool water.

She slid down from the horses back into James's arms; he held out his hands to catch her. She caught her breath as she descended. He put his arms around her shoulders and led her to the water's edge, suggesting she enter the water first. He went back to the horse and tethered it, so it could drink its fill of water. While Elaina was disrobing, he quickly walked around the side of the rock, where he could reach the cave behind the waterfall. James quickly retrieved the items he sought and brought them back to where the horse was tethered. He hung the sword from the saddle and put the small pouch of personal items in the saddlebag.

Elaina was now submerged in the pool of fresh mountain water and loving the feel of the rippling water upon her skin. James quickly disrobed and joined her. He walked round the rock ledge to stand under the waterfall and fell backwards with a large splash into the pool below. He surfaced where Elaina was treading water at the deepest point of the pool, as she was not as tall as James.

The water would cover her head if she was to stand with her feet upon the bottom. James caught her around the waist and propelled her to the pool side, where it wasn't as deep. Neither of them wore any clothes, so this contact of skin to skin stimulated their desire, which was ready to explode. One minute, they were playing together, and the next, they were locked in a passionate embrace. Neither could wait, so their bodies came together, with Elaina clamping her legs around James's waist as he drove into her with unrelenting and uncontrolled passion. They climaxed together, and their emotions slowly subsided, as the heat generated between them became cooler with the cold water around them. It was difficult to think rationally, but the cool water sobered them enough to realise it was time to get out of the pool to dry.

There was a horse blanket under the saddle on James's horse, so he put it under the trees so he and Elaina could take their siesta. The noise from the waterfall was a constant hum, which lulled them into a peaceful doze. Sometime later, they both awoke at the sound of birds in the trees. There was a chill now in the breeze, and James instinctively wrapped his arms around Elaina. He loved this woman, who could evoke such responses from him just by touching him and inviting him with her eyes and hands. He would have to speak to her father very soon and get the monks to marry them in the next few days.

If White Water's words came true, and there was nothing to suggest they would not, the information he had imparted had confirmed what James had already been told. Elaina's eyes half-opened as she felt warm and loved being held in James's arms. She held his gaze as he looked down into her eyes and felt herself swimming in a sea so beautiful and peaceful, that she offered herself up to the feelings that were building. James felt the change within her and found his body was responding to hers. This time, he would take things slower, he thought, but no sooner had passion engulfed them than instinct took over, and they were writhing on the blanket like two animals in heat. Their joining was just as explosive as it had been earlier.

By the time they came back to reality, the breeze was much cooler, and they dressed quickly and saddled the horse. James had told Elaina they would be leaving the mission soon and they should get married before they left, so it would be easier to travel together through the American lands. Elaina had not got round to telling James about her intended trip to her grandmother's, nor of the fact she couldn't get married without parental permission until she was twenty-one years old, which wasn't for three more months.

She agreed with James and said all could be sorted out when they met with her father later that evening. James and Elaina made their way back to Fernando's farmhouse, where they made themselves at home in Consuela's kitchen. They had some bread and cheese dipped in some chili mix, which was very tasty. Elaina suggested they go and look through the trunk in the barn for any clothes that would fit James. Because he was so tall, some of his clothes were short in the leg. This didn't matter if he was working in the fields, where no one important could see him, but he needed clothes to be more presentable in outside society. His one and only outfit other than working apparel was the long trousers and long waistcoat that Fernando had first given to him, that made him look like a Mexican grandee.

A further half an hour was spent in discovering the delights hidden in this chest of assorted clothes. Two more trousers were found to be a perfect fit for James, having long legs and a trim waist. One pair were American denim and very hard-wearing, with the other a beautiful light doe leather skin made with fine cream stitching on the sides, and a design upon the pockets made of the same cream stitching. Someone had put a great deal of love and time into making these trousers, and Elaina wondered what story they could tell. There were three shirts, one coloured, one white, and another which had ruffles down the front. This went with a short black waistcoat that was the same material as a long coat with velvet lapels. Next, there was a lovely emerald-green velvet jacket. This would pair up with the cream trousers and make a smart, expensive-looking outfit. Amongst the clothes were some hats and a straw trilby, worn by many Easterners.

Elaina gathered these together and packed them neatly in a carry bag. In another trunk, she found shoes and leather waistbands with varying buckles. Elaina picked a pair of leather sandals and a formal pair of soft leather slip-on shoes, which would be ideal to wear with the light beige trousers and emerald jacket.

She knew they were the right size as she had measured them against the canvas loafers James was already wearing. They had just got back to the buggy to load their things and were hitching the horse back into the reins, thinking that Fernando's family were running late, when noises were heard and the wagon came into view, full up with produce and people. Lena and Pedro came to greet them first, followed by Consuela, carrying baby Phillip. Fernando saw to the horses before getting down from the wagon to add his greeting to them both. He insisted they celebrate in style by having a drink and brought out a bottle of fine wine.

Although both James and Elaina told him they did not drink alcohol, he had poured them a glass each, so they both had to drink this beverage. It was a red wine, which was not unpleasant. James felt the liquid burn his throat and stomach, and he experienced warmth flooding through him. If this feeling occurred after only one glassful, goodness knows how it would affect a person if they drank a whole bottle. James now knew how others must feel when they drink more liquor than just a single glass. James could feel his face redden in warmth and said they must leave, as it would be dark shortly.

Lena and baby and the rest of the family were in high spirits and perfectly healthy. There was no need to do a formal examination, as Lena reassured both Elaina and James that baby Phillip was fit and well. They exchanged farewells and promised not to lose track of each other. They all knew that they could get word to each other via Emile or Joe. The mission was a central point for communications, and forwarding letters and messages to most places occurred by one means or another.

Fernando took only minutes to load some produce into the buggy and wave goodbye to James and Elaina so they could start back. It wouldn't take so long getting back to the mission, as it was all downhill. With both James and Elaina fortified with a glass of wine, the chill of evening went unnoticed, and the horse and buggy seemed to float down the hillside with ease. By the time they reached the mission, James's mind was once again clear, and the purpose of confronting Jonathan Westwood about his daughter's future was once again uppermost on his mind. He unloaded the produce from the buggy into the kitchens, bedded down the horses in the stable and stored the buggy in the barn.

James had arranged to join Elaina in the infirmary, where they hoped to meet with her father. When James arrived at the infirmary, he found Jonathan Westwood entertaining a very attractive older woman. They had obviously had dinner and were finishing off a bottle of wine. Jonathan invited James over and introduced Camille as a new assistant to the clinic. James said he didn't know that the clinic needed another assistant, but Jonathan, not realising that James was uninformed, said that when Elaina went back East, he would need to replace her. James's face fell at the news of Elaina leaving the mission; she had not told him this. It was like a bowl of cold water being thrown on his face. Why was she leaving? Why hadn't she told him? He needed answers. He got up and left Jonathan and Camille, who watched his abrupt departure with opened mouths.

He found Elaina coming down the stairs after changing into a dress. He was angry. He had never felt so angry. His emotions were out of control where she was concerned. Without provocation, he accused her of deceiving him and using him and then trying to leave him. He was so fired up he wasn't making sense, as he had reverted to his Indian dialect, which Elaina could not understand. What Elaina did understand was that something had upset James to the extent he had erupted, and his emotions were all over the place. She placed her hand on his arm and lifted her lips to kiss him, which calmed him down. This act was to reassure him that everything was alright between them. Elaina knew that James was emotionally vulnerable in situations not under his control, and that today had unlocked emotional depths that even she had not fully understood. She was in full view of anyone passing by, but she didn't care anymore about propriety. She was James's woman, and that was that. She was concerned about him, as she had never seen him like this before.

As luck would have it, Father Carlos arrived on the scene and wondered what on earth was happening. He took command of the situation, as he could see it was emotionally explosive, and walked the couple into the infirmary, where Jonathan and Camille were sitting. Father Carlos, being old and wise, suggested that everyone calm down and start talking about what troubled them, as talking was a good way to get things sorted. Father Carlos said that he had lived this long and survived wars and hostilities, and at the end of the day, it was about sorting problems out by talking, which had brought peaceful solutions. He was stretching the truth, but it didn't matter, as it was the thought that counted.

Father Carlos asked what had made James angry. Jonathan believed it was something he said without thinking, and he rightly thought it was the fact that he had mentioned his daughter was leaving the mission shortly. What he hadn't explained was that she visited her grandmother back East every year, and it was coming up to that time when she would do so again. It was also a time when Elaina could source certain medicines which were only available in the Eastern states and bring supplies back with her, as she had done last year. He apologised to James if that information made him angry, but he had hoped that the relationship between James and his daughter was such that James would accompany Elaina as her protector in the absence of himself, who could not leave the mission without a doctor for the three-month vacation that was envisioned. James finally understood; he was relieved but embarrassed that he had jumped to conclusions, without knowing all the facts. James assured his future father-in-law he would accompany Elaina, not as her protector but as her husband.

He had every intention of marrying Elaina before she departed on a journey that would take her away from the mission. James stated very firmly he would marry Elaina without delay, as it was decreed by the Sky Spirits that they should. It was the only way to protect Elaina from circumstances existing outside the mission; he would protect her with his life if he had to. He didn't know about American ways or culture, but he did know what he felt to be true, and he knew without any doubt whatsoever that he was right where Elaina was concerned. He looked straight into Jonathan Westwood's eyes and said that he had made certain that Elaina was his woman, and if he had any doubt, he could ask her. It wasn't very often that Jonathan could be flustered or embarrassed, but somehow, James had been so blunt in telling him that he had taken his daughter, in the physical sense, that he had no choice but to agree to their marrying.

By rights, Elaina's grandmother should agree to her marriage as well, as it had been her mother's wish before she died. Jonathan was sure Father Carlos could get around this small technicality. He took a look at his daughter, who nodded, confirming James's words and giving her agreement. It was therefore agreed by all that they would marry, and Father Carlos seemed pleased with the outcome. He suggested a quiet wedding with just the family members, to be held as soon as it could be arranged.

The priest was relieved that events were turning out as he had planned and that the God he prayed to was looking after his mission folk and sorting out yet another intrigue. The dialogue between James and Jonathan Westwood had not gone unnoticed by him, and he had noticed it had been conducted in the American language on an equal term basis. This had surprised Father Carlos, as it had been James who had kept his control and therefore the upper hand.

It never surprised him more than when one of his prodigies showed unknown depths to their character. He rustled the envelope in his pocket to remind him to reread the letter he had received today. It was time to write more letters and set more plans in motion. He hoped his invitation to Camille, to attend the wedding ceremony of Joe and Lois, had had some positive effect, and it seemed on the surface that it had.

Father Carlos loved matchmaking and performing the marriage ceremony, as he felt that it was the way God worked, to keep goodness revolving, by forming families in loving relationships, all of whom upheld the mission complex in financial and actual prosperity. Father Carlos believed in happiness of the inner soul.

"God works in mysterious ways his wonders to perform." This was Father Carlos's favourite saying.

CHAPTER 10

CONSPIRACIES
AND CHANGES

Father Carlos and Dr Westwood were in conference the next morning. Father Carlos was verifying that Jonathan's mother-in-law, the mother of his late wife, was sister to the Marianne who had married Captain Prentice, and whose new son-in law was now a prospective senator for the state of Virginia. Marianne Prentice was mother to Samantha Prentice, who had married Walter John Adams, her first husband. Marianne was therefore Julianne Adams's grandmother. This heritage meant that Julianne and Elaina were second cousins. Their grandmothers were sisters; both were still alive, living in Virginia and holding large stocks in many financial and industrial businesses. Both girls shared the same great-grandparents of Theodore and Annie Edwards. It had been Theodore Edwards who had started an engineering enterprise which had then switched to making armaments during the Civil War. This had made their fortunes, and then by a stroke of good luck, their landholdings in Texas and other Southern states struck oil, and more money poured into the family coffers.

Hence, after Samantha married Walter Adams, investments were made to make the ranch a success, by using the family's contacts with the Army. Subsequently, oil was discovered, and now oil was one of the most profitable streams of income for the Edwards business empire, bringing in a continual and uninterrupted flow of revenue, which had accumulated for the shareholders over the last twenty or more years. Maria Silvano and Samantha Prentice had been cousins who had been as close as sisters while growing up, as both had been educated together when attending an exclusive girl's schools back East. Both had inherited shares in the Edwards Companies, from which dividends had been paid or accumulated, if not drawn. Both girls had travelled West with Samantha visiting her father while he was serving in the Southern Army Corps at Fort Worth, and it was there where she had met Wesley Adams. Maria had met Jonathan Westwood and had followed the newly qualified doctor out West, to serve the frontier communities.

Maria caught one of the fevers which had spread throughout the country after the war years, succumbing when her daughter was eight years old; Elaina attended school in the East, so her grandmother Catherine took over the child's upbringing; and it was Catherine who had arranged for Elaina's schooling and paid for it. Catherine allowed Elaina to visit her father during the summer holidays, and she corresponded with him by letter during the rest of the year. When Elaina reached eighteen, she decided to stay with her father to train as a nurse, rather than attend the finishing school her grandmother had chosen for her.

Elaina declined to return from her annual visit to her father and stood firm in her resolve. She had found a vocation to help people, where it mattered and make a difference. She also found it filled the vacant space in her heart, which had occurred after her mother's death. Catherine did not like the arrangement, but she did understand and gave in gracefully, making sure Elaina visited her each year and thereby reversing the arrangement she herself had put into place, from the time her own daughter Maria had died. Jonathan explained to Father Carlos that Elaina would inherit substantial amounts of money from her grandmother on her twenty-first birthday, which would be in three months.

These monies and investments from the Edwards grandparents were held in trust by Catherine, as they had been her mother's property, bequeathed to their grandchild. Maria had never used her inheritance, as she had journeyed West with Jonathan against her family's wishes. Dividend payments were never drawn, so a small fortune had accumulated, which was Elaina's by right, irrespective of any shares or other inherited property, stocks, or bonds. The inheritance of Maria passed to her daughter,

Elaina, and could be claimed upon marriage if it occurred before her twenty-first birthday, assuming that parent and guardian agreed. That meant that both Jonathan and Catherine must agree to Elaina's marriage to James prior to her birthday. Marriage before the twenty-first birthday without parental and guardian's permission would negate the automatic rights to the inheritance and revert it to Catherine's discretion. Catherine was known to waver with her mood, which could blow hot or cold. Her mood could change according to how strong or weak her opposition was, and whether the idea or notion at hand was to her liking. Catherine was an adversary that many lesser individuals found difficult to overcome.

Father Carlos and Jonathan agreed they had to keep the marriage secret so Catherine would not hear of it until after Elaina's twenty-first birthday. By the time Elaina and James reached Virginia, it would be near her birthday anyway, when her inheritance would pass to her automatically, with no one being the wiser. They could get married again, and this time with Catherine's approval and blessing; then, all would be well. However, if events did not go as planned and an Eastern marriage ceremony did not take place, and a child was subsequently conceived, the child's legitimacy would be preserved by the fact of a recorded former marriage certificate, which Father Carlos would hold safe at the mission. Father Carlos would give a copy to Elaina to keep in a secret place, just in case it was needed. Father Carlos suggested she sew it into the hem of a jacket or shirt when she travelled, so it would not get lost or stolen.

Jonathan and Father Carlos thought they had covered all eventualities as best they could. Now they had to explain it to the couple in question and hoped they would understand and agree to this small subterfuge. James was covering for Jonathan at his clinic and found he liked the work of administering to these locals, whose ailments were general and mostly preventable. To his surprise, he found many of the people he treated were work-worn and depressed; they were not very happy with farming and ranching. It was all because of the overseers who treated ethnic people as slaves to do their bidding. They liked power and status, and they flashed their money around, to show how great they were.

The ordinary workers were not interested in status or power; just finding food and shelter for themselves and their families was sufficient. A number of men worked with horses and suffered deep bruises and grazes from the many falls suffered when breaking in a horse. James was surprised there were no bones broken. Once he had instructed how to make compresses to alleviate the pain and discomfort of bruises and grazed skin, that would considerably lessen the swelling, the patients went away happy. One man had to have a tooth pulled and another, a toenail removed. Elaina was busy mixing some medicine to settle stomach upsets and bowel disorders, as these were always needed in substantial volumes. Strong spices and food affected by the heat were contributors to many stomach problems.

After the last patient left that day, Father Carlos, James, Jonathan, and Elaina sat around the desk in Jonathan's office. Father Carlos tried to explain to James the terms of Elaina's inheritance and told him her grandmother was a very influential and important person, who was not to be angered. Father Carlos would marry them both tomorrow, which would be perfectly legal, but this was without Catherine's consent, as she was not physically present. Catherine could be difficult if she found out about it.

If Elaina married without consulting her grandmother first, she could withdraw the substantial financial donation she always made to the mission, and that could affect its everyday operations.

James understood, then, that this woman, who was Elaina's grandmother, sponsored the mission financially; he saw that many peoples lives and living could be at stake, if she was angered.

It was best to keep their marriage a secret, until after Elaina's coming of age, which was in three months. After that, it would no longer matter. James stated that they didn't need Elaina's inheritance, as he was quite able to provide for a wife and family, but then Father Carlos pointed out he should not dismiss Elaina's inheritance, as he had future children to think of, who might be glad of the inherited wealth, as you never knew what the future held in store. That information made a lot of sense to James, so he decided he would reserve his judgement until he met this grandmother and saw for himself how affairs stood. He knew elderly grandmothers could become very obstinate, particularly when all their children and grandchildren had grown up and left home. They had to exert their authority somehow and boss someone around, which usually were those they thought were weaker or more vulnerable.

James was only really interested in making Elaina his legal wife in the eyes of the American nation, so they could be joined as one, and then no one could take her away from him. The Sky Ancestors had been adamant that they should marry before setting off on any journey, and now James could see why this was necessary. It was a long way to go and a lot of land to cross from the mission near El Paso, Texas, to the town of Richmond in the Eastern state of Virginia. A night's sleep would clear everyone's head, and so all departed to finish any outstanding chores and think about all that had been said.

James kissed Elaina good night before walking to his sleeping quarters in the barn. Tonight, he would sleep inside the barn and not outside it. He might have to start changing some of his ways, as by all accounts those who lived in the Eastern states lived inside buildings because the climate was wetter and cooler than in the warm South. If he was to have Elaina as his wife, he must learn her ways and customs before he taught her his ways. He had already said that he would follow her, until she decided to follow him. This he firmly felt was what the Sky Ancestors had decreed, and they had always given him good guidance.

It was not necessary to understand everything the Sky Ancestors related, but to trust the knowing of Sky Spirits, so that his life and Elaina's would flower in its fullness, at the right time and place. James remembered his vision that had yet to be fulfilled. He saw it again: Elaina holding a blond-haired baby that he knew was his son, standing in front of a ranch house, with some mechanical pumping contraption in the background, which he could not explain or understand. He knew this must be at least a year from now, so he resigned himself to follow life's fated circumstances and allow events to unfold. Little did he know just how transforming the next year of his life would be.

Years later, he would sometimes review this period of his life and thank the Sky Ancestors for their assistance and wise directions. James and Elaina were married the next day in the chapel, with Jonathan Westwood giving his daughter away; Camille was invited to attend as bridesmaid. Milo stood beside James with a big grin upon his face, as he had procured another wedding outfit to fit James, which was very similar to that which he had sourced for Joe only a few days before. Elaina wore a simple white dress, with a flower as decoration in her hair.

Father Carlos conducted the service, with Father Frederick, a young monk, assisting. Papers were signed for recording in the national register and a copy given to Elaina, in case of need. Again, Father Carlos donated two plain gold rings for each to wear as tokens of their commitment to each other.

CHAPTER 11

CENTRAL MADNESS

It was decided that Camille would take Elaina's room as soon as she departed on her journey East, as she would be taking over her job and helping Jonathan care for the community's health and welfare. There were just three days before James and Elaina began their journey East, to meet with her grandmother and other relations. They were asked to carry a box of correspondence from Father Carlos relating to business matters, they were told, which should be given to Michael Silvano, who was Elaina's uncle and a respected lawyer entrusted with the Silvano family affairs. They carried two large holding bags containing clothes and personal items, blankets, a supply of dried food suitable for the journey's overland start, and a water container. They would take the buggy and two horses to travel the first part of their journey, which they could use as a sort of honeymoon, as they would be on their own, travelling overland through the central plains to Oklahoma City. At the rail station, they would pick up a train to transport them north-east to St Louis, and then east to Richmond. The train journey would take a week, as would the overland trek to Oklahoma City.

James stayed with Elaina in her allotted room for a few hours, making love in a soft bed which he found an interesting experience. However he could not settle, so once he was satisfied Elaina was asleep, he left the room to find his own sleeping place outside of the barn under the stars. He found being indoors too enclosed and needed to sleep in the night air.

By dawn, he was wide awake and washed in the bathing pool nearby. He was excused from working during the mornings prior to his departure, so he helped Jonathan in the infirmary. There were patients who had appointments with more stocks of ointments and medicines to be mixed and put in containers for future use. Elaina finalised her affairs and carried out last-minute packing and made sure she carried the open-ended train tickets she had procured from the railway agent in El Paso. The train line had not been connected yet to El Paso, but one day it would be, which would make travelling over the large distances of the interior much quicker and safer. There were still some groups of Indians residing on the central plains who lived as their ancestors had lived and who showed no respect for white settlers or travellers.

James had assured Elaina that all would be well and that he would protect her. He would show her how delightful it was to sleep under the stars and to embrace the experience with joy, as she would remember this time in years to come. Elaina trusted James and knew his instincts were strong in natural surroundings, but his life had been limited, and she worried sometimes if he was as capable and knowledgeable as he made out he was. He certainly was not as worldly wise as she, but she felt certain that together, they could overcome most things. She would teach James all the new things he needed to know about life in the East, which she looked forward to with some interest, just to see his reactions. They had decided to speak American from the time they left El Paso so the language would become second nature to James, and as they travelled, he would absorb more words into his vocabulary as he saw different sights and met different people, living different lifestyles.

Elaina hoped James would enjoy the experience and not be intimidated by so much newness to absorb. They began their journey after saying their farewells, travelling a good distance on their first day across the dry plains. They were treated to a grand sight of a rainbow stretching across the dry earth, bringing colour and exhilaration to their journey. They took the rainbow as a good sign to wish them well.

The first night, James and Elaina made camp besides some rocks to shade them from the strong breezes which picked up from time to time. The wind often stirred up the sandy earth and made it difficult for the horses to travel, so they would have to stop and wait until the wind subsided. By starting early in the cool of the morning, they covered more ground.

Afternoons at high sun time were spent in a Mexican siesta, with the horses uncoupled from the buggy, fed, and watered. In this land of arid dryness, the waterholes had to be picked carefully. They often found a pool between two boulders, and if all failed, then cactus leaves were chopped and the insides eaten as refreshing nourishment. James remembered what White Water had told him about desert conditions and recognised the prickly cactus, which most folk overlooked, as being a life-saving plant.

By the third day, conditions were very hot and sticky, so James found a place amongst some rocks and trees to stop the buggy; he looked around and found a hidden pool, which was ideal for restocking their water supplies, watering the horses, and having a bath themselves. He unhitched the horses from the buggy that allowed them to dress at their leisure. Both James and Elaina were dusty from the trail, so they disrobed to enjoy the coolness of the water … and each other. There was a little shade from the few trees around, which made it a wonderful place to frolic.

James and Elaina indulged their mutual passions, enjoying the sensory delights of making love. They gloried in the intimacy of each other, thereby cementing their personal feelings and making each other feel loved, warm, and safe. After they dried off and dressed again, they tidied up their belongings and then reloaded them on the buggy.

As James was hooking up the horses, he suddenly froze and said very quietly to Elaina, "Do not make any sudden movements."

She became aware they were no longer alone and looked up into the faces of three Comanche braves, wearing no more than breechcloths. A sudden feeling of trepidation came over her, and she looked at James beseechingly.

The braves all held bows and arrows in their hands, and one addressed James in his own language. James replied without looking directly at the one who had spoken, returning the greeting, and then Elaina recognised him as the Indian messenger Fast Walker, who had come to the mission to find help for his father, White Water, who they had treated for a snake bite. James looked at Elaina and told her to get her things into the buggy quickly, as they would have to go with these braves, who had requested they return with them to their camp. You did not refuse such an invitation, so they had no choice but to do as they were bid. For the rest of the day, they followed Fast Walker on his horse travelling west, while the two other braves followed behind the buggy. Around evening time, they came upon a small campsite of a dozen tepees situated amongst some high ground just inside the forest tree line with mountains in the distance.

Who should come to greet them but Chief White Water. It had only been six days since he had been bitten by a snake and here he was, up and about again, residing with his own family in the freedom of the countryside. White Water still had a dressing on his leg and was using a stick to help him walk, but his vitality and life force was once again back to normal. He apologised to James and Elaina if the manner of their greeting with his son was not to their liking, but he had followed their progress upon the interior plains and wanted a chance to thank them both for saving his life. He invited them to dine with him and then spend the night in a spare tepee situated next to his.

The other two braves had gone away with instructions to put on a great display and to get their women to cook some food for their guests. He told James that the Sky Spirits had spoken to him again and had instructed him to carry out a marriage ceremony the Indian way, so that the union between James and this yellow-haired woman could be blessed by the Sky Ancestors. This way, both sides of James's heritage would be satisfied, and it would show he was truly joined to the woman of his choice.

When Elaina heard this, she was surprised but flattered that this old man had taken it upon himself to involve his tribe in James's affairs. James seemed to have a dramatic effect upon people, whoever they were. Shortly, drums could be heard, and James suggested they put on their finery once again for another wedding. He just wore leggings and the long waistcoat but no shirt, as it was still very warm. Elaina put on her white sundress again and found some flowers to make a headdress.

An old woman entered the tepee and smudged some coloured paint upon Elaina's face and did the same to James, which made them looking more Indian. A red headband was placed around Elaina's head and her flowers placed into it. James was given a similar headband with a white feather in his. They stood outside, ready for the ceremony, and were invited to stand before White Water and Fast Walker, who was holding his father upright, so he would not fall. James told Elaina they had named her Sunshine Woman because of her hair colouring; the ceremony that was to take place would be between White Feather and Sunshine Woman.

White Water chanted and waved his pipe over their heads, blessing them, Elaina assumed. He took their hands and nicked their wrists, putting them together and entwining them with a leather cord, wrapping it between the two hands as symbolic of joining as one. The blood of the two would now flow as one; the joining was done.

Merriment began by dancing around the campfire; pipes and drums supplied the beat. Food and drink were passed round. Elaina did not know what she was eating or drinking, but she felt she had to take some of this food, as it would be disrespectful to do otherwise. It was all overwhelming, and Elaina began to feel drowsy, and she looked upon the entertainment as if watching a dream. Before she knew it, she had been picked up and taken into the tepee and laid upon a buffalo skin. Somehow, her clothes disappeared, as she found she was now naked. The buffalo fur felt so soft and warm; she was so comfortable, and then James joined her and wrapped the buffalo fur around them both.

If she had enjoyed her wedding night at the mission, she was enjoying this occasion even more. She certainly was transported to new heights within this tepee. It was magical and enchanting to be loved in such a manner, with the freedom and love generated by people she didn't even know. The music of drums and pipes carried on for a long time, and so did their lovemaking. The pair did not sleep until early morning and were not up and about until midday of the following day, when the sun was at its highest. Knowing looks were given by those they passed when packing up to leave.

Fast Walker advised James to take a slightly different route to his destination and pointed out the water holes he should aim for. In another two days, he should pick up a cattle trail which would take him directly into Oklahoma City. They set out again on their journey at early evening, when the sun was sinking, and as there was a full moon overhead, they were able to drive through the plains for most of the night. It was light and cool for both man and beast, and ideal for covering many miles. Their horses had enjoyed a good rest and had eaten their fill of forest grasses and some grain, so they were ready for a good run.

White Water had given them another horse, so White Feather could ride while Elaina drove the buggy, or one horse could be rested while the other two were pulling the buggy. This was a mighty fine horse and very similar to the one Grey Arrow had brought from Strong Arrow's village in the high hills. It was dark brown with white hair and a white blaze upon his forehead. It was decorated with some white and black feathers in its mane, to show it now belonged to White Feather. It was a larger horse than the two horses pulling the buggy and galloped like the wind. James was very pleased with his present, as he had reluctantly left his own horse at the mission.

The languages of the central plains Indians were slightly different from that spoken in the hills, but it was surprising how you could make yourself understood. Much of the dialogue was done in signs and signals where meaning was transferred. With Fast Walker, who also spoke Mexican, any differences could be clarified and corrected. James was able to ride ahead of the buggy and survey the land. Early next day, he took off on White Blaze and returned with two rabbits. He had used the bow and arrow Fast Walker had given him as a wedding gift, as he wanted to show his skills at trapping and hunting game out in the open country. Dried food was adequate in emergencies, but if fresh food was available, it should be hunted and used, as it was never known what circumstances lay ahead which might produce the need for using the stored dry food.

During the next day, James and Elaina rested by a small waterhole between two rocks. The rocks offered limited shade, so they used the buggy to cast a larger shadow so they and the horses could have a short rest. They decided to ride in the evening again so they could cover as many miles as possible. The land began to change to a greener landscape with trees and grasslands, and they were soon on the Oklahoma cattle trail. Now they could ride and rest at leisure as there was always water and food readily available for both them and their horses.

Over the next few days, they covered the distance of the trail and arrived at the outskirts of Oklahoma City. Drawing near to this town, there had been a number of farmsteads fenced off to keep the cattle from wandering into common lands. As they drew closer, the number of buildings began to increase, until they had reached the town itself, which was a bustling cattle town, housing the railroad junction.

PART 3

ANOTHER WORLD

CHAPTER 12

AMERICAN CIVILISATION

James had never seen so many people gathered in one place. He had never seen such a town with so many houses and so much noise. Elaina directed James to the stable depot, where they could leave their buggy and two horses. Mr Williams had done previous business with the Silvano family and was interested to see who was requesting his assistance. He was an elderly gentleman and commented that Elaina took after her grandmother in looks, as he had met Catherine Silvano many years ago, when she was inspecting some land nearby.

Elaina signed the tab so he could claim his fees for stabling the horses and housing the buggy. If they did not return within three months, he had instructions to sell the buggy and horses and forward the balance to Richmond. Mr Williams was being well paid for his services and dutifully complied with the young woman's wishes. He stored their baggage in safe keeping until the morrow, when they would catch the early morning train. James would be taking his horse, White Blaze, with him on the train, and a baggage car was booked to accommodate him.

Meanwhile, Mr Williams would look after this fine animal, even if it was decorated Indian style. He had given James a questioning look at his choice of horse, but James had not responded, as it was none of this fellow's business, so he did not have to explain anything to him. James had dressed in his American clothes of trousers and shirt, which he left open so he could feel the breeze. Elaina and James walked to the hotel, which was not far from the horse depot. Elaina knew they would get a decent meal here, as she had visited the place on her last trip.

James couldn't keep his eyes off all the people walking up and down the street. They consisted of various nationalities besides the cattlemen who were American, Mexican, Gringos, and European. Elaina said there were some people who were as fair-haired as she. James looked at a funny man who was small with yellow skin and slanted eyes; he asked Elaina what that fellow was called. She explained he was a Chinaman who came from the country of China, which was across the Atlantic Ocean. China was another land mass as large if not larger than the Americas.

Elaina told James the Chinese were industrious peoples and had come to this country to flee oppression and find a life of freedom, where they could work and build a new life. Chinamen were good healers, as they used needles to alleviate pain and knew other ways of healing people's ill; they believed each person was a whole unit, and you had to treat their ailments as part of that whole. Otherwise, if you cured one part, another problem would surface, and so it would continue until you found the original cause. These people were also good at cooking and used different foods that were similar to Mexican dishes, since they used rice and noodles and plenty of spicy vegetables. James wanted to know more about what the Chinamen did with their healing. Elaina said she would introduce him to one shortly, when they had booked into their hotel and had eaten.

The couple only had their holding bags to carry, so as soon as Elaina had booked them into the hotel, she took him next door to a Chinese diner, so he could sample Chinese food. The place was a bit rough and ready; many cattlemen and women frequented this establishment, as it provided the cheapest menu and was the best filling meal you could get in town. Wong's Diner was well known on the Oklahoma Trail. They dined on rice and vegetables and China tea with lemon. James found the food interesting, as it was tasty and warming. Then Elaina took James to visit Dr Lee Wong, the diner's owner's son, whom she had met in Richmond three years earlier; they had travelled West together. Dr Wong had stayed in Oklahoma City while Elaina travelled on by stage to El Paso to meet with her father. Lee was an accomplished doctor, using Western and Eastern techniques, particularly acupuncture. When they knocked on his door, Elaina found him at home on his afternoon off, so he was pleased to receive visitors. Elaina introduced James as her husband and explained that he was also a doctor, using natural medicine much like an herbalist, and he was interested in what Chinese medicine could offer.

Lee showed James some interesting charts of the human body, with lines drawn from head to toes, which he called meridians. He explained that these lines were invisible but carried the life force energy around the body. If conditions were inflamed or required stimulating, points on the body could be poked with a needle (this was called acupuncture), which released the energy flow and brought the body back to equilibrium. Lee also showed James the art of cupping, using the vacuum of a jar to bring out bodily poisons and draw the offending juices to the surface of the skin, where they could be cleaned off and cleared.

James reciprocated by telling Lee how he would cure a similar condition, using natural vegetation, particularly river weeds, as they contained high volumes of minerals washed down by the mountains. Together, they passed three hours in talks; the afternoon was soon over, and Lee had to start his evening surgery. James asked if he could sit in to see how he treated his patients, and Lee consented. Elaina returned to the hotel to rest, and James continued with his medical research until evening when all the patients had been dealt with. Lee and James walked back to Wong's Diner, where Lee introduced him to his parents, who ran the diner and were the cooks. James was then given some information about how beneficial bean shoots were for the digestion.

The Wongs showed him how they cooked the food quickly in a wok, sealing off the nutriments and flavours, so the people would benefit from maximum nutrition. James thanked the family for their good advice and promised to visit them on his return journey from Richmond. James went next door to the hotel to find Elaina, who had spent the time resting, for it would be another long day tomorrow with an early start. He did not like sleeping indoors, as he found it too confining, but tonight, it was preferable to what was outside in this town, with so many people about. The hotel bed was large and soft, which made a change from the hard ground, so he took advantage of indulging himself with softness around him, which included Elaina's voluptuous curves.

At sunup, James and Elaina were ready to leave. They managed to have a quick breakfast of eggs and toasted bread with tea for Elaina and a glass of milk for James. They both made their way to Mr Williams's delivery depot to pick up White Blaze, James's horse, and the rest of their belongings, which were now stored in the travel bags hung over the horse's back. The railway depot was bustling with activity when they arrived, as four carriages were being loaded with prime steers and cattle. They were being transported East for breeding purposes. The front baggage carriage was next to the passenger carriage; this was the carriage booked for James's horse. There was plenty of hay and grain for White Blaze to eat, and buckets hung on the wall were filled with water. White Blaze was coaxed into the travelling carriage, and James made sure he was comfortable and at ease. With the commotion outside of people loading the remaining carriages, the noise from raised voices was so loud that James had to raise his voice to bring calm to the horse's agitation from being in new and strange surroundings.

There was a connecting door between the carriages, so Elaina went through to the passenger seating area, leaving James with his horse.

Their carry bags were packed on upper shelves above their seats, so they had easy access to them and their belongings. James's sword was covered in sacking, and so was his bow and arrow. These items had been left with White Blaze in the horse carriage. The journey to St Louis would take another two days, which meant they would sleep on the train as they travelled through the night. They would have to change trains at St Louis before travelling on to Louisville, which would then take them through to Charleston and then on to Richmond. The train had to stop at the towns to fill up with supplies of fuel and water.

For the next twenty-four hours, James had nothing to do but to look out at the passing landscape. He had never seen a train or ever travelled on one before, so everything about this mode of transport was new and wonderful. Elaina had explained that the train had an engine at the front, with a fuel carriage behind it. The train was fuelled by coal and the driver and his assistant had to continually stoke up the fire in the boiler for steam to be generated; the pressure of that stream would drive the wheels of the train on its track.

The train could travel over lowlands and highlands if it had a track to follow. It was a very quick way to travel, compared to horses and wagons, and could transport many things from one place to another. There were mines in the hills which had their own trains for transporting mineral ore, coal, and rocks used for making roads. Roadways were big constructions called highways, which were permanent tracks that passed through large expanses of land to connect the East of the country to its Western shores. Roads and railways had been constructed east to west but had not ventured as far south yet as El Paso, which was a border town. Soon, however, the railroad would reach El Paso, and journeying to other parts of the country would finally be possible, as all major towns of the American country would be connected.

This was what progress was all about, as far as the American white man was concerned. American industrialists had visions of reaching the hidden resources within the continent and building towns and cities for people to live in. They believed in the industrialisation of this new country, as it would bring prosperity to ordinary American citizens throughout the new United States. Richmond was a hub of new ideas, new industries, and new prospects, which dominated the Southern states. Since the Civil War, the country was rebuilding itself with a policy of equality for all. Ethnic immigrants like the Wong's were bringing in new cultures and new talents for all to share.

Everything was in a melting pot, so on the one hand, you had old prejudices still evident, while on the other hand, progress was leaping ahead, when everyone accepted everyone else's right to a living and allowed each other to have their own space to live in peace.

James was thoughtful as he digested these new concepts. He liked the part about a melting pot of new people and ideas, for he was part of that newness in a way. His brand of healing was as old as the Ancestors, but these white people had knowledge that did not include an ancient understanding of identity, for they were new to this land and were beginning their own heritage and culture, by combining parts of everyone else's, both old and new.

The stop at St Louis was just sufficient to give White Blaze some exercise while the train was refuelling. Elaina had first thought they would have to change trains, but the cattle were being transported to the eastern shores so would be travelling straight to Richmond as they were. In the passenger carriage, two farmers introduced themselves to Elaina and James. They were brothers who ran a ranch outside of Charlottesville, a small town in the Blue Ridge Mountains. This was a hill stop before you reached Richmond, as the big township was located farther downhill on the coastal inlet of the St James River.

Amos and Anthony King invited James and Elaina to visit them any time while they were in the district, as they would like to show them around the local countryside, which was teeming with potential. The brothers were very proud of the fact that they lived in a wonderfully fertile hillside valley that produced rich grasslands for cattle grazing and fertile earth for growing vegetables and vines. They also told them that a monastery nearby was run by nuns and produced Dutch Gouda cheese. The two brothers had bought breeding stock from the cattle barons of the Midwestern states to strengthen the durability and robustness of their herds; they hoped the physical bulk and virility they displayed would produce strength in their progeny. They had also bought three horses to augment their stables. James volunteered to assess the horses, to ascertain their worth regarding their hardiness for hill country. He would do this while the train stopped at Charlottesville, as there would be a delay while the majority of the cattle and horses were unloaded.

The journey was now beginning to be tiresome, but the company of interesting strangers was stimulating, so they spent time in conversation, with James perfecting his language skills to include local knowledge and attain the more Eastern accent, which was slightly more refined and less broad than a Southern accent. James was a brilliant mimic, and it was second nature for him to adopt the local accent wherever he found himself.

Once he heard Amos and Anthony speaking, he adopted their accent in replying, and they never thought to question if this suntanned Americano from the mountainous West was anything other than what he appeared to be. He was certainly knowledgeable on many subjects and friendly and helpful to them, and there was something about him that was truly likable.

When they at last reached Charlottesville and the cattle were being unloaded, James took a look at the three horses as promised. He found these prairie horses were good sturdy workers and would give solid service if treated well. They were all young mares with good temperaments, but one was more skittish than the others, so would need extra attention on arrival. They could be trained by their riders and moulded into congenial animals if their owners were firm but kind, and if they had plenty of grassland to graze upon, they would be fit and robust.

In James's opinion, they were ideal brood mares and suggested they could be serviced by White Blaze. When he showed his stallion to Amos and Anthony, they were impressed by the superiority of James's horse. A definite visit was required once these mares were settled in, so they invited him to visit them in a few weeks. James and Elaina waved goodbye to Amos and Anthony, who left the train well pleased and with smiles on their faces. They settled down for the last part of their journey, which was only a few hours away. It had taken them nearly a month to reach Richmond from when they had first left El Paso. Elaina wondered how her father was getting along with his new assistant, Camille.

In fact, they were getting on very well indeed, as each was taken by the other, both professionally and personally. Camille was turning out to be a very competent nursing assistant; she picked up procedures and treatments very quickly. Jonathan taught her about mixing the medicines and making ointments so stocks could be replenished. Father Carlos had popped his head around the door to say hello one day, and seeing as everything was progressing along nicely, with two heads close together, he left, smiling to himself and knowing that God was doing his miracles, to the satisfaction of all parties. He just hoped that James and Elaina were progressing along as well as Jonathan and Camille. Give it another month or so, he thought, and there might be another wedding. He did so enjoy weddings.

CHAPTER 13

RICHMOND

The train pulled into Richmond around mid-afternoon, and it took another hour to disembark from the carriages and make sure White Blaze was able to cope with the noise and bustle of town life. Rail junctions were always busy places with people, freight, and animals coming and going. Elaina led James, who was holding White Blaze's reins, to the road outside of the station yard gates. A carriage with two horses was waiting; the black carriage driver remained in his seat while another man alighted from the carriage and waved to Elaina, who rushed forward to embrace this elderly white-haired man, her grandfather, Phillip Silvano.

Elaina was about to introduce James as her husband when she remembered about keeping their marriage a secret until after her birthday. She therefore introduced her grandfather to Dr James Adams, her fiancé. She saw her grandfather's eyes light up in surprise, as he was obviously not aware that she had pledged herself to marry. Elaina briefly explained that James had been working with her father at the mission, and that was where they had met. Phillip saw in front of him an imposing figure of a young man who was obviously self-assured, as he had no trouble with eye contact. He was scrutinising Phillip to get the measure of him, while Phillip was doing the same to him.

James knew that Elaina's grandfather was of Spanish origin, so he greeted him in his best Spanish-Mexican. Phillip noted that his speech was very clear and understandable, but he noticed the slight drawl of a

Southern accent. Pleasantries were exchanged; Elaina enquired about her grandmother and was told she had taken to her bed with an infected leg. She was waiting for the doctor, so that was why she was unable to welcome Elaina home and so had sent Phillip to meet her at the station instead. Their holding bags and saddlebags were transferred to the carriage, and White Blaze was tethered to the back of the carriage. The three of them got into the carriage, with Phillip giving instruction to the driver to take the scenic route home. This was for James's benefit, so he could get a good look at the town. Various notable buildings were pointed out to him, as well as the fast rapids of the St James River, which were a sight-seeing attraction; Phillip also pointed out a new entrance gate showing the name Botanical Gardens.

The civic leaders were bringing culture and class to this fine colonial town; they designated areas for parks and good walking trails beside the St James River that were safe and free for everyone to enjoy, for Richmond was a free city.

The city was self-governing and offered religious freedom, adopted after the Civil War with a philosophy of treating all as equals, regardless of ethnic origins, and it was developing as a centre for free-thinking individuals. James noticed that many flowers were displayed in window boxes and on front garden borders, which made the buildings and land very colourful. There were many people walking and riding up and down the main road, but they turned right and entered into a residential road, where there were large mansions, and the carriage entered one of the gates which took them into a courtyard of a large, imposing building. The carriage pulled up in front of the entrance steps to big wooden doors.

Elaina held James's hand and squeezed it in reassurance, as she knew he had never seen such a place as this. The house was palatial. It was the Silvano headquarters as well as their Richmond town residence. The doors were opened by servants, and James noticed that those who worked in this house were of mixed races. The man who opened the door was a black Negro, with silver hair very similar to the carriage driver.

His name was Tomas. He welcomed the master home, and Phillip Silvano enquired if the doctor had arrived yet to see his wife. The answer was not yet, but it was expected that the doctor would be calling within the hour. Elaina and James were shown to two rooms adjacent to each other; when James entered his room, he found an interconnecting door, which was at present locked. He found that Elaina had the key on her side of the door. Neither James nor Elaina had a great deal of luggage, as they had travelled light, so as soon as they had deposited their travel bags in their respective rooms, Elaina call James to join her, so they could go see her grandmother together.

Tomas led the way upstairs to a front bedroom and ushered them into a large airy room with an imposing bed in its centre. Elaina's grandmother, Catherine, was sitting up in bed, propped up by numerous pillows and looking somewhat subdued, compared to her normal forthright self. James noticed that this woman looked very youthful for her age, as she must be over sixty but looked much younger. Her hair was golden like Elaine's, and you could see the likeness between them in their facial features. Elaina kissed her grandmother on the cheek and introduced James as her fiancé, explaining that he was a natural healing doctor she had met while working at the mission.

Catherine gazed steadily at James and found his dark looks reminded her of her husband, Phillip, when they first met. Phillip was Spanish and in his youth had very dark hair, almost black, and skin weathered by the sea and sun. The outdoor life had given him the air of someone tall, dark, and handsome, and Catherine had been enamoured by his delightful manners and deep, intense eyes. Phillip was white haired now, but he still was a handsome man.

Catherine wondered if James could look at her infected leg, as being a doctor, he should know what to do, and old Dr Raymond was late again. She asked Elaina if it was alright if James could look at her leg and proceeded to push back the bedcovers to show him her right leg. It looked awfully inflamed and swollen, and there were two boils which looked like they were coming to a head. James asked Elaina to fetch their medical bag and to have someone supply him with two jars of hot water.

While Elaine was organising these things, James asked Catherine what she had done to get herself in such a condition. She explained that she had taken one of her grandchildren to the riverbank, where there were rock pools. She had taken off her stockings and shoes and gone paddling in the rock pools with her grandson. She had missed her footing and scraped the side of her leg against a rock, which was covered with a green, slimy substance, and following this incident ten days ago, the leg had since festered to the state she found herself in today. Dr Raymond had taken a look at her leg three days ago and just told her to rest and keep the wound clean, but her leg had got worse, and she was now feeling unwell. Because she was unable to get around, she had to cancel all her social engagements for the next few weeks.

Using the American and Spanish languages, James was able to inform Catherine that her leg had become infected and poisons had entered into her bloodstream, and that was why she was feeling unwell. If she would like James to treat her, she would have to do everything he told her and accept his treatment in its entirety, for her condition to respond effectively to begin to heal. Catherine was fascinated by James's American drawl and was surprised at his command of Spanish, which wasn't at all bad, even though she could detect a slight Mexican accent. Catherine was conversant in American, Spanish, and French, as these were the languages of the surrounding peoples, and some of the colonial elite still used Spanish or French in their official meetings. Catherine was fed up of waiting for Dr Raymond, so was glad to agree to anything at that moment, as she was feeling rather poorly.

James explained he was first going to get the poisons out of her leg by using hot water in the jars to ripen the boils. This treatment allowed the puss within to seep out. He had some medicine that would help the blood to purify itself; he explained that she may have to pass water frequently, as this was a good sign that the body was eliminating the poisons from within. James told Catherine he needed some special herbs to use for a wound dressing to fight the infection, but he would scout around the local district to find what he needed. In the meantime, he would use the dried herbs they had in the medicine bag, and this would take away much of the pain associated with the injured site, as it was red and inflamed.

James really needed some river weed to fight the infection and reduce the swelling, but he didn't have any. He had noted on their tour of Richmond that the Botanical Gardens might be the very place to source plants useful for his requirements. He would have to take a trip there tomorrow. Elaina returned to the room with the items requested, and James procured the bottle of medicine from the medical bag. He gave Catherine instructions to drink a spoonful of this medicine with a glass of water every two hours during the day and then every four hours thereafter, until the inflammation receded.

The treatment of the water jars would sting and be painful, but this was the best way to draw out the poisons and not leave any unsightly marks upon the skin. This seemingly unusually method did make sense and was much preferred if it worked to good effect, as the lancing that Dr Raymond advised would leave large scars and take forever to heal. The treatment began by placing the jars filled with hot water over the boils. This soon softened the skin at the upper points, and within seconds, you could see a small spiral of puss emanating from the boil into the water.

During the treatment, Dr Raymond arrived to see his patient and found her surrounded by her granddaughter and her fiancé, undergoing some peculiar treatment. By all accounts, Catherine was enjoying the attention, although she protested somewhat at the discomfort of this self-imposed torture. Dr Raymond was of the opinion there was no gain without pain. James and Dr Raymond exchanged a few words, and the young man explained his diagnosis and treatment plan.

Dr Raymond, not one to look a gift horse in the mouth, welcomed this young man's medical assistance, as he was extremely busy with too many patients. If this was a treatment that would work, he was all for it. After all, medicine was an unknown science, and each doctor had some unique treatment he called his own; if it proved beneficial, who was he to deny benefits that might arise? The older physician was very interested in what James had to say and what he was attempting to do. Catherine was a prestigious client of his, so keeping her happy was the main aim.

Dr Raymond asked James to let him know how things worked out. He gave James his card and asked him to call upon him in a few days to give his report. The hot water jar treatment was carried out a number of times over the next two hours, each time keeping the water temperature hot enough to draw the poisons out. When the skin was pressed on either side of the boils, it squeezed the puss out; when a little blood began to flow, it indicated that most of the offending substance had been eliminated. The leg was dried and bound with a herbal dressing. After another glass of medicine, Catherine was ready for sleep, and she did sleep deeply for the next six hours. This was the first time she had slept properly in the last week. Catherine awoke again in late evening, feeling as if a great burden had been lifted. Her mind was clear, her leg was more comfortable, and she did feel a little better. She pulled the bell cord, and Wilhelmina, the house servant, came to her bidding.

Catherine asked for some coffee and something to eat, but Wilhelmina told her that Dr James said she was to "have nothing but medicine water to drink, and if she was hungry, then a bowl of thin soup could be taken." No stimulants were allowed, and that meant no alcoholic drinks, no coffee or tea, only fruit juices, medicine juice, and water. Catherine's immediate response was one of defiance, but she checked herself in time and told Wilhelmina that she had forgotten about the instructions James had given, so could she please have some soup and some more medicine juice?

"Yessa, ma'am," was Wilhelmina's reply, and off she went to do just that.

Meanwhile, James and Elaina were having dinner in the dining room with Phillip and Michael, her uncle who was a practicing lawyer; Uncle Michael looked after the Silvanos' business and personal matters. Uncle Michael dined at his parents' house at least once a week, as he kept them up to date with various business matters. He discussed marine affairs with his father, concerning his ships and shipping business, which Phillip's other son managed full-time. Catherine had her own affairs to discuss, business interests both of her own and capital she had inherited.

Oil and commodities were discussed, and the current prices and availability of supplies were always of interest, as they determine the volume of sales in any one quarter.

James and Elaina were tired after the day's events, so they left father and son to talk on. This was after James had asked Michael if he could call upon him regarding a personal legal matter, so Michael gave James his card. James suggested to Elaina that they should look in on Catherine before retiring for the night, and they found her taking some refreshments which Wilhelmina had supplied. James noticed there was no coffee or alcoholic drink to be seen. He determined that her leg was still clear and beginning to dry up, and he saw that Catherine looked and felt a little better than before; they said good night and arranged to meet again in the morning. Phillip had given them a message to say he would look in on Catherine once Michael had left after their talk.

James and Elaina made their way to their allotted rooms. James followed Elaina into hers, went to the side door, and turned the key to open the door to his room next door. They had never yet spent a night apart since they had married a month ago, so James did not see why they should start now. If they worked it right, they could sleep together in one room and look as if they were using the two. The interconnecting door would be locked each day from Elaina's side to keep the servants from knowing what when on behind closed doors. James still found it strange to sleep indoors but did like the wonderfully soft big beds, where you could snuggle up in your own world of dreams.

James was tired, but not that tired, so once within the pristine white clean sheets of this big soft bed, the sweet love of two who were attuned to each other became a pleasing sensuous delight that surprised them both. Soon they were fast asleep and did not wake until the first sunlight streamed through the window. James awoke first and knew it was daybreak, as it was this time of day he usually awoke. He wanted to source some medicinal weed for Catherine, so he thought he would ask one of the servants to take him to the Botanical Gardens, which he assumed would be a good place to find what he needed. He dressed and left Elaina still asleep.

Once downstairs, he found Tomas and asked him about getting to the Botanical Gardens. Tomas instructed young Gordon, who was a white American of German extraction and about the same age as James, to drive Dr Adams to the Botanical Gardens. Gordon was the son of the stable master and was attending one of the universities, studying commerce and finance. He was on leave in his final year to compile a thesis on some business project of his choosing. At present, he was visiting his father, who lived within the grounds, as he had done, up until attending the university.

They lived in an apartment over the stables. Gordon was a true American, with grand ideas of advancement. He had seen the trappings of the wealthy and vowed to be a part of any up-and-coming commercial enterprise; he aimed to get recognised and somehow obtain some stake money. James heard all about his dreams while they travelled in the open wagon up the high street and round to the Botanical Gardens. The gates had not been fitted yet, and the place seemed deserted. Gordon drove up as far as he could, and then the two of them left the wagon and horses, which Gordon tied to a tree.

The place was relatively new, and the land was staked out with display beds. Some areas had been planted, and there were three lakes connected by a stream joining them together, and allowing the running water to flow between them. In some display beds, new plants were flowering and taking hold, as they had filled out and were displaying strong growth as bushes and clumps of related plants, herbs, and general localised vegetation. James made for the waterbeds and found some plants similar to those he had used back at the mission. The stream was small compared to the nearby rapid river, but it was sufficient to grow waterweed, algae, and edible water greens. James picked some water greens and waterweed, sufficient for his immediate use, and put them in a sack he carried. He then focused upon another display of foliage where local plants had been planted.

The young healer placed his hand above each plant, and from the tingling effect upon his palm generated by the power of the vibrations of the plant, he could tell if it was a medicinal plant of value or one not worth considering. He was looking for other plants that could prevent the spread of infections and found upon an uncultivated patch of land a common leaf which looked like a fleshy dock leaf; that might do to normalise an acidic stomach or area of inflamed flesh. He grabbed handfuls of this spotted weed and piled them into the sack.

There was a glasshouse against a nearby wall, where he found two gardeners potting plants. James didn't want anyone to think he was taking something he shouldn't, so he introduced himself as a natural doctor looking for medicinal plants amongst those displayed in the garden. Tom and Frank Gister, who were father and son, were the resident botanists in charge of planning for this botanical site. Tom, the father, was a botanical planner, as he had done this job for most of his life and moved from one town to another when a new botanical site was started. He was teaching his son the wider issues of planning and displaying the plants which reflected local and foreign species of vegetation, from as wide a range of localities as possible, including rare and exotic varieties of tropical plants.

Both Tom and Frank were interested in what James had picked out as medicinal plants, as they said they could document the variety and establish its correct Latin name. James showed them the plants in his sack, and Tom wrote some things down in a notebook. They arranged between them that Gordon would bring James back to the Botanical Gardens the next day, and they would give James a proper tour of the whole site and explain what they did and their long-term purpose and goals.

James thanked the Gisters for their help and returned with Gordon to the Silvano household, just in time for breakfast. As he entered the house, Elaina was descending the stairs and was surprised he had been out and about so early. She was amazed at what he had accomplished in so short a time. She had been afraid he would not find Richmond to his liking and feel out of place, but already he had ascertained where he could obtain natural plants and had arranged for Gordon to take him into the hills surrounding Richmond, to get more water plants from the naturally flowing streams. Breakfast was taken in the dining room, which was a grand room with a long table and many chairs.

Fortunately, a buffet had been laid upon the sideboard, and you could help yourself to what you wanted to eat. James ate simply with eggs, milk, and toast, which he found acceptable. He did smell some meat and found some kidneys cooked, so tried these as well, which was more his style, for he was used to eating meat for strength and vigour. His table manners were still questionable, as he would revert to using a spoon or his own hands when no one was about. James knew he must conform, so made himself wait until he was seated at the table before eating and used a fork and a spoon to eat, which he did quickly, as he found he was indeed quite hungry after his early morning travels.

Elaina smiled, as she knew how much he tried to conform to more civilised Eastern ways; she marvelled at his natural skill of finding his way around using his own initiative. Gordon had taken the sack of botanical plants and left it in the kitchens, so after breakfast, James went to retrieve his plants. Gordon was still in the kitchen, finishing his breakfast, as he knew all the staff, and Mrs Williamson, the cook, was his father's lady friend, since his mother had died three years ago. She looked after him and his father, and both had a great affection for this homey and kindly woman.

James retrieved his sack and arranged with Gordon to meet up again the same time tomorrow, so they could take the tour of the Botanical Gardens. James and Elaina visited Catherine again to dress her wound and pack it with fresh waterweed, which would reduce the swelling and inflammation much quicker than the herbal poultice.

They found Catherine much improved but not too keen on taking more of the medicine James had prescribed. They found a compromise by combining the medicine with some fruit juice, which gave it a sweeter taste. James suggested that Catherine get out of bed and try walking to get the circulation going. He left Elaina and her grandmother together, working out how she could get washed and dressed to look normal with one leg heavily bound in bandages. An hour later, Catherine was up and about, and with the help of servants, she was carried down the stairs to the large lounge with ground-to-ceiling windows overlooking the gardens.

The sun was shining outside, and it looked as if the day would be bright and sunny. Once comfortably seated in her favourite chair, Catherine decided to attend to her correspondence, which had piled up while she was out of action. Catherine suggested that Elaina show James around the house and gardens, and after lunch, she could show him the river rapids and the town's museum depicting the history of Richmond and surrounding areas.

Elaina led James outside into the large gardens, where a large lawn with flower beds was surrounded by bushes and trees. Behind the lawn area was a vegetable patch, and to one side was a fruit orchard. In the opposite direction were the stables; that reminded James to visit White Blaze to see if he was alright. He met the stable boys, Toby and Ron, who were the grandsons of Tomas, the elderly butler. Gordon's father was in charge of the horses and stables; he had an office at the side of the stable building. He was also a mechanic of sorts, as he dealt with the maintenance of the carriages and wagons the Silvano household used for their transport.

James found White Blaze well fed and rested, and Toby informed him he had received a workout this morning when he and his brother went exercising the horses. They had ridden White Blaze and Black Knight, as the brothers had decided to ride the best horses in the stables. James was pleased with his horse's condition and asked how they dealt with horse welfare.

Gordon's father admitted he did the best he could and took the horses to a blacksmith when they need to replace horseshoes. The horses around town needed horseshoes to ride on solid surfaces, as otherwise, the horse's pads would wear out quickly. The horses would go lame if they did not have horseshoes, as the wear and tear upon their hoofs was demanding on hardened ground.

CHAPTER 14

THE CAPITAL CITY

James and Elaina took a leisurely ride on their horses, White Blaze and Black Knight, down the high street and stopped off first at Dr Raymond's to catch him before he left on his house calls. James informed him that Catherine was on the mend and had come downstairs today. The doctor asked James if he would consider taking his afternoon surgery to deal with some of his patients who had minor injuries, ailments, and infections, while he concentrated on the more serious cases.

After some discussion, it was agreed that James would work in the afternoons, to arrive after Dr Raymond's morning surgery, so he could brief the young healer on what patients he would likely meet. If James held the afternoon surgery, then Dr Raymond could carry out some house calls and look in at the local hospital. Dr Raymond promised to show James the local hospital, which was about to open; it would be the most modern and best equipped in the district.

If James could help him out for a few weeks, then the volume of patients requiring attention would drop, once they had caught up with backlog. The new hospital, when opened for business, would take the pressure off local doctors from having to make so many house calls. There had been an unusual increase in digestive problems lately, and people were getting infections from grazes incurred when paddling at the water's edge, cutting their feet and legs on sharp stones and rocks, so there was plenty that James could do to help Dr Raymond.

James and Elaina continued to the museum, where James found pictures and artefacts of the local Indian population which used to live near the river. They had since migrated southwards, although some had integrated into Richmond society, where they were treated with reserved respect. There were so many different ethnic cultures in Richmond, being migrants or descendants from colonial European countries. This created a colourful and vibrant society where men were encouraged to excel in education and commerce, and so bring culture and class to a city which was fast achieving respect from the other American states. Many state meetings were being held in the fine colonial buildings, which made Richmond a striking-looking capital city.

Elaina and James returned to the Silvano mansion in time for luncheon, which was cold meat and fresh vegetables. Catherine was still in her lounge, giving orders to staff and taking her light repast on a tray. She had received some visitors who had enquired about her health, and she was bemoaning the fact that she had to visit the water closet every hour, as the medicine was having a dramatic effect upon her personal waterworks. This was good news, James said, as it showed the poisons caused by her infected leg were fast being eliminated.

"Another day, and you will be back to normal," James predicted, and Catherine looked relieved.

Elaina said she would stay with her grandmother this afternoon to keep her company and would change her wound dressing, so if James wanted to go back to Dr Raymond's to see what patients he could treat, he could do so, and so James did just that and began his afternoon treatments. The next few days followed a pattern of James getting up early and travelling with Gordon to the Botanical Gardens to look over all the plants and vegetation there. Tom and Frank were very knowledgeable about the plants; James would assess plants for medicinal properties by passing his hand over them, and the Gisters made detailed notes of each plant, listing down their properties and medical applications. James explained that he only needed the outer leaves of some plants, so the plant itself was not destroyed but encouraged to grow more vigorously. These leaves and plant and flowers were crushed and could be made into a paste, liquid, or lotion.

Some plants were not exactly medicinal but favoured the aesthetes or inherent beneficial properties to bring smoothness to skin after sunburn, irritation, pigmentation spread, rashes, and sores. James showed the Gisters how he mixed the plant juices and mulch into a cream or paste, so that it could be spread upon the skin to affect a cure. Tom and Frank thought they could grow specific plants in volume using the glass house, so that certain plants would be available in quantity, if this cream were to be produced to sell as a cosmetic aid.

Gordon suggested they all go into business together, with James being the expert medic, the Gisters being the plant growers, and he being the businessman who could market any products that the four decided would be medically or commercially viable. Gordon knew where he could obtain glass jars and bottles suitable for creams, potions, and medicines. He suggested they form a plan and concentrate at first on six main products. Gordon had found his university project and was raring to go. From what he had learnt so far, creams for the skin would be of interest to the ladies and anyone else who had any skin eruption or discoloration.

Digestive medicines were always in demand, and herbal ones without any adverse symptoms, other than passing impurities out of the body by natural elimination, were far better than vomiting. The use of waterweed for a base in an ointment would guarantee to be of interest to all medical men when they sought to reduce inflammation, swelling, and infection. Combined with wound dressing, the paste could revolutionise the healing capabilities. The new Richmond hospital would become famous if such treatments could be used; patients would spend less time in the hospital as a result. This was a wonderful idea, with Gordon, Tom, and Frank becoming quite excited.

James was still thinking and came up with a suggestion (he always liked to see things logically); he suggested they begin with samples he could use on his patients. The first priority was medicine for digestive problems. Then the river or waterweed ointment, as this could be used universally for many applications, including infections, irritations, and aggravations of the skin.

Meanwhile, the Gisters could experiment with a compound of creams using the cacti plant flesh and sunflower seed oil, which would appeal to women hoping to clear their skin of spots, blemishes, and adverse colouring. James said he would continue assessing the botanical plants each morning, which might add more to the list of plants which could be used as natural healing remedies.

"That's it," said Gordon. "We will market these products as Adams & Gisters Natural Healing Remedies. I will bring an agreement tomorrow for us all to sign." He knew they were on to something good. Everything had to be done properly if a business was to grow and become successful. Going into business with a Silvano family member had to be a good thing, and Gordon could see his prospects rising fast. Gordon was full of what they could achieve, given that James would be able to find the right plants to furnish the creams, potions, and medicines for remedies. He even asked James if the same remedies could be used on horses and was surprised when he said they could, as this was how he had first learned if certain plants were harmful or acceptable to humans.

The river weed used down south at the mission was ideal for horse sprains; it quickly alleviated swelling and discomfort. Gordon was impressed with James's knowledge. They would need some stake money to get started, and he wondered if he should ask James if he had access to some. Being full of enthusiasm, he came right out with it and explained that a little bit of money may be needed to provide bottles for the medicines and for marketing by giving away some free samples to try, so people would be willing to purchase after using the sample. Once they had tried the herbal remedies and had found them beneficial, he was sure they would be inundated with orders.

Gordon explained to James that he could see there would be two sides to the business, the medical side and the commercial side, which was where the ladies' creams and everyday remedies for stomach upsets could be supplied. James was impressed with Gordon's grasp of what natural products he used and told Gordon he could get some money from Elaina; he also suggested that if they needed a lawyer, they could use Michael Silvano, who was Elaina's uncle.

That evening, James asked Elaina if he could have some money. Thinking he wanted some pocket money, she was about to hand him some when she asked how much he needed, or if he had something in mind he wanted to purchase, and how much it cost. James didn't know how much money the stake was that Gordon had referred to, so he asked Elaina if he could have enough to buy some bottles and jars so he could make up some more medical supplies.

Elaina was full of apologies, as she had forgotten to tell James she had arranged for a bank account to be opened in his name, so he could draw upon funds for business and personal uses. James didn't understand about money matters in a commercial way, or so she thought, for he had never shown the slightest interest in money, for it meant very little to him. His life did not involve money, unless he visited a town, for all he wanted and needed could be sourced within the natural countryside. This is what she had liked about James for he was totally self-sufficient and capable of walking through life with just his own self and capabilities. With that thought, she remembered they ought to stock up on clothes, shoes, and personal items while they were here in Richmond.

James also reminded Elaina he wanted to visit with her uncle Michael to discuss his personal identity and wondered whether they should enlist the help of her grandmother, as she knew almost everyone of importance in Richmond. Elaina was glad that James had asked her about these things, as he had begun to immerse himself in all things medical, and that meant they did not get to see so much of each other. Elaina had her suspicions that she was pregnant, as she had been feeling a little wheezy in the mornings of late. She did not want to tell James just yet, in case she was wrong and it was a tummy upset affecting her, as stomach problems had recently affected many others in the city.

Elaina was amazed at how quickly James grasped modern understanding and particularly the quirks of modern speaking and language. He seemed to be able to tune into the airways around him and very easily copy the status quo. James had mastered the Eastern dialect and was now speaking in a pure American dialect with little trace of a Southern or Western accent.

The patients at Dr Raymond's clinic all spoke highly of James and many were surprised how quickly they recovered from the remedies he had given them. Little did they know that the batches of medicines were only hours old, having been made up in the glasshouse at the botanical gardens by Tom and Frank. Gordon was always dashing here and there, distributing some concoction they had managed to produce, based on James's recommendations only days before.

Catherine Silvano was now her normal busy self and had resumed her social engagements around town. After returning from one of her coffee mornings, she breezed into the luncheon room to find Elaina and James seated at the large table. Out of her handbag, she produced one jar of cream and another medicine bottle which looked suspiciously like the one James had used when he had treated her a few days earlier.

"Are these anything to do with you?" she asked, looking straight at James rather accusingly.

James replied that the medicine bottle looked like one he had used, but he didn't recognise the jar of cream. Catherine informed him she had been given these items at her coffee morning as the latest cures on the market. Her friends were going wild over the jar of cream. Once applied, it left the skin feeling smooth and clear and was even eliminating wrinkles in dried skin. James smiled as he realised that his recommendation for ladies' face cream was now a reality, and Tom and Frank had made it happen. Of course, Gordon was the one with the contacts, as he had asked James for a list of names who were Silvano visitors and friends.

James surmised that Gordon had distributed free samples amongst Catherine's friends, and they were all trying them out. James had got a list from Tomas the butler, as he knew everything that went on in the Silvano household. He even knew about the latest money-making scheme involving Gordon and James and how the two from the botanical gardens were involved; he had suggested if they needed further financing, they could offer shares in their company.

Tomas said he would invest some of his savings, as he knew James was a good man and liked to think his instincts about people were correct.

James faced Catherine and admitted that the two items in her hands were samples he had allowed to be distributed on the open market, in readiness for a full-scale production, if the products were liked and had a demand. Catherine was delighted to encounter another potential entrepreneur within the family, and what a surprise it was. She would never have thought that this young man from the backwoods of Western America could be so talented. He was growing in her estimation, and she wanted to know all about his business enterprise.

James told her in a matter-of-fact manner that he had gone to the Botanical Gardens to find some river weed and certain plants, which he had used to treat her leg inflammation and digestive problems. After meeting the Gisters, who were botanists at the Botanical Gardens, they had all decided that James's natural remedies would be good products to market commercially. Gordon had the business expertise, as he was completing his university degree in commerce and had suggested they form a company and market the more non-medical remedies for general consumption and use.

In the process, it had been found that some creams used to treat skin eruptions were equally effective in a lesser consistency, which produced a smooth and clear complexion in women who suffered skin blemishes and decolourisations. It seemed that pink skin would return to its rosy pink colour, brown skin would become less muddy, yellow skin clear and smooth, red skin shining and healthy looking. Much sun damage to lighter skins would clear up in a matter of days; this cream could also act as a barrier, to keep the sunshine from affecting the most sensitive of skin types. This meant that many women who for cosmetic reasons did not go out in the midday sun could now venture forth, knowing their skin was protected from unnecessary burning and decolourisation.

Catherine was momentarily speechless, as her mind was galloping away with ideas for the promotion of such products. She suggested to James that when he met with Michael, the Silvano lawyer, who also dealt with the Silvano business empire, he should ask him to look over any documentation to see if his business agreements were sound; if necessary, Michael could act on his behalf in any legal or financial matters.

Catherine had been worried when Elaina had said she intended to marry James, as she was concerned about the risk to her granddaughter's inheritance. It was for this reason she wanted to know who exactly Elaina was marrying. She had reservations at first not knowing this young man, but James had assured Catherine he did not want a penny of Elaina's money because he was quite capable of providing for her and any family they might have.

She had taken this statement as bravado but was now realising James had meant every word. James had been forthright when he had told Catherine that any accumulated monies Elaina might inherit should be made over to their son and heirs, whenever they arrived. He also asked when they could be formally married in Richmond, as the sooner they were, the quicker any family would be forthcoming.

James had become quite animated; Elaina was surprised at the passion in his voice, as he rarely showed this side of himself. James felt very strongly about family matters and was very protective of her, which she liked very much.

CHAPTER 15

THE UNRAVELLING

After this heated outburst, Catherine said she would arrange a meeting with her son Michael for the following day, so matters could be resolved. On the morrow, James returned from his early morning trip to the Botanical Gardens, where he had been introduced to a Mr Adrian Shaw, a chemist, who was prepared to stock his products. Furthermore, he had experimented with a jar of skin cream and reduced it to a powder, so it could be stored and preserved. This way, stocks could accumulate, and the powder could be reconstituted by adding water, which would return it to its creamy state. There was no loss of nutriments, as Adrian had tried both compounds on his daughter, who suffered sores to her arms; one arm was treated with the fresh cream compound and the other reconstituted compound, and both arms had cleared up nicely. There didn't seem to be any differences in their effect. James was impressed and asked if Tom and Frank would send samples to the El Paso Mission for the attention of Jonathan Westwood, the resident doctor there. He also asked him to send instructions about the reconstitution process.

James also wanted some supplies of the digestive medicine to be shipped to El Paso, and in particular the medicine which made people sleepy, so they didn't feel any pain or hurt from the administrations of a doctor when he was cleaning wounds or digging out unwanted material. Pain and hurt from a doctor's attention was one reason why many patients feared going to see a doctor in the first place, and they would leave a doctor's visit until it became absolutely necessary and unavoidable. James believed that patients should see a doctor earlier if they developed a hurt or condition, so their ailment could be treated at the beginning of their symptoms and not when the condition had gone past the state of hopelessness. James told Tom and Frank what Gordon was doing regarding his marketing and distributing activities, adding that many ladies were keen to receive supplies of the skin preparations, which would improve their complexions from the ravishments of the outdoor weather.

James told Tom and Frank to expect an increase in demand the following week, as he knew for certain that many influential people were promoting the products. James left his friends sorting out the Adams & Gisters Natural Healing Remedies while he attended to matters closer to home. He knew Elaina had been feeling unwell in the morning, and he suspected she was carrying his child, but she had not said anything to him yet, so he would bide his time and just keep watch. There were only three weeks to go before Elaina's twenty-first birthday, and he wanted to arrange the Richmond wedding for this date. By doing this, no one could object, and Catherine would not be angered or upset in any way.

James had come to know Catherine quite well and recognised a strong protective mother's influence, which was understandable in the circumstances, as she was compensating for the loss of her own daughter, Maria, who had been Elaina's mother. When they arrived at Michael's office in town the next morning, it was apparent that Catherine wanted to sit in on the meeting, and so it was that James, Elaina, Michael, and his mother Catherine heard, in graphic detail, the story of James's birth. James chose not to identify Black Buffalo as his natural father's killer, as Black Buffalo was still alive; James thought it best to tell the essence of the story without disclosing all the facts. He had altered the story to that of a group of Indians who had wanted Black Elk's body returned, and it was they who had attacked the soldiers, killing them all as a result of a retaliatory fight.

Michael and Catherine were looking at each other questioningly, for something in James's story had struck a chord. Adams was the surname of Walter Adams, who had married Catherine's niece Samantha when Wesley failed to return from his last mission. If what James had said was true, it meant that Julianne, who was Catherine's great-niece and her sister's granddaughter, was James's half-sister, for they shared the same biological father. The hair colouring between the two was very similar, but that could be coincidence. Catherine could also see a resemblance to a young Wesley in James's look and mannerisms, but her memory was not as good as it was, and she could not be sure her memory was reliable, as it could just be her own imagination running wild. It was all a long time ago.

While Catherine and her sister Marianne had been blonde, both their husbands had been dark haired, and their respective daughters had inherited dark hair, as had their sons. It was only the grandchildren's generation, of which Elaina was one, who had inherited the blondness like her grandmother's and great-aunt's hair colour. Julianne, who was Marianne's granddaughter, had golden brown hair and was headstrong like the Edwards sisters.

The Adams side of the family were also influential people in the Eastern states, as one branch of the family was into politics in upstate New York, and that was where Samantha Prentice Adams had met her second husband, while she visited some family relations. James showed Michael his artefacts, including the sword which had been taken from Wesley Adams, and the letter which Father Carlos had read which proved the relationship of Wesley Adams to Samantha Prentice. In addition, there was the timepiece containing a white woman's picture, which at first no one could identify. It was Catherine who came to the rescue, for she stared at this small cameo image and then said she thought this was a picture of Wesley's mother, Amy, in her younger days, but she hadn't known her that well.

She did know Amy's mother, Isabelle Van-de-Vault, who was still alive and living in Richmond. Isabelle was in her middle eighties and still active; both Michael and Catherine knew her. Isabelle's nephew, a highly respected lawyer and judge, had recently retired.

Catherine noticed that the image seemed rather thick and wondered if there was something underneath the picture. Using a fine lever from her cosmetic bag, which she carried in her handbag, Catherine lifted the image from its seating and found another photo underneath in pristine condition, as it had been kept hidden for many years. As if to confirm Catherine and Michael's thoughts, there in front of them was a picture of Isabelle Van-der-Vault in her younger years, with Amy, her daughter, as a young girl standing beside her. This was a mother and daughter picture, as they would have appeared just before Amy had married Walter Adams.

Michael with his legal mind suggested they contact Isabelle to see if she would be prepared to recognise James as kin, as by all accounts he was her blood great-grandson. It wasn't known if the Van-der-Vaults held any inherited funds on behalf of daughter Amy or Wesley, who had been Isabelle's grandson. It was worth finding out.

Michael further suggested that he would write to the Adams's lawyer, who he knew quite well, as he had previously dealt with him regarding Julianne's inheritance from her grandparents, as a settlement document was presently being drawn up to cover inheritance issues for when she married. Walter Adams, her father, was keen for Julianne to marry his nephew, Donald Caraway, as such an alliance would keep inherited assets within the immediate family. Walter's association with the Edwards family through his marriage to Samantha Prentice had brought about investment monies used to drill for oil. This had been the making of the continued prosperity coming from the ranch lands.

Unfortunately, Julianne was not to be persuaded to marry anyone other than the man she chose herself, as she had her own ideas for a husband, and this only cousin on her father's side was too weak a character for her to consider. Donald did everything his mother told him to do. There had been some friction between the family members, but Julianne had continued to stay at the ranch, as she was in her element when around horses. Julianne may be a female, but she had earned the respect from all the men who worked as stable and horse-hands on the Adams Ranch, which was more than could be said for Donald; her cousin as he had a knack of rubbing people the wrong way. Nobody respected him, as he was insolent and surly in his disposition and drank too much. He was also known to have roughed up the local tavern wenches when visiting the local township; more than once, bribes had to be made to keep quiet a messy situation that Donald had created.

Julianne was disgusted with his behaviour, and Donald hated her because she was the legitimate heiress, whereas he felt he should have been. This was the trouble created by Walter, who had brought up Donald in place of his dead son Wesley, because he was the only boy within the Adams family. Donald would never in a thousand years make the grade as a ranch manager; it just wasn't in him. He was just too much like his own father, Ed Caraway, who had been a drifting cowboy, who fancied he could turn his hand to horses and had come unstuck. Prudence Adams Caraway, Donald's mother, was the poor relation and relied on her brother Walter for everything. Prudence had married late in life and had produced this son when she was nearing forty years old. He was only a couple years older than Julianne and had lived on the Adams Ranch all his life.

Ed Caraway had been killed shortly after his first birthday, when thrown from a bucking horse he was breaking in. Prudence had no means of support and turned up at her brother's ranch. Walter had recently remarried and had a daughter. Prudence and Samantha never did get on, as there was friction between them from the start, and Walter was split between the two women, as he wanted a son desperately.

Samantha had refused to be a proper wife to him and only agreed to stay with him because he had married her to legitimise her daughter Julianne, who was his blood granddaughter. As the two children grew, Donald became a good horseman, but Julianne, who went East to school when her mother left the ranch, returned with a brain full of knowledge and had acquired an exceptional expertise in horsemanship.

This was not only a natural gift but included things she had learnt from dealing with the best horsemen from Europe, who had emigrated to the American East Coast. Julianne had been privileged to fraternise with the best colonial horseman newly arrived in the American Eastern shores, and she knew everything there was to know about the best horseflesh. Julianne knew she may eventually be left to run the Adams Ranch, so with her business skills as well as her horsemanship, she was a force to be reckoned with. Even Walter had to admit she was far more competent with business affairs and also a superior horsewoman, who could outwit a local cowboy with very little effort. She certainly could outwit Donald anytime; his only advantage was manly strength, which just meant he used bullying techniques to get what he wanted.

James did not know about the history of the Adams family or how the family tied up to the Silvano family. Michael just stated he would look into things and asked James to trust him to look after his artefacts; until they could be authenticated, he would lock them in the office safe. This meeting did produce one or two good things, as the marriage ceremony between James and Elaina was fixed for her birthday, which fell on a Saturday. This meant all friends and nearby relations could attend the wedding function to be held at the Silvano mansion.

Elaina was also informed that she was entitled to receive a substantial yearly income from accumulated funds. These arose from the interest on her mother's inheritance, which Maria had never claimed. This was irrespective of any inherited funds and property she would inherit in her own right, and of course any wedding gifts made to her and her new husband by relatives.

James stated again that they didn't need a lot of money and that he would be willing to waive away any legal rights to Elaina's inheritance in favour of the children he hoped they would have in due course. With regard to the yearly income from Elaina's mother's assets, he was glad that Elaina could have her own monies to use as she wished, but he would make sure that she had all she needed for daily living. Money was already coming in from the Natural Healing Therapies, and James felt sure the Sky Spirits had directed him to engage in this business enterprise in order to make some money and be equal to Elaina.

James knew that by having an income of his own would mean he could then choose the lifestyle he wanted and be free to choose where his family would live, which could be in the East, West, or South of the country. James knew that money was needed for certain things, but in the real world of living, and that was in the countryside within nature's big garden, the Great Sky Spirit provided all that was required.

James knew he had to go back to the West at some time in the future, but it would be after his visit to the Eastern states. His travels so far had showed him there was much to learn, and he was assimilating new things each day, so he would not leave this area until it had taught him all he needed to know. First, he was going to get married again, but he did not tell this to anyone, as everyone else was under the impression that he was Elaina's intended.

James remembered Black Buffalo's teaching: to never volunteer information unnecessarily, as it was the Indian way to see how the land lay before committing yourself to anything. It was always wise to keep your own counsel; a wise man was a listener and not a talker. This wise counsel had been proven many times over the years, and James was well aware that you gained more information by listening to others.

The next day found James back at Dr Raymond's afternoon surgery. Dr Raymond had gone out on his house calls, which were reducing as the hospital had just opened, and those who needed bedside attention had gone there to sample the new surroundings. Resident doctors and nurses were on hand, so patients could be attended to faster than when doctors had to pay house calls.

James treated a number of children with sores and infections on their legs and arms. He showed their parents how to put pressure on certain parts of the child's body, which were the sites of Dr Wong's acupuncture points. James had found children automatically trusted their parents, so they were more willing to have them involved in the treatment.

When James had to squeeze a boil or sew up a cut or attend a nasty infection by applying a poultice, it helped to offer pain relief. The pressure points that were utilised were able to numb the surrounding area. This enabled the doctor's administrations to be undertaken with diligent speed and the patient made comfortable in a bandage or wound dressing that would safeguard the problem area from further contamination.

Once the administrations were complete, the release of the pressure point would return normal feeling in that limb or contaminated area. This was much better than knocking out a patient to achieve the same ends. Children were very responsive and very sensitive, and James learned much from the ordinary people who attended Dr Raymond's afternoon surgery. This afternoon, Dr Raymond returned early and found James immersed in his work with the children. He was impressed that many families waited for James to be available, as word had spread that he was caring and able to treat the young, pain free.

Dr Raymond was middle-aged and had long forgotten the enthusiasm of youth and being new to the wonderful techniques of medicine, as they arose in man's developing understanding. James had renewed his interest in medical methods outside the mainstream, accepted avenues, and he had been introduced to a modern development which was becoming something of a new way to treat many cases, without the trauma and side effects of conventional treatments. Certainly these creams that James had brought along were clearing up infections, sores, and abrasions, and the face creams for women were ideal for curing sun blisters, emotional rashes, spots, and other eruptions.

Dr Raymond was just amazed at the new things James had introduced and was now copying him in some of his ways and approaches, as they were more humane than anything he had encountered before. He cringed when he thought of the war years and the many limbs that had been amputated because of infected wounds. So many men became cripples when they may have been treated differently, with no loss of limb. It was a pity James would not be staying in Richmond, as Dr Raymond would have liked him to become a partner in his practice.

As promised, Dr Raymond took James to look over the hospital one day, and that was a day he would remember for a long, long time. The first patients had arrived, with men in one ward and females in another. Four women were about to give birth, and for one reason or another, they had problems which were better dealt with in a hospital. A caesarean was the last resort to save a baby and its mother, and this usually resulted in the mother being unable to bear any more children, because of the damage rendered by this kind of surgery.

James had never seen an operation of this kind before and arrived when one woman was being carried into the operating room. Ether was used to put her to sleep, and it smelt horrible. The surgeon was a Mr Blackmore, who was an ex-army surgeon of many a campaign. He was a large man with large hands and wielded a knife as if he was avenging a demon. Although the baby was delivered alive, the mother's body was grossly cut, and a great loss of blood ensued. The mother was in a poor state when she regained consciousness and was violently sick, making the stitches in her belly open up again, with more blood lost. The baby had to be fed on goat's milk, as the mother was not in a fit state to attend to her new born child, so no bonding could take place. It was some three weeks before this woman could be discharged from the hospital.

James was informed of this sometime later, and it was doubtful if this new mother could bear any more children. After witnessing such horrific sights, he asked to examine the remaining women and questioned why it was necessary for them to undergo such an operation. He discovered one woman's child was in a breech position, so the feet would come out first; another was having twins, and the last woman was having palpitations in fear of what was to come. She was in a most tense state and had been in labour all day and was beginning to tire. James asked if he could attend to this woman first, as she was the one who was about to give birth.

This woman was named Sarah; she was a mature woman who had six children already: all girls, and was content to leave it at that. Her husband had persuaded her to try one last time, to see if they could have a son. Her pregnancy had been difficult, as she had felt unwell for most of the duration, contrasting to her previous pregnancies, when she had felt fine throughout, with no trouble at all. James found all this out in five minutes, just by asking the right questions. Already she was beginning to relax, and James asked her if she would allow him to help her through a natural birthing, which he was sure he could accomplish with her cooperation. Sarah agreed, and James called a birthing nurse over to be ready to see to the child when it was born. He asked Sarah to focus upon him and listen to his voice, for he would chant and give instructions for her to follow.

James began talking in a strange language which Sarah found hypnotic, so she forgot her tenseness and relaxed. As soon as James realised she had relaxed, he touched her forehead, and she momentarily fell asleep. Meanwhile, her belly muscles began contracting fiercely. When the nurse indicated that the baby was about to be born, James tapped Sarah's forehead again and engaged her eyes with his. He told her quietly and calmly to start pushing her baby out and to stop when he squeezed her hand. James told her she would feel no pain, just the motion of her baby coming into the world.

After four or five more pushes and stops, little Ben arrived in the world. Sarah was delighted and cried in gratitude. The nurse was amazed to see such a smooth delivery, when it had been expected to be a difficult one. All this had happened in the space of one hour; shortly afterwards, the word got around that Sarah was fine and had birthed a healthy son, so everyone was pleased, especially Sarah's husband, who could not stop smiling and wanting to shake hands. Two other doctors beside Dr Raymond came to see how everything was proceeding; they heard how James had taken charge and used some tribal treatment which had resulted in a pain-free, natural birth.

While the hospital medics were discussing the birthing techniques, James went to see the other two ladies. They had heard the good news about Sarah and were relieved that they may not need an operation to give birth to their babies. The next lady who was in the throes of labour was Annie, whose baby was in the breech position. James explained the procedures he was going to use and asked Annie for her cooperation to follow his instructions completely. He explained it was necessary to be quiet and calm; this encouraged the baby to be relaxed because if the mother was tense, it affected the baby, who had to struggle and fight to get born. The anxiety of the mother was transferred to the child, who could show distress when born. Put this way, Annie understood and was prepared to accept James's help and guidance.

He told Annie that because the baby was positioned upside down, it could take a little longer for it to exit her body, so it was particularly important that she follow his instructions of when to push and when to stop, as this made the passage of entering the world so much easier for her child. The same birthing nurse came to help James again, as she was really impressed with his manner and expertise. She had never seen such competent command of the birthing procedure, as most doctors left the women to get on with their labour and were only present for the actual birth, which was loud and noisy, with the woman yelling in pain until it was all over.

James managed to keep everything quiet and orderly. Even his voice was soft and haunting, and the atmosphere changed around the birthing mother to one of quiet acceptance and anticipation. The nurse was interested in this delivery because it was a breech birth, which usually led to difficulties. Babies born feet first often got stuck and had to be pulled out of the mother's body; as a result, they often died.

Dr Raymond decided he would stay to oversee this birth, as he was also interested in what James could do when faced with the difficult and unusual. James went into the meditative process for Annie, who fell asleep naturally to allow her body to work on its own in the final stages of labour. While she was in this sleep state, James continued talking to her, giving her the instructions she needed for when the time came to push.

All of a sudden, some big contractions occurred, and Annie opened her eyes with fright. James took her hand and turned her head so she was looking straight at him. Their eyes locked, and he began taking her through the birthing process. Each contraction heralded a pushing action, and when the contraction eased, she was to pant and breathe quickly and regularly.

Half an hour passed before James gave the instruction to push hard, and within seconds, little feet were emerging from the woman's body. He gave the signal to stop and pant, and then another contraction took hold and with it expelled the baby's body. Another violent contraction, and the baby girl emerged, yelling as she took her first breath.

The birthing nurse cleaned the baby and placed her in her mother's arms. Annie was all smiles and full of thanks for James, who had not let her down. Dr Raymond held his own counsel but was pleased to see everyone happy with the outcome. James needed a rest after two births occurring one after the other. The baby was wrapped up and put in a cradle to sleep, and Annie was also ready for a sleep, so the doctors left her with the nurse, who was tidying around the patient. The two doctors were joined by Mr Blackmore, the hospital surgeon. They discussed the two births James had conducted; both Mr Blackmore and Dr Raymond were curious as to what exactly James had said to these women to make them focus so strongly upon him they forgot their pain and discomfort.

James explained his process to the doctors, which rendered a mother only aware of the birthing process to deliver her child. They had to follow James's vocal instructions by aligning their mental focus. The woman's instinct responded willingly and was eager to follow his voice and instructions to bring about a congenial birth experience for themselves and their child. This was because the natural processes were being endorsed with support in place to alleviate their fear. James explained that the words of his meditation were an old Indian chant and said that when he lived with the natives, they had taught him to harness the mental and emotional energies of someone who was hurt or injured. This took their mind and feelings to another place, where they forgot what was immediately troubling them, so that the healer could get on and do the practical treatment needed.

This could all occur while the person remained in an altered state of mental focus; she would not feel every twinge or hurt that came from the remedial treatment. The same procedure and application worked for birthing mothers, for their pain stemmed from muscle cramps, which the body induced to birth a child. If excessive pain was to be reduced so as not to overtire the woman, the mind's focus needed distracting. Chanting a repetitive song produced a rhythmic tempo. This somehow had an equalising effect upon the patient's mental rhythm, so her focus was temporarily moved elsewhere, while the practical administrations were applied.

Dr Raymond and Mr Blackmore nodded in understanding and marvelled at the simple explanation for something that was so profound. The two new mothers who had birthed babies under the guidance of James were able to return home within hours. The other mother who had received surgery was still unwell, and the baby had to be looked after by a relative. This left one other mother-to-be, who was the lady who was expecting twins. Her name was Mabel, and she already had one daughter who was five years old.

Mabel was a large woman who was a baker's wife. She was fortunate that she could help herself to bread and cakes at any time, and this had added to her large frame and large girth. She began to swell up considerably, and it was obvious she could not get about by herself, as she was just too large. Her belly carried a rather large baby, or it must be more than one child, as the doctors had detected more than one heartbeat. Mabel had been brought into the hospital, as the doctors thought she may have to be artificially induced to give birth, as the swellings were now reaching every part of her body. It was feared her heart may give out under the strain, and she was not that old, as she was only in her early thirties. James was consulted. Dr Raymond and Mr Blakemore were undecided as to the best way to proceed and wondered if James could give his opinion.

He spent a little time with Mabel, asking about her family history to see if there had been anyone else who had twins. Mabel thought her husband had been a surviving twin, but she wasn't sure, as his parents were both dead, but on her side of the family, she did know that she had twin aunts who were identical twins. They had never married but had kept house for their parents and now looked after Mabel's youngest sister, who was disabled. Mabel went on to say her youngest sister had broken her leg, which had healed crookedly, so one leg was now considerably shorter than the other. She had to wear special shoes to compensate for the height difference, and this made her movements difficult.

While Mabel rambled on, James felt her abdomen. He could feel a clump of tangled legs and arms and thought he could feel two heads but couldn't feel which way round these babies were lying. They seemed a reasonable size, and James asked how far along she was in her pregnancy. The calculations were about thirty-four weeks. James suggested to Mabel that if this was correct, she should try and keep rested for as long as possible, so the babies could keep growing another week or two, to give them the best chance of survival.

Meanwhile, James wanted to try a treatment which he hoped would reduce the swelling. This would make Mabel feel more comfortable and ease the tension on her heart, as it was in her best interest to be as fit as possible for the birthing time. James recommended some of his medicine for purifying the blood. He hoped that by eliminating toxins built up in the blood, the natural water elimination process of the body would automatically reduce the overall swelling. In addition, a daily massage of her body to encourage the expulsion of fluids was also advised, as according to Lee Wong's teachings, this could prove beneficial in increasing the body's energy flow. Dr Raymond and Mr Blackmore agreed to follow James's suggestions.

Mabel was told the medicine would flush away the water content in her body, so she could expect to pass water many times in the process of eliminating the offending toxins. James and Dr Raymond left the hospital to the medical staff and said they would visit again. Dr Raymond long remembered that day, as it was the start of a new way of treating pregnant women, which was all down to James and the techniques he had employed and shown them.

It was now only three days before the wedding; Elaina was busy finalising arrangements with florists, caterers, and musicians, and sending numerous invitations to friends and families in Richmond and the surrounding area. The invitation list including all the influential friends connected to the Silvano family, whether they were known to the marrying couple or not.

On this day, a meeting had been called by Michael for an update on James's affairs. They again met at his offices in town, where they were introduced to the elderly Isabelle Van-der-Vault and her nephew, the lawyer, Andrew Van-der-Vault, who had come to see this young man who claimed to be a relative. Elaina had taken James on a shopping trip a few days before and had bought a range of new clothes which were serviceable, traditional, and expensive, being of the best quality.

James was looking very handsome with a new haircut, trimmed neatly to his collar, a fresh plain white shirt, which accentuated his suntanned skin tone, and trousers which were the best beige calfskin. Isabelle had been surprised when Michael called to discuss the matter at hand. They had already had two meetings without James to discuss him and his story and to investigate what might well be an inheritance of sorts. Isabelle had seen the images in the timepiece and confirmed that the pictures were of her and her late daughter Amy, who had married Walter Adams and was the mother of Wesley Adams, her deceased grandson.

Isabelle had recognised the timepiece, as it had been a gift from her to Wesley on his twenty-first birthday. She also recognised the ring, as it had been her daughter's wedding ring, which originally belonged to Isabelle's own mother. She did not recognise the key but suggested it might be a key to a trunk, as all Army personnel had one to store their personal effects. Isabelle had heard the story of how James had been conceived and was immediately struck by the similarity in looks to Julianne, her other great-grandchild, who was the same age as James (only six weeks separated their birthdays). Michael had told Isabella and her nephew, Andrew, who was representing Isabelle's interests, as you would expect, that James was not a fortune hunter and was only interested in his heritage because of his marriage to Elaina. It was of interest to him to find out who he was related to, as even in Indian custom, the Ancestors were important, and it was this aspect of his heritage which had brought him here, with a prophecy from a shaman of finding his true root heritage.

It turned out that Amy Van-der-Vault had inherited from her grandparents title to land which was adjacent to that of the Adams Ranch in Texas. This was originally intended to be a wedding gift for her eldest child, but Amy died before her son, Wesley, was full grown, and he died before he married, so the property and land in question was tacked onto Walter Adams's landholdings and had become part of his cattle range. As far as it was known, the original property had consisted of a wooden ranch-house, which was used as accommodation for employed cattle range managers. Isabelle presently held the title to this land and received a peppercorn rent for its use from the Adams solicitor in Austen.

Isabelle had recently found out that the oil wells drilled on the Adams land, which provided a substantial income to the Adams and Silvano business empires, also included three oil wells situated upon this land. Isabelle had brought this to the attention of Michael Silvano so he could sort the matter out. There was some redress to be achieved for the missing twenty years-plus of income from these wells. Income should have been paid into the Van-der-Vaults's business funds, and not into the Edwards's coffers.

CHAPTER 16

CONSOLIDATIONS

Michael was sorting this aspect out with the Adams lawyer, who he was presently in contact with over Julianne's marriage contract. Isabelle had never benefitted from this land lease other than the peppercorn rent she had received. Isabelle didn't want or need this land title, as the Van-der-Vaults were well provided for. She was considering giving this land to James as a wedding present, which she would be pleased to do, as she was too old now to battle with the likes of Walter Adams. Isabelle had never liked her daughter's choice of husband, and as it turned out, her grandson Wesley was equally as bad a character as his father.

The family knew about Julianne being Wesley's real daughter and not Walter's. Julianne would have her own inheritance from both her mother's family and from Walter Adams, when he died, as she would inherit the ranch outright and all that went with it. Isabelle knew what Walter Adams was up to in trying to get Julianne to marry his nephew, Donald Caraway. Walter just wanted to get his hands on all the inherited assets. Well, this one she was determined he wouldn't get. It would be fitting that brother and sister should own two halves of what was now considered one property, and the income from the three wells and its income for the last twenty years would be separated into a new fund, to become the wealth and income of James's new family line. Isabelle was strong on family and thought this arrangement would be a fitting outcome for all the hurts she had incurred by the loss of her only child and grandson so many years ago.

Wesley had always been a spoilt child, but if nothing else, he had left two good-looking great-grandchildren, even if they were illegitimate.

On seeing James, Isabella was impressed with his looks and personality, and having heard of this Dr Adams, who was new in town, she was even more impressed when meeting him face to face. James may have only been in his early twenties, but he was definitely a man who knew his own mind. Isabella liked a man to be self-assured, and James was. She was convinced he was related to Wesley, as she could see the eyes of her father very clearly in James's eyes. The eye colouring was different from Wesley's but the same colour as her father's, and the shape and expression in the eyes were similar.

They were compassionate and caring eyes, so Elaina would be very lucky in life, by having James as her husband. James knew nothing about what was being arranged behind the scenes; he socialised with Isabelle and Andrew, and made sure they were invited to the wedding. When they sat down eventually to talk, it was a surprise to Elaina and Catherine that James would be a wealthy man in his own right, whether he wanted it or not. Isabelle gave Michael full authority to make the transfer of property and land and all the income appertaining to this land title. James had wanted a heritage, and now he had got one, with land and money to spare. The Sky Spirits had come up trumps. James did not know what to say. It was beyond his present understanding, and all he could say was thank you to two most charming people and especially to Isabelle, as he respected his elders and could see her mature spirit shining brightly.

Andrew Van-der Vault offered to help Michael sort out the legal paperwork, as he had more time to spare now that he was retired, and Catherine thanked him for helping out in this matter. Before Isabelle left, Catherine gave her a jar of skin cream and asked her to try it out, as it was proving wonderful for tired skin, and wrinkles were fast disappearing with additional rejuvenated skin tone. They would all meet up again in two days' time at the wedding.

The next stop was to meet Catherine's sister, Marianne Prentice, who was Samantha's mother and Julianne's grandmother. Marianne lived on the other side of Richmond, when she wasn't visiting Samantha in New York. Marianne had married Lawrence Prentice when he was a dashing sergeant major (he later became a captain) in the Southern Army Regiment. It had been when he was stationed at Fort Worth that Samantha had visited her father there and had met Wesley Adams. There had been a right rumpus at the time, when Samantha had found out she was pregnant, and then Wesley failed to return from his mission. Samantha had travelled from the fort to the Adams Ranch to await Wesley's arrival. After waiting a month, it was obvious Wesley was not going to return, and everyone feared the worst. Samantha waited as long as she could, but at five months' pregnant, she succumbed to Walter's pressure to legitimise her child by marrying him instead.

Marianne was waiting for their arrival in a colonial white townhouse, which was not a mansion but a comfortable family home. She had only just returned from New York after visiting her daughter and was still unpacking. Marianne was unacquainted with the recent developments of Richmond society so was not expecting James or Elaina, as she had only received a message to say that her sister was about to pay a visit.

Catherine always called upon her when she least expected it, paying a flying visit when it suited her. When she met James for the first time, she was momentarily bemused, as he seemed remarkably familiar to her, but she didn't know why.

When James first met Marianne, he was somewhat taken aback, as Marianne was a twin sister to Catherine, and they looked very much alike. It was obvious that Catherine was the elder of the two, as she was the dominant one. She handed Marianne a wedding invitation and introduced James as Elaina's fiancé. She emphasised that James was Dr James Adams and explained that they had met when Elaina was working with her father at the El Paso Mission. Marianne was nodding, taking in all that Catherine was telling her. Suddenly, she perked up and said to Catherine that when Elaina married James, she would become an Adams, keeping the same name in the family.

Julianne, on the other hand, was going to lose her Adams name when she married her fiancé, Antonio Rossi. Marianne made a comment never getting rid of the Adams name, as Walter had never been her favourite person. She had battled with him on many occasions, and there had been many arguments over the years. Catherine took this opportunity to take Marianne aside and fill her in on the latest findings regarding James's heritage. Marianne suddenly exclaimed that she now knew why he looked so familiar, as of course he looked like Julianne; the hair colouring was the same, and they had a similar look. Catherine didn't tell her sister about any inheritance coming to James via the Van-der-Vaults but did say that everyone who was anyone would be attending the wedding. Marianne could be a gossip, so Catherine only told her what she wanted her to know.

Catherine and Marianne were really the best of friends as well as sisters. Since the death of her husband, Lawrence, over ten years ago, Marianne had taken a new lease on life, as she could come and go as she pleased. She even had a new man in her life but was wise enough to keep him at arm's length, as she didn't want to be beholden again to any man. Louis de Claremont was of French extraction and a real gentleman. He would be escorting Marianne to the wedding, of course, and he was welcomed, as both Marianne and Catherine had known both him and his wife for years before he became a widower five years ago. Louis had two daughters, who were both teachers at the universities in Richmond. Louis was very knowledgeable and could talk on any subject under the sun, and you would never get bored. He was excellent company and a lovely human being.

He would marry Marianne tomorrow if she would say yes, but Marianne maintained his interest by keeping him on a string. She enjoyed her life, and this was a time she treasured; she was determined not to miss out on anything. Too many of her friends had given up on life, and within a few years, she had seen how life had beaten them. She was set on living life to the full while she had time and energy to do so. Spending time in New York had opened her eyes. Her daughter, Samantha, had married a man involved in politics, and on her recent visit, she had entered a whirl of socialising that had swept her off her feet. She still hadn't come down to earth, and here was something else to get excited about.

A wedding on her doorstep, with an element of mystery and magic; it couldn't get any better. Just think, Julianne had a brother she didn't even know. What a surprise. From what Marianne had seen of James, she knew that he would be a match for anyone, and with Elaina as his life partner, they would make a formidable team. Marianne had always liked Elaina and had felt sorry for her when her mother died, as she knew Elaina had felt lonely. She had often pointed this out to Catherine.

Grandparents did not make up for real parents, and Marianne had often questioned Catherine about her controlling attitude, but she knew Catherine meant well, when all was said and done. Sometimes, Catherine just couldn't let go of what she thought was the last remaining fragments of her dead daughter. Elaina was the link to Maria, so Catherine had piled all her love and hopes onto Elaina. Catherine was secretly glad Elaina had found someone so wonderful, just like her Phillip. James was certainly unique and would make an impression wherever he went. Catherine knew Elaina would travel back to the West, as the mission and her nursing was a part of her vocation, and she knew Elaina needed to be where she could make a difference to the people around her. Elaina was a wonderful nurse and a great asset to James, as he was to her.

When the visiting party arrived back at the Silvano mansion, they were all exhausted. The evening meal was taken in the formal dining room, with Phillip and Michael attending, and all the day's events were discussed yet again. It was hoped that after the marriage, James and Elaina would journey to eastern Texas on their return trip, to survey their inheritance and meet with Julianne. It was known that Walter was not in good health and that Julianne was running the ranch with the help of Antonio Rossi, the son of a neighbouring ranch owner; he worshiped the ground she walked on. Julianne would make an alliance that could be capitalised upon, as she would double her acreage and landholdings by merging the two ranches together.

The day before the wedding was one of rest and last-minute checking for Elaina and James. It was just the immediate family who would be attending the church service, and that included newfound members who loosely qualified so they could witness this union. By doing so, the relationship was legitimised, witnessed, and agreed to by the main players of the Edwards, Silvano, Van-de-Vault, and Adams heritages. Uncle Michael brought round some paperwork to be signed. James signed where he was told to, not really knowing what it was, but trusting Michael to do all that was right and proper.

Gordon arrived to update James on the latest happenings regarding their Natural Healing Remedies; he told James that the stocks held at the chemists shop had sold out in a week. The ladies' creams were selling well, and the hospital had asked if they could be supplied with a complete range of medicines. James informed Gordon to charge a special rate to the hospital of cost plus one dollar, so they would always know how many bottles of medicines were sold, by the amount of dollars received as profit. It would cut out the need for a lot of accounting and calculating.

James advised that the other products should always be made affordable to the common folk, so everyone could benefit from their range of natural remedies. The chemist, Mr Adrian Shaw, had hit upon a good idea when he had rendered the cream into a powder. Gordon had instructed him to powder as many of the other concoctions and potions as was possible, so they could be stored and reconstituted the same way. It was obvious that fresh mixtures could not be made in great quantities, so if demand were to overtake the ability to supply, stocks would run out. It had also become obvious that some plants were seasonal and could only be harvested at certain times of the year. These supplies had to be harvested and stored when they were available.

James gave his input to Gordon, who brightened up and went away with some more ideas to further the supplies of the enterprise. Phillip Silvano had offered a vacant warehouse by the river's edge, to be used for packing or mixing supplies, and this offer was taken up almost immediately. Phillip had got involved with this latest activity, as enquiries were being made to his own business about shipping overseas. Phillip had even taken a secret visit to meet the Gisters at the Botanical Gardens when asked by Catherine to find out how this business was really doing. There were plenty of potted plants now housed in the glasshouse, and more were planted out in the display areas.

Tom and Frank were starting work earlier and leaving later to fit in the hours of harvesting leaves, crushing ingredients, and mixing compounds to create more supplies, just as James had instructed. The fresh supplies had a limited lifespan of freshness, so new batches had to be made each week to feed the demand. New supplies for testing were also required, as James kept coming up with new products for different remedies.

The Gisters had taken James to a hillside river where marigold flowers grew, and nearby, there were fields of mushrooms, as they liked the damp humid atmosphere. James was soon harvesting mushrooms to make a creamy paste and adding marigolds. This gave the cream a golden colour, and so a new skin lotion was born, for the two properties proved beneficial to curing all sorts of blemishes. Soon they would have a medicinal range for most general ailments, with some specific conditions also catered for.

The Gisters had everything written down about the ingredients, quantities, and qualities each plant or compound contained. They consulted a recipe each time they made a batch to keep the same consistencies. Gordon would arrive each day and take away any bottles or jars they had filled. He made sure each container was labelled correctly and would leave them with more supplies of unfilled containers, ready for the next batch.

Business seemed to be booming, so much so that there weren't enough hours in the day to fulfil all the activities. Gordon had written up his thesis, giving projected outcomes for the next ten years. He had asked Phillip to be his business mentor and had given him a draft copy before he submitted it to the university faculty.

Phillip was impressed with Gordon's understanding and what amounted to a ten-year projected business plan, and he realised that James had hit on a winning formula, which was taking the city by storm today and could become a standard product used by everyone within the foreseeable future. Once the city of Richmond had been saturated with Natural Health Remedies products, other large cities and smaller towns could be similarly targeted as distribution depots. There was no reason why distribution could not go even farther, perhaps overseas or Mexico.

Phillip could see potential in the recipes that the Gisters had recorded, as where the physical vegetation differed through geographical locations, different ingredients could be substituted to provide the same or similar compounds. Phillip knew that Jonathan Westwood would be greatly interested in mixing his own compounds with locally grown produce and vegetation, as the supplies of medicines to this outpost of a township, had always been somewhat erratic.

Thoughts turned again to the following big day, as this was to be quite an event in the Richmond social calendar. Amos and Anthony King from Charlottesville were arriving to attend the wedding and to take James's horse, White Blaze, back with them as a stud for their mares. This would save James and Elaina an unnecessary visit, as they had other plans. Amos and Anthony had heard about Natural Health Remedies and wanted some ointments to use for their horses. Gordon would be in his element, canvassing for business from the wedding guests.

That night, James and Elaina cuddled up in the big soft bed in Elaina's room. Elaina was now sure she was with child and told James so. He was delighted and kissed her lovingly. They decided to stay another month in Richmond before setting off on their travels so they could make sure the business was able to continue without James's presence, and by that time, Elaina would be over her initial discomfort and escape before she began to show any noticeable enlargement. It would be sad to leave Catherine and Phillip, as they had been as good as parents, but the pull of the mission and the work there was compelling, and even James agreed they couldn't leave Jonathan on his own for very much longer.

Little did they know that the relationship between Jonathan and Camille was blossoming into a passionate romance. Father Carlos was smiling every day, as he sensed that another one of his match-making schemes would soon lead to a wedding.

Jonathan Westwood was delighted with his new assistant and marvelled at how quickly Camille had fitted into the regime at the mission hospital. She was attractive, and he had to admit she had taken him by surprise. He had not expected to be attracted to another woman after so many years of being on his own. He felt rejuvenated, and all because of Camille's presence. Jonathan and Camille worked closely together for a couple of months, so it became logical to eat their meals together. Each evening after work, when the clinic closed, they would eat al fresco at a table in the courtyard.

At this time, the workers were eating in the cantina, and Milo acted as waiter, as he now had help in the kitchens from a Mrs Weaver, the cook, and her daughter, Vanessa. Mrs Weaver was Mexican; she had been married to Jules Weaver, an Americano who had been a soldier in the Civil War. He had been injured and only recently died, leaving her and her daughter in poverty and without a home. She had arrived at the mission asking for help and had volunteered to work for her board and her daughter's keep. Both women were hard workers; they also did the laundry between mealtimes. This was a great help to the mission, as help was received and given, pleasing both parties. The women did not feel they were receiving charity, and every effort was being made to find them a permanent home. Meanwhile, the cantina took on a lively ambience, with mother cooking and daughter serving and clearing up. That left Milo to see to any other personnel who needed a meal, and this was how he came to be the one serving Jonathan and Camille outside in the courtyard.

Father Carlos had given him instructions to foster the relationship between these two, so Milo's idea was to couple them at mealtimes.

Occasionally, a bottle of wine appeared on the dining table. A pleasant evening followed with the consumption of good food and good wine, and the conversation was enhanced by the ambience of a warm, starry night.

Thoughts of Jonathan were abandoned by James and Elaina as they snuggled down in their comfortable bed. The heat between then flickered into passion, and soon they forgot about anyone else but themselves. Their lovemaking was followed by pleasant dreams, and all too soon, early morning broke, which signalled the start of their great day. James had to retreat into the room next door, and Elaina remembered to lock the interconnecting door. Brides were not supposed to see their bridegrooms until the wedding time, so they said goodbye to each other until later on in the day. By eight o'clock, the servants had brought breakfast to their rooms on a tray. This was just as well, for Elaina was unwell first thing and couldn't stomach the smell of food in any form.

Dry toast and coffee was as much as she could manage. James, on the other hand, ate a hearty breakfast, as he knew lunch would be a long time away. The wedding ceremony was scheduled for midday at the church, but it would be nearer two in the afternoon before guests were seated for the wedding meal. A large marquee had been erected in the garden for dining, with a musical group of six to play classical tunes. The marquee was decked out in white and yellow tones with flowers and ribbons, tablecloths and chair covers following the same colour scheme. The whole place smelt of fuchsia's which seemed to be the predominate flower used for this occasion. The ambiance was heady but sophisticated at the same time and masked any odours that came from the close proximity of a crush of peoples.

After eating a superb luncheon, followed by liquid toasts to celebrate this union, Catherine and Phillip circulated amongst their guests. Catherine came upon some women discussing the medicinal qualities of the Natural Healing Remedies and offered herself up as an example of how effective these products were, for they had cured her problem exceedingly well. Even Dr Raymond had been impressed, and everyone knew he was as traditional as they come.

Gordon was not far behind promoting the healing products and gaining orders and recommendations from all different sources. A number of free samples of the latest marigold cream were distributed, with the perfume itself very pungent and appealing.

James was introduced to Catherine and Phillip's youngest son, Jason, who was married to Anabelle. They had three sons, all taking after their father and grandfather, being tall, dark, and good looking. Jason was the son who ran the Silvano shipping line now that his father had officially retired. Jason's sons were sixteen, eighteen, and twenty years, and were either at school or university studying commerce, shipping, and finance. During the holidays, they worked in the shipping offices near the docks to gain experience. They were a loving family, and Anabelle was a most supporting wife.

PART 4

THE NEW LIFE

CHAPTER 17

FOLLOWING THE RAINBOW

The wedding was a fine occasion, where many contacts were made, and the elite of Richmond society came out in force to support this newly married couple. The Van-de-Vaults were most gracious people with good manners and consideration. They exuded wealth, power, and old-style colonialism. Isabelle looked magnificent in her cream gown and overcoat, decked with pearls and diamonds. Her hat of cream stiffened lace was reminiscent of an age gone by, that was wholly elegant and fashionable. Marianne, Catherine's sister, and her beau, Louis de Claremont, were entertaining characters, as Louis liked to dance and parade Marianne around, as if to show her off. Louis was forever bowing to ladies and making them laugh at his small jokes, which never offended. All the ladies loved Louis, and Marianne beamed in appreciation of the fact that he only had eyes for her.

New to the city was Dr Jenner, who originated from Europe. The Swiss man was in his mid-forties and was a business friend of Phillip and Jason, as he imported many medical supplies from overseas. He was interested in the work James was doing and offered to share his expertise, as Americans were crying out for natural and herbal supplies, as they were very difficult to source and supply. Dr Jenner was a biochemist and carried out research for government and medical organisations. He wanted to approach James to get his permission to licence some of his medicines, ointments, and creams. Licensing the recipes would provide a lucrative source of income; they could be made anywhere in the world.

Catherine was responsible for introducing Dr Jenner, as she knew he was influential in high government circles. Anything that was endorsed by this man was guaranteed to be successful, and Catherine could see the potential of herbal supplies being shipped overseas by her husband's shipping line. This would benefit everyone. With permission from James, the Gisters were invited to liaise with Dr Jenner over the different recipes to everyone's encouragement and satisfaction. The financial negotiations were left to Michael Silvano, who added a sharp and confident manner to the proceedings.

All was set for a prosperous future that would benefit all those involved with the Natural Healing Remedies. Catherine promised James and Alana to provide legal and financial assistance for research and development and to keep a continued eye on their interest.

With Catherine involved, the business took off quickly; the following month, sample shipments were sent overseas via the Silvano shipping line, and with the sales of licences and recipes, the financial rewards began to fill the bank account substantially, in a very satisfactory manner.

James and Elaina decided it was time to head back West to the mission in El Paso, Texas, as they wanted their baby to be born there, with Elaina's father, Dr Westwood, and James in attendance. With a necessary stop at Austin, to discuss oil and land rights with the Adams lawyer, it would take them at least a month or six weeks to reach the mission complex. This meant that they would have been away from the mission for over four months. Elaina was starting to put on a little weight, but at the moment, it did not show to any great degree. She was now feeling well and fit, so it was a good time to travel. Passage was booked by train and overland stage, as the route back would be different from the one they took to Richmond. Farewells were difficult, with Catherine actually tearful at the parting. James said farewell to all his staff, who had become personal friends, and gave his workers assurances that the Silvano's would govern wisely with his proxy and that he would visit Richmond again in two years' time.

James and Elaina set off upon their journey and made remarkable time, getting to Austin in ten days. Their visit coincided with meeting Julianne and her new husband, Antonio known as Tony, who had come to the lawyer's office to attend this business meeting. It transpired that Walter Adams had died three weeks earlier, and Julianne had come into her own inheritance. Her marriage had brought more landholdings, so she didn't need the land bequeathed to James. Further papers were signed to capture the oil income, and instantly, James became an independently wealthy man.

Julianne and James had eyed each other up, recognising a kinship between them. Their looks and hair colouring were very similar, and you could see straight away they were related. Once they began talking, it was apparent they had similar qualities and interests. Horses were a common subject, and herbal remedies for horse ailments were also discussed. Once the business side of things had been dealt with, and the change of ownership papers signed and sealed, social discourse ensued.

Julianne told James and Elaine that she had married Tony the moment Walter had died. Walter had become bedridden in his final weeks of illness and had died after running out of energy to fight anymore. He had been a difficult man to live with, so this was a relief from the encumbered past. Julianne and Tony agreed to continue to care-take James's new landholdings until the following year, after Elaina had given birth and James promised to visit and view his inherited land, once the baby was born and able to travel. Julianne had received information about James and Elaina from her mother, who had written at length on all the recent developments in Richmond. Catherine had written as well, detailing the business matters requiring her attention.

Julianne had inherited a lot of Catherine's personality, and that included a good head for business matters. By the time James and Elaina reached El Paso, both were weary from travelling, and Elaina seemed to be enlarging quite noticeably. There was great rejoicing at their arrival back at the mission, and no one was that surprised to find Elaina expecting. What was a surprise was that Camille and Jonathan had decided to get married, so yet another wedding was scheduled in a few weeks. This meant that James and Elaina would have to take over the mission infirmary while Jonathan and Camille took their honeymoon. They had decided to take a trip into Mexico to visit Joe and Emile to see how they were progressing in their new lives. The mission monks were using their visit to send a case of Bibles to their brothers over the border. Jonathan and Camille didn't mind, as the monks had been good to them, and it was all about spreading the good word of God into fertile regions, to educate and bring about acceptable moral standards.

The wedding between Jonathan and Camille was a low-keyed affair, with only close family members attending. As Camille did not have any close relatives, Milo and Juanita came to the rescue again and produced family as supporters and wedding garments just right for the occasion. It seemed Milo and Juanita were forever conspiring together, as between them they seemed to have a wonderful way of obtaining things from unknown sources, as they knew the right people to ask who could fulfil their requests.

While Jonathan and Camille left for their visit to Joe, Pedro, and Emile in Mexico, James and Elaina filled the needs of the clinic. James had acquired new skills in medical understanding from his travels to the East, and with new techniques for pain control suitable for both the young and old, the effectiveness of his administrations were enhanced substantially, when many of his clients became thankful for his personal approach, reassurances, and know-how. His herbal remedies were very popular, and in particular, the women were all keen to avail themselves of the creams to aid their complexions.

The overhead sun was both a blessing and a curse for complexions of native peoples who were constantly outdoors. Their skin aged and dried, so youthful looks were very transitory. Sun-barrier creams were sought after by the lighter skinned females, who fought a constant battle to keep the sunrays from ravishing their complexions.

Elaina bloomed in health and increased considerably in size. She was concerned that she was carrying a lot of water, but each time James examined her, he heard a healthy heartbeat and detected a growing baby with active arms and legs. It looked like she would have a large, healthy baby, as her slender frame was ballooning around her. She felt fantastic, and James made her feel so special and loved; it was a wonderful time to be together and be fulfilling her dream of helping the locals, particularly the poor and underprivileged. Never before had she realised how lucky she was, in never having to want for anything, including love, which was in abundance all around her.

CHAPTER 18

DOWN MEXICO WAY

Joe and Lois, with baby Eve, were given the overseer's bungalow, which was recently vacated by the horse manager when he was recalled to Mexico City. Joe had never lived in a house before, and while Lois thought this whitewashed bungalow with a red tiled roof was the prettiest she had ever seen, Joe wondered if he would be able to settle here. He was prepared to try, so left Lois to settle in while he was shown the stables and horses.

Pedro and Lena and their baby son were back at this plantation and living in another white bungalow across from the stables. The Cortez plantation was massive in size, with the main house, stables, and outhouses at its centre. The journey from the border had been pleasant enough, through highlands, scrubland, and then more plush surroundings of trees, then the lowlands opened to cultivated fields, fenced off from open paddocks, housing cattle and horses. This was a wealthy estate, with many families working and earning their livelihoods from the landholdings of this grand hacienda.

Joe had learned that the horses he was to manage were not prairie horses but purebred Spanish horses used for ceremonial and dressage purposes; Emmanuel Cortex was very proud of them. Joe had heard of these fine horses but had never seen any, so he was anxious to assess their superiority for himself.

What he found both pleased him and saddened him. The stables were superb in their construction, and the horses were indeed superior, but the condition of both left Joe surprised and worried. No one here had attended to the horses or seen to their welfare since the horse manager left, as no one was in authority to give instructions. The horses had been fed and watered, but that was about all, and Joe doubted they had been exercised. Pedro told him that the Mexican workers had been afraid of the horse manager, as Fernando Perez was a hard master to please, and they had been afraid of working on their own initiative, in case there were repercussions from the big house. They were waiting for someone to take charge and give them their instructions. In addition, many of the stable workers seemed to have stomach flu in the last few days; they were sick and unable to attend to their duties.

Pedro was in charge of dressage and the training of paired horses to perform sequence activities according to Spanish cultural heraldry. Joe had picked up the Mexican language very well at the mission but realised he may need additional help from Pedro, as his vocabulary was the everyday variety and not specialised for horsemanship and all that associated with them, especially regarding Spanish heraldry.

Joe noticed a lot of rubbish stacked beside one of the wells and asked if this was the well that the stable workers used. He sampled the water and spat out the rank-tasting liquid. This water was contaminated and, at present, useless to man or beast. This must be the cause of the stomach sickness. He found out this was the well, used by the stable workers, so he asked Pedro to have some workers clear the rubbish away. It was the poisons coming out of the rubbish that were seeping into the ground and affecting the water underneath which supplied the well.

He also said they should cover the well with a wooden lid, to stop anyone from throwing rubbish into it. Just to make sure nothing else was contaminating the well. Joe asked them to dredge it. They found a rotting dog's body, which was obviously the main source of contamination. Once a lid was in place on top of the well, no more rubbish would be thrown down the hole.

Joe also instructed that the two other wells around the main house were to be similarly cleaned and dredged, to make sure they were clear from any contamination. He also suggested they should be fitted with wooden lids, so the water beneath could be retained and not allowed to evaporate. Joe had copied the setup he had seen implemented at the mission, which he observed always had a clean supply of water.

Joe then called the workers into the courtyard; he noticed they were a mixture of Mexican and Indian heritage. They were surprised to see a pure Indian taking charge. Joe, who was usually unassuming, was angered by the state of affairs he had encountered. Even a poor Indian looked after his horse better than these most valuable prime specimens, which had been left in a decrepit state.

Joe was wise enough to realise that these workers knew no better, so he controlled his anger, changed it to assertiveness, and began his management regime, as he meant to deal with these people in a firm and fair manner. Joe gave instructions for all the horses to be led out into the paddock, while the stables were cleaned from top to bottom. This took most of the day. The horses were mostly greys, having been bred from the Andalusian bloodlines that came over from Spain with the original invaders. These horses had been given as gifts from the reigning Spanish kings.

These Andalusian horses were strong warhorses with fine features, beautiful manes, and usually sturdy constitutions. Andalusians are often called the horses of kings. Joe then inspected each horse at it was returned to its stable. Several horses had ticks upon their skin, others some sores. Their mane and tail hair required brushing, and many were in a tangled mess. Each beautiful horse definitely was in need of some loving care and personal human contact. Joe attended to each horse personally, whispering in his native tongue the horse's friendship song, which his father had taught him when he was but a youth. Having done his best for each horse, he used some of his own horse ointment and was glad of the bag of river weed James had given to him, to use for any cases where inflammation was present. The horses were fed and watered afresh, and everyone was pleased that someone had taken control at last and knew what they were doing.

It was twilight when Joe eventually returned to Lois, now installed in the little white bungalow. She had opened all the windows and shutters to allow the air to circulate and somehow had found flowers to decorate each room, to give it a better smell than that of dust and staleness. There were four rooms, being a kitchen, two bedrooms, and a general room, housing a wooden table and chairs. There was a front door and a back door, which led to an outhouse used for ablutions. Beyond this was a small garden with a cultivated area to grow root vegetables. This was beyond a small terrace and grass area, overhung by a sunshade of growing vines, which provided an open-air sleeping and eating area.

The climate here could be changeable, with hot dry days and nights, or cold nights at times when it would rain continuously for days. It was tropical weather one minute and then desert weather the next.

There was a general food store at the big hacienda that supplied meat and produce to the workers. They could source what they wanted from the main house for meals to cook at home. At other times, anyone could go into the main house kitchens to be fed, as all were either guests or estate workers. No one went hungry on the Cortez plantation, so all who were employed gave their best service for what they received in food and welfare.

Within three days, the stable workers were all back at work and doing the jobs they were employed to do. Each morning, Joe would supervise the grooming of each animal and assess their condition to see if they were free from tics, sores, and distress. Within a week, the horses were in a better condition and ready to start their workouts. Joe instructed that the horses should be led outside to walk in the sunshine or trot in the paddock, before formally receiving dressage training.

Joe was not familiar with dressage and was fascinated by the wonderful movements these beautiful horses could perform. His job was to keep the horses in good condition so they would respond enthusiastically to the dressage training. This was where Pedro came in, as he would instruct stable riders in the art of parade formations, under the directions of Antonio Lorenzo, who was a Spanish horseman of some renown. It was to Antonio that all the stable employees reported. He was a man of impeccable dress and a showman to the core. His knowledge of horse welfare was not extensive, however, as his expertise lay in training the horses to perform for public display.

Antonio could, however, see if a horse was well cared for and when it was happy and when it was not. He had been greatly impressed by this Indian, Joe Fox, who had quickly taken command of the men and the situation he had found. He treated him and everyone else as an equal and had not at any time acted subservient to anyone. This had earned respect from Antonio, who knew that a man's worth was seen by how he acted and conducted himself. Antonio had begun life as an orphan, being brought up in poverty by his aunt. He had been lucky, as he had been adopted as a youth by Juan Lorenzo, a stable worker who worked at the royal stables and had taken a liking to him. His adopted father had been a dressage trainer, and all he now knew had come from him.

Lois and Lena became friends, as each had a young baby to attend to, so they pooled their resources and spent time with each other every afternoon, while their respective husbands were at work. They also swapped stories surrounding their childbirth experiences, as both had been assisted by James; what a difference he had made to the whole process and to their lives. Lois was now growing in confidence as she was responding to the loving given to her by Joe, who was so kind and gentle. She really had to pinch herself sometimes to feel if she was real, as she was so happy.

Baby Eve was growing into a bonny lass, and besides her lighter coloured skin and hair, she looked very much like Lois, with a dainty round face and fine features. Within a few weeks of being at the Cortez estate, Lois thought she might be expecting another child. She would know for sure in another month, and this would please Joe, as she knew he had always wanted children of his own. The days passed in happy contentment while the women carried out their work around the home; their children growing, and the men progressed with horse welfare and training.

They made friends with other stable workers and their families, and each week, the workers came together to socialise. Women would cook food, and the men would drink and play their musical instruments. Inside the big house, more merriment was taking place, as visitors had arrived from Mexico City. Entertainment on display for the dignitaries and their families they had brought along. Tomorrow, the stables were to be inspected, and a rehearsal of the dressage would take place, as part of the afternoon entertainment. Joe and Pedro would have to rise at sunup to see to all the arrangements. All the horses had to be groomed and dressed in their finery.

Emile would be included in the audience, as he had been accepted as the son and heir and was now a man of importance. This would be the first time Joe and Lois met with Emile since they arrived over eight weeks earlier. Emile had been absorbed within his father's family, and there had been much to learn, see, and assimilate regarding the working of the estate. Emile had to learn about the responsibilities he had regarding estate families and the obligations he had inherited. The obligations were from the royal connections the family had established, with those residing at the capital, so that was why he had little time to contact his friends up until now, when their paths crossed once again.

The sun was shining the next morning, and the horses put through their paces as a rehearsal for later. Lois dressed little Eve in her best dress and herself in her finest outfit. This afternoon, they were to fill the stalls in the stable theatre for the display taking place. This formed part of the formal ceremonial celebrations to welcome Emile as the heir to the Cortez plantation, and this was his formal recognition into the ranks of the influential Mexican elite. When the visitors arrived, it was noted that Emile was escorting the ambassador's daughter.

She was very beautiful, with long dark hair piled high and covered in a lace mantilla headdress. Her gown was white, and she looked very regal. Emile was dressed in black with a white ruffled shirt, and a red rose was in his lapel. Once his party was seated, he excused himself and came to say hello to Lois. He commented on how baby Eve had grown and asked her if her accommodations were satisfactory.

Lois noticed his speech was more refined than it had been back at the mission and knew he was speaking proper Spanish rather than Mexican Spanish, which was considered a slang version of the language. Joe came to join them then, and the two friends shook hands and asked each other for their news. Joe told Emile what he had been doing with the horses, and Emile said he had been busy with rounds of official gatherings, seeing the estate, and learning how it was run. Emile explained that the young lady he was accompanying was Katerina Valdez, only daughter and child to Ambassador Eduardo Valdez, who was another wealthy landowner from farther south. In addition, he was the agricultural minister to the current Mexican ruling government.

Emile's grandfather was a major contributor of cattle, horses, and farm produce to the markets at Monterrey and Mexico City. Katerina was an heiress, and it seemed there was matchmaking in the air. Emile said he liked her very much, as she was a genuine person and not stuffy, as some of the young ladies he had been introduced to. Once you got to know her, she was fun and down-to-earth. She had managed to look after her father for a number of years after her mother died giving birth to her dead brother. Her father had been devastated at the loss of his wife and son, and it had been down to her to instil some normality, for life to continue on. She had taken on the formal duties that came with the ambassadorship, which otherwise a wife would undertake, and had enjoyed learning so much while having her father as company, when at court and touring the countryside's large estates.

Katerina's looks and dress were formal, as she had to represent her father's interests while they toured the country on government business, but underneath the formality, she was a young girl, who very much wanted a family of her own, and to live in the style and manner that she had been used to. Katerina needed someone who could understand her and who could take some of the life burdens from her, so she could just be herself, with the freedom of safe surroundings. Emile admitted that he might marry her, as she was a favourite of his grandfather, and he was always a good judge of people and horses. The visitors were staying on for three weeks, but Katerina had intimated she would like to stay on for a few more weeks, to get to know Emile better.

Her father and Emile's grandfather sanctioned her extended stay, as both families were keen to unite their families, by the union of these young people. Emile admitted he was living in total luxury and found it somewhat disconcerting that his every wish was attended to. While he did not dismiss his good fortune as unimportant, he did realise that his friendships to people who knew him well were indeed valuable, for good friends were made for life. Emile wanted Joe and Lois to know that he remained their friend, and at any time they needed help or assistance, they could contact him. Emile assured them he would never let his friends down, for they had supported him on his quest to find his heritage, and they should share in his good fortune, so anything they needed, he would be there for them, and that also included White Feather. Joe and Lois were deeply touched that Emile felt this way and thanked him. They told him they were delighted with the bungalow accommodation, and Joe loved looking after the horses which were the best he had ever seen and handled. They were both enjoying the friendships of the workers and told Emile that Pedro and Lena had become their firm friends.

The horses began to assemble in the display area, so Emile returned to Katerina's side. The dignitaries were seated in the high seats under a canopy providing shade, so they had the best view of the arena. Joe and

Lois sat near the front so they could see the horses close up, as they passed by in their sequenced dances. By being nearer to the horses, you could feel the tension and delight when the animals performed as they had been taught and displayed their steps, synchronised to the music. The afternoon was a wonderful experience for both the riders and spectators, as the display was both colourful and enchanting. The riders and horses became as one operating unit, so the exact movements of dressage and group synchronisation was wonderful to watch.

The elite spectators were won over by this display, and the dignitaries left their seats in a glow of pleasure. All those who had contributed to this performance were satisfied that their hard work and weeks of training had paid off; the positive way that this display had been received was the proof that the standards set had been surpassed beyond all expectations.

Antonio Lorenzo came to thank Joe and Pedro for their hard work and told them that the ambassador had invited them to Mexico City to provide entertainment to royalty. This meant they would be travelling as a troupe of people and horses to the Mexican capital; it was expected that Joe and Pedro, together with their families, would accompany the travelling troupe when the time came.

The Mexican royal family held a countrywide competition to determine the best of the dressage troupes, and the winner would be bestowed with royal endorsements to ensure a financially successful future. If the Cortez troupe won this accolade, it would ensure the prosperity of their horse breeding lines for generations to come.

They spent the next two months training and perfecting new moves. Joe's job was to keep the horses in tip-top condition; each day, they were expected to fulfil a regime of grooming and exercise. Joe would ride the horses; he was learning some of the moves used in the display, as Pedro had instructed him. Joe also suggested some new moves that Pedro could incorporate in the display, and he did. Joe understood the horses and knew which of them would complement another when choosing pairs to operate together. With the compatible coupling of like horses, the overall performance had become improved, as there were no longer any personality conflicts.

Pedro and Antonio were impressed by Joe's knowledge and horse expertise. Antonio felt that Joe fitted in well with the team members who managed the horses and their training. He recommended him for a raise in salary, for he had proved his worth and was continuing to become an invaluable asset to the Cortez empire. Joe was enjoying this life experience, especially since Lois had informed him she was carrying his child. A child of his own was all he had dreamed of, and he gave thanks to the Great Sky Spirit for bringing his dreams to fruition and making his life worthwhile, after it had been devastated by the death of his first wife. Joe's thoughts moved to his nephew, White Feather, and he wondered if his life was emerging as productive as his own.

Lois was proving a wonderful loving partner, and Joe was greatly pleased with his choice of wife, especially now she was blossoming and bearing fruit.

----- xxx -----

The journey to Mexico City was to coincide with the marriage of Emile and Katerina. Katerina had stayed on after her father had left the Cortez plantation, and the friendship which started with her visit had blossomed into love for each other. Katerina and Emile would be married at the Cathedral Metropolitana de la Asunción de la Maria, which was the Metropolitan Cathedral of the Assumption of Mary in Mexico City, and the Cortez horse show would be entered into the royal display competition. Anticipation was high from all quarters of the Cortez plantation regarding the proposed trip to Mexico City, and more than one person was counting the days for their departure. This adventure was part work and part holiday, for the capital city of Mexico would be a new experience, and it was hoped that there would be time for some sightseeing.

> In present times, the breeding, showing, and registration of the Andalusian horses are controlled by organizations such as the Association of Purebred Spanish Horse Breeders of Spain (*Asociación Nacional de Criadores de Caballo de Pura Raza Española*or, ANCCE), who use the term "Pura Raza Española," or PRE, to describe the true Spanish horse and claim sole authority to officially register and issue documentation for PRE horses, both in Spain and anywhere else in the world. Sourced (APSHBS)

CHAPTER 19

MEXICAN HISTORY

The Porfiriato (1876-1911)

Order, Progress, and Dictatorship

Porfirio Díaz became Mexico's new president in 1876, and thus began a period of more than thirty years' stability (1876–1911), during which Díaz was Mexico's strong man. This period of relative prosperity and peace is known as the *Porfiriato*. During this period, the country's infrastructure improved greatly, thanks to increased foreign investment and a strong, stable central government. Increased tax revenues and better administration brought many improvements, including the development of a national health service, a better communications network, investment in infrastructure, and development of a national educational system. Under Díaz, the population increased to sixteen million, and life expectancy reached sixty years. Although illiteracy diminished greatly, the period was also characterized by social inequality and discontent among the working classes. Foreign capital helped build Mexico into an industrial and mining power, but the wealth did not trickle down to the masses, as they remained in abject poverty. Much of the nation's infrastructure was owned by foreigners, and Britain once contemplated running its navy off of Mexican oil.

By 1900, it was obvious to all concerned that Mexico was an economic satellite of the United States and little more than a source of raw materials for the great powers. Slavery had been abolished in 1824, 1835, and 1857, but in the 1880s, it was estimated that thousands (especially in the south of the country) were still held in bondage. Some farmers were paid labourers, but most were little more than serfs on great estates. Disease and starvation were commonplace on the plantations, and working conditions were little better in the cities. All attempts at unionization were quickly suppressed, and injured workers were frequently thrown out into the street to die. Those too old or incapacitated to work were reduced to beggary, and periodic protests were suppressed with force. (sourced: History of Mexico)

The Cortez party arrived in Mexico City by invitation of the ruling Díaz administration and were housed on the outskirts of the city in various rented houses, while the horses and their riders were taken to the display centre which formed part of the palatial grounds of the Palencia de Suma. This was not very far away, as it was within walking distance, but the horses needed the large paddocks that backed onto the Palencia grounds, so most of the riders stayed with their horses and bedded down in the stables; they slept in the haylofts. The riders had the advantage to eye up the competition and become friendly with the other riders who were in reciprocal positions.

Joe and Lois, together with Pedro and Lena and their respective children, shared one of the allotted houses, and this was where they stayed for the duration of the equestrian displays, covering the next three weeks. The first week was to allow the horses to become adjusted to the higher altitude, for Mexico City was situated on a high plateau over seven thousand feet above sea level. It had once been the home of the ancient Inca people, and the grandeur of the city was apparent to everyone. The city had recently been fitted with tramlines, and the carriages pulled by horses provided transport around the city roads. This was in addition to independent horses and carriages. While Joe and Pedro were working, Lena and Lois took their children on a trip to see the city sights.

They travelled in one of these trams and passed the cathedral in which Emile would be married. It was a magnificent building, with spires and grand marble arches. Lena and Lois were wide-eyed at the scenic delights, as they had never visited a big city before. They had never seen so many buildings in one place. If the tramline hadn't gone round in a circle, they would never have found their way back to their starting point.

Besides the grandeur of buildings and apparent prosperity of some shopkeepers, there were still many natives who were begging in the streets. Both Lena and Lois looked at each other and realised how lucky they were to have husbands who were employed by a benevolent landowner. Compared to some, they were well off, as they had a roof over their heads and sufficient food to eat, and their welfare was considered as part of the conditions that governed the employment of their husbands.

Lois now understood why Lena and Pedro had wanted to return to the Cortez plantation, as life on such a grand ranchero was a good existence for a family. While Lois and Lena had been sightseeing, Emile and Katerina had been rehearsing their marriage ceremony within the great Metropolitan Cathedral. Their actual marriage ceremony was scheduled in two days, just before the horse competitions began. They would use this time in Mexico City as their honeymoon and hopefully enjoy the family's success in the competition stakes. There was great excitement among everyone who was connected with this expedition. The ceremony would be attended by local dignitaries as well as the Cortez workers who were presently located within the capital city.

The ceremony would take place late morning, so by the time they had returned to the Palencia de la Suma, the grand reception would be waiting for them. They were expecting about two hundred people to attend, and Emile's grandfather was finding he had a new zest for life, as all his dreams were coming true. Winning the horse competition would complete his dreams, and he could then sit back and begin to relax, knowing his grandson would continue his family dynasty and take over the responsibilities of his empire. He hoped that there would soon be a great-grandchild, and that would be a wonderful bonus in his autumn years. He would be seventy-eight shortly and wanted to live a bit longer to see another generation born.

Emile and Katerina's wedding day arrived. Everyone who was anyone crammed into the cathedral. It seemed as if the whole city was attending this marriage ceremony. The Cortez family were dressed in their finery, and Katerina looked beautiful in a pure white lace gown with a matching white mantilla. Her dark hair glistened in contrast with Emile, who looked handsome in pure black silk with a pristine white ruffled shirt. He too was wearing white lace upon his shirt, at the cuffs and neck.

The service was lengthy, and after two hours, everyone was beginning to fidget. Eventually, however, the doors opened to allow everyone outside, and while most people made their way to the reception at the Palencia de Suma, those who were part of the wedding group had to stay behind for photographs. This was a new visual recording device which involved a man who looked into a brown box and told you to keep still, while he took the exposure. The exposure was a picture image produce by the light imposed upon a dark plate. Other men were artists who were drawing the grand gathering and individuals within the assembly.

Pedro and Joe, together with their families, managed to reach the reception in time to get a seat at the main table. There was a grand central table for family and close friends, and they had been invited to this table, which was a prestigious appointment. Emile had not forgotten his friends, and sure enough, their names were placed on seats which had been reserved for them. There was another wait until everyone had arrived, and then the grand feast for two hundred people began.

From out of nowhere, servants arrived with fruit delicacies to start with. The main course followed with deliciously cooked meats and vegetables, followed by an array of sticky pastries. Wine was liberally drunk, but water was available for those who preferred. Pedro had one glass of wine as part of a toast, but Joe was not used to wine, so he remained content with water. The women had a sip of wine just to say they had taken part in the experience, but they reverted to water once the tasting was over to clear their palates.

The day was lengthy; once the formal dinner was over, the orchestra started to play and people danced the night away. Lois and Lena had to go home to see to their young children so they left after the grand luncheon, fully satisfied. Pedro and Joe decided to leave with their wives as they had risen early and were now tired from all the activity.

The next few days were to be devoted to the horses, so any rest they could get should be taken when the opportunity arose. The competition started in two days, and last-minute alterations were necessary to make sure everyone knew their role and requirements. Just as everything seemed to be in place, disaster struck.

After leaving the wedding feast in an inebriated state, Antonio Lorenzo was confronted by a disturbed horse and tried to pacify it. He got too close and was kicked in the arm, breaking it, so he couldn't ride at the dressage. Pedro was needed to direct the horses, so it left Joe to take Antonio's place. He would be required to lead the opening ceremony as the front rider in the group of horses, who would then go on to dazzle the crowd with their expert moves and synchronised dancing.

Joe was not comfortable in the limelight, but Pedro said it would be just like at home, when Antonio wasn't there, and Joe would take his place and front the dressage team. The only difference would be that Joe would be wearing his finery and not dressed in work clothes. Joe was nervous, but Lois assured him he would be fine, as all the horses knew him and knew his scent, which was most important to animals.

That is why the horses were more compliant for Joe than they ever were for Antonio, who tended to overlord the proceedings and forget he was dealing with sensitive animals. Lois, of course, was biased, but she happened to be right. This settled Joe's thinking, and so that is how it came about at the competition display. The two other teams were from nearby plantations and were extremely good in the classical way. They executed their moves in a traditional and time-honoured manner, which made it difficult to distinguish who was better than the other. Antonio was in great pain with his arm and really couldn't do much. The doctors advised him to rest, so he just told Pedro to do his best.

The night before the Cortez display, Pedro and Joe deliberated on some moves they had themselves originated and decided to include them in the display as extra and different moves, which displayed heightened command of the animal and a closer relationship with its rider. The time arrived for their display, and everyone was briefed about the extra moves. This would either make or break them as a team, but it was a chance worth taking to distinguish them from the others in the competition.

Joe was dressed in a traditional Mexican outfit, with a broad black hat that gave him a dashing appearance. No one who had seen him as an impoverished Indian would recognise him now. He expressed an air of stateliness and dignity which shone out for all to see, and when he led the horses in their movements, he was precise and light fingered in his directives. The horses knew their leader was Joe, and the way they responded to him in unison was magical. The spectators were spellbound and delighted by the extra moves included in the programme, which certainly made a memorable difference. Joe finished with a flurry of his hat and curtsied from his horse, and the onlookers responded with pure delight.

There was a grand applause. Joe had upstaged every other rider in the competition. When all was over, the riders saw to their horses and had to wait for the judgement to be announced. There was a buzz in the audience which fell to silence as the master of ceremonies stood up to announce the winner. Everyone waited with bated breath, and were on tender hooks, as all three teams had shown superb horsemanship. When it was announced that the Cortez team had won the competition, the spectators let out a great roar of pleasure, and Joe was asked to accept a trophy given by the Mexican government. Along with the trophy came endorsements and economic aid, to ensure that the breeding line of Andalusia horses would continue, together with continuity of dressage trainers and skilled riders.

Emmanuel Cortez was thrilled his dream had come true, and he was most generous in personally thanking Joe and Pedro for carrying on after Antonio's injury. Emmanuel had been impressed with Joe's ability, for he had a true empathy with the horses, and this was quite noticeable to anyone who knew what was involved with such work. Emmanuel hoped Joe would be around in three years, when the next round of competitions would commence. Antonio was now past his prime and may decide to retire and become a ranch owner himself.

If this happened, Emmanuel could see that Pedro and Joe would work as a good team and take Antonio's place at any time. Emmanuel felt good that life was being kind to him. He felt truly blessed at that moment when all in his life was perfection. The participants of the display team celebrated after the win, but Joe and Pedro went home to celebrate with their wives. They could now rest for a few days while the team prepared to return home to the Cortez plantation and while Emile and Katerina were finishing their honeymoon.

The next two days, Joe and Pedro, accompanied by their families, toured the city and surrounding area. The men had been given two extra days' holiday, which they spent with their families and each other. It was a magical time for all concerned, and the conversation revolved around the last act of the display, when Joe had carried out his flurry when his horse had curtsied. They were the actions most people talked about for days after. Ordinary life would seem mundane in comparison to the last few weeks, but Joe was looking forward to normality, as Lois would be presenting him with his firstborn child in the coming months, which was something even better to look forward to.

When this child was born, Joe would have to journey back to the mountains to visit his elderly mother, for she would want to see her new grandchild and hold the baby up to the Sky Spirit to be blessed by the Ancestors. Only she could do this, as she was now the senior family member. Joe was suddenly homesick at the thought of his mother and wondered about his brothers' family, thinking of the new grandson born just before his leaving the village and starting on this new life journey the previous year.

The Cortez troupe returned home to the hacienda and settled down to normal life activities. Emile and Katherina followed a week later and took their place in the big house. Katerina's father returned to his own plantation in the company of a new housekeeper and her husband, who were distant cousins. Maria and Gomez were kind people and goodhearted and would look after Katerina's father as they had looked after his brother-in-law, their father, who had died in reduced circumstances only the year before. They had jumped at the chance to live in luxury surroundings and be part of elite society. Their standing in life would be restored, for which they would be eternally grateful.

As the weeks and months passed, Joe and Lois settled into domestic life, with Lois increasing in size as her growing baby began to show in her rounded body form. Lena found that she too was expecting another child, and so the bond between these two women was cemented even more strongly.

One day, Lois received a message to say that Dr Westwood and his new bride, Camille, would be visiting for a week and staying at the big house with Emile and Katerina. By the time Jonathan Westwood arrived with Camille, both Lois and Lena were six months into their pregnancies. Even Katerina was now with child, having made the formal announcement only a week ago. They all agreed that Jonathan could give them a check-up and do the rounds on all the plantation workers to make sure everyone was in good shape. This service to the workers would be his payment for their stay and leave workers confident and assured of their personal welfare.

When Jonathan and Camille arrived, they were overjoyed with their greeting from Emile and Katerina and spent a day of leisure strolling the grounds and pastures after their long journey. The following day, Jonathan insisted he start work by setting up a temporary clinic, where he could meet workers and their families and tend to any needs that arose. Camille was now a working nurse and she assisted Jonathan, making sure potions were mixed and medicines given where necessary.

Camille was also able to dispel the fears of women who had problems that only women understood; she made everyone feel comfortable and at ease. The first customers at Jonathan's clinic were Lois and little Eve, with Lena and her son following. The children were checked out first and seemed fine, so while Lena looked after the two children, Jonathan examined Lois, who complained of feeling tired and different from her first pregnancy. This was explained by Jonathan that she was now looking after an energetic child which meant she was not resting as much as she should be, and the greater heat was taxing her strength. The first indication that she might be carrying a son was the fact she felt the pregnancy was different but didn't know why.

Jonathan explained this could be down to hormones having their effect, as in every other respect, Lois was glowing with health and happiness. This explanation seemed to satisfy Lois, who went to look after the two children while Lena was examined. Lena was a very down-to-earth person and did not usually complain about any health issues, but she had developed puffy ankles and found during this pregnancy that she was more emotional and tearful. Again, Jonathan suspected she might be carrying a daughter, rather than a son like her first child. Lena was not one to be normally overemotional, so this was something new for her. Again in all other respects, she was fit and healthy; she loved her life and home on this grand plantation. Jonathan was pleased to see these two young ladies well and happy, and was heartened by the fact they were well cared for and content.

Jonathan saw many other families that day, and all were happy and content with their lot, showing only mild ailments which were commonplace in every society. Only one person on the estate required treatment, and that was from a stomach upset caused by eating food from outside the plantation's boundaries, where it was suspected the cook had reheated food and served unwashed salad items.

Jonathan and Camille dined al fresco one evening with Joe, Pedro, Lois, and Lena. They learned that James and Elaina had returned to the mission after their trip back East and were running the mission clinic in Jonathan's absence. Jonathan told them about James and his herbal remedies and said he was using many of them in his own treatments. They were informed that Elaina was expecting as well, so Jonathan was anxious to be there at the time of birth, to see the arrival of his first grandchild. This would be in a couple of months.

If this came about as expected, Jonathan agreed he could make another trip to visit Joe and Pedro to coincide with their expected births, or the two women could visit the mission, where all three families could meet up again. This was food for thought and needed further consideration.

It was holiday time in three months, so it was possible to take a trip away from the plantation if organised cover could be arranged to see to the horse's welfare. Emile would have to be consulted over this arrangement, but the more everyone thought about it, the more attractive it became that Lois and Lena should visit the mission at the time of their expected deliveries, which were only ten days apart.

Both wanted to have James around, as they had experienced his ways with their first child, and he had made it a memorable experience. Lena and Lois agreed between them that they would work on their husbands to bring this about. By the time Jonathan and Camille left the hacienda to return to the mission, they were thoroughly pleased that everyone was prospering and life's rewards were visible happiness and contentment.

CHAPTER 20

WHAT HAPPENED TO BUFFALO HORN?

After James and Lone Eagle left the village, Black Buffalo and Morning Flower lived through many days of sadness and loneliness, but not long afterwards, life resumed its fullness, and their two eldest daughters became interested in the two eldest half-brothers of Lone Eagle's family. This occurred from the visits made between each of the family members, who commiserated after the departures of their sons.

Buffalo Horn, the natural son of Black Buffalo and Morning Flower, kept to himself at this time and did not interact with his family, preferring the unemotional company of the old shaman Rainbow Man, who made no unnecessary demands upon him. He preferred his own company for most activities and couldn't see what all the fuss was about. He found he had little in common with White Feather but did not harbour any ill will towards him; they were just very different personalities. White Feather had a purpose in life, but Buffalo Horn had none and was content to drift along with no direction.

Bright Star visited Morning Flower a number of times and gave her some interesting information. Bright Star told Morning Flower that White Feather had met the blonde-haired woman who would change his life, and as a result, he would be travelling with her to the far eastern shores of the country, which was a very long way to go. This was White Feather's destiny, his journey of discovery, and she should not grieve for his absence, as one day, he would return with a family of his own and riches beyond belief. Bright Star also told her there were more changes to come regarding her family, and that she might lose her other son to an unknown female, but her daughters would always be around to support her and would provide Morning Flower with sons-in-law to replace both departing sons.

They would love her as much as her own true sons, and this would compensate for the life journeys that had to be taken by each of her sons as part of their own personal experience. The Sky Spirits had told Bright Star that some people have to journey far to find their dreams, while others have their dreams placed right in front of them.

And so it was that Morning Flower's two eldest daughters, Morning Blaze and Evening Dew, became the wives of Lone Eagle's half-brothers, Grey Owl and Red Hawk. Grey Owl was now the eldest son of his family and a serious-thinking young man; he was traditional in his beliefs and solid in his understanding of cultural life. He was friends with Bright Star; they often talked about spirit matters and the importance of right relations. His interest lay with Morning Blaze as she was homey, practical, and artistic, using paints to decorate and needles to sew and make garments. She was also womanly like her mother, who had taught her the arts of herbs and spicy plants used in cooking. She was not as serious as Grey Owl, as she was bright and jolly in her personality, but she did like his quiet ways and felt safe within his company, knowing he was solid and wise. They were similar in lots of ways and a good match for compatibility. Fortunately, none of the brothers had inherited the bandy legs of their father, but they had inherited his lustiness and robustness.

Red Hawk was the adventurous one; he was an excellent hunter, a proud athlete, and an expert archer, being proficient with the bow and arrow. He was also accurate with a knife and could run like the wind. He had a fine physical body, and Evening Dew appreciated what a fine handsome man she would be getting in a husband. Evening Dew had inherited her mother's beauty and delicate ways, which appealed to Red Hawk, who loved femininity, women's softness, and all things beautiful. Evening Dew was his opposite in many ways, but together, they made a whole. This couple were demonstrative in their courtship, unlike Grey Owl and Morning Blaze, who were quiet and secretive and never made a fuss. At the combined wedding ceremony of Black Buffalo's two eldest daughters, the village swelled with visitors from the mountain groups who had come to attend the celebration. Amongst them was a father and daughter en-route to the western hills; these travellers, Shadow Man and his daughter Storm, were peculiar-looking people.

The father was tall and thin, with a long nose and large droopy eyes, while his daughter was very small, like a young child in height who had not grown up. She had a large head, which was at odds with her body structure. She was definitely stunted in her height. They were both magic people, having some shamanic powers, and Buffalo Horn became enamoured of this young lady, who could command the will of those she locked eyes with, and she locked eyes with him. It was celebration time, and Buffalo Horn loved the liberal amounts of corn juice available.

For some unknown reason, Storm took a liking to Buffalo Horn and set out to catch him. Her father had told her he was dying and she should avail herself of a husband as quickly as possible, so that she would be taken care of after he was gone.

They were travelling to see Storm's aunt, her father's sister, who had married a Mexican and lived in the Albuquerque district. Storm was not shy about coming forward to get what she wanted. Her father had always indulged her, ever since her mother had died ten years earlier. She had picked out Buffalo Horn as a man she could control and manoeuvred herself to be at his side throughout the evening, and she soon felt he was warming to her. She believed she had magical ways to entice a man and touched him here and there, rubbing up against him to generate feelings familiar and accessible. Buffalo Horn felt himself becoming aroused and looked down on this little woman to find he was attracted to her.

He felt a wave of protectiveness come over him, which heightened his sexual arousal, and he found himself directing their steps to wander outside of camp, where the shadows hid their presence. When in the shadows, he sat on a mound, ready to confront Storm, but she was too quick for him, for she had taken the advantage and was standing in front of him, standing between his legs and feeling under his breechcloth. He felt her little hands upon him, warm and firm, and was nearly undone. He had been used to visiting a widow lady for his sexual releases, but this was something else. He had never had a young marriageable girl do this to him or show that she wanted him in this manner. He could not stop his hardness and momentarily closed his eyes to savour the moment of exhilaration.

Storm covered his lips with hers, and he instinctively lifted her up onto his lap. She put her legs around his waist. Her skirts flared out to cover their lower parts, and that was when he realised she was naked beneath her skirts. She exposed her little breasts, which were perfectly formed, and he fondled her. He was enjoying this intimacy. Storm shifted her position and impaled herself upon his hardness, surprising Buffalo Horn with her fit. He was again thrown into sexual delight when she began to move, swaying this way and that, and he found he was powerless to prevent the explosion of his seed pouring into her hidden depths. The sensations of the swaying and rocking had just been too much for his control. He couldn't remember when he had last felt like this, transported to sensual paradise.

This woman, Storm, had caught him right enough, but he didn't mind at all, if she was prepared to do such things to him, as he found it greatly evocative and sensually satisfying. He thought that if he could become her protector and provider, it would suit him fine. She could service him at her leisure, and that would make him a happy man. When sensations had subsided, he looked at her, and she smiled.

She flattered him by telling him he was a lusty man and she wanted him again, so she could see what he could do. He may have been satisfied by this sexual act, but she was not, she stated with a twinkle in her eye, so the next few hours were spent in experimentation to satisfy them both. Storm had an insatiable sexual appetite, and Buffalo Horn was the exhausted one, after the marathon orgy had run its course. Storm invited Buffalo Horn to join her and her father on their travels west to visit her aunt and told him he may even get to see the big ocean. Buffalo Horn was hooked on this enchanted woman, who held her charms just for him. She had bewitched him. He knew she was different from other women, but he acknowledged to himself that he was different from other men, so it may be that the wise Sky Spirits had brought them together because of their differences.

The next day, Storm introduced Buffalo Horn to her father, who turned out to be blind. He made up for his loss of sight by developing his insight into people's spirit and soul. He thought Buffalo Horn would be ideal for his daughter, so he asked the village elders if they could perform another wedding before they left on their travels. He wanted to be transported to his sister, after which the couple could choose where they wanted to live and make their home.

Buffalo Horn told his father, Black Buffalo, that he had to accompany Storm and her father, as they needed him to help them on their journey to visit the sister before he died. He would return to the village after they had seen to Storm's father. The journey would give Buffalo Horn some experience of other places, and he might even get to see the big ocean on the western shores.

Black Buffalo was surprised at the turn of events but was pleased that his son had found someone who was willing to be his mate. It was better than spending a sterile life attached to Rainbow Man. Granted that this Storm and her father looked a bit different from normal, but looks could be deceptive, and it was the spirit within which was more important. In some ways, Morning Flower had been prepared for this departure of her natural son, as Bright Eyes had informed her only days before that this may occur. And so it was that Black Buffalo's three eldest children all got married around the same time and settled down to family life.

Buffalo Horn travelled with Storm and Shadow Man, journeying towards Albuquerque. Buffalo Horn hunted for food during the day and did all the manly chores needed when they made camp each night. Shadow Man would fall asleep after his meal, and that left the night for Storm to entice her lusty husband to indulge in sexual fantasies. This they managed to do each night. Storm liked to be ridden by this giant of a man who was showing insatiable stamina to match her own; she never tired of his attentive behaviour, as she had worked out early on how to handle him, as he could become insolent if not firmly commanded and controlled.

She used her female wiles to keep Buffalo Horn in suspense; by doing so, his interest was always aroused, and he found he could not get enough of her. It was not long before Storm's belly began to swell, but she did not stop the nightly sexual delights; she just used some imagination to continue the most stimulating times of each day, for as long as possible.

One night, Shadow Man died in his sleep, so he never got to visit his sister. They buried him under the tall pines within the forest hillsides. As there was no purpose now to continue to Albuquerque, they just drifted around in a circle; as the months passed and the seasons changed, they made permanent camp in the forest where food and water was plentiful. It was a good time for them both, just being alone together with the natural environment and the Sky Spirits.

Each day, Storm would connect to the Ancestors and receive daily instructions on what they should do. Some days, she would tell Buffalo Horn that he should hunt elk, and on another, it was rabbit or fox. When the weather began to cool, Storm told him to construct a shelter for when the autumn coldness came and to stock wood in a pile. She was so fat now that she could hardly walk, as her belly was huge in comparison to her little body. Her breasts had enlarged considerably, which Buffalo Horn found most erotic and stimulating. Even in this state, Storm would entice him to her, by sitting in his lap and getting him to fondle her enlarged breasts, so he would engorge his member and spill his seed within her still. Buffalo Horn could not say no to her desires, as he found her the most erotic person he had ever met.

She told him things about other people over the far side of the mountains and shared stories about their different cultures and habits. She told him of different belief systems and said that it didn't matter what you thought, as all spirits served the one Great Sky Spirit. She was as weird as Rainbow Man had been, but different and more exciting. Buffalo Horn just loved it all and realised he loved this little woman he had taken as his wife.

She moaned and moaned and kept on moaning all day and all night of the next day. Storm told Buffalo Horn to get the baby things from her bundle, as the child was on its way into this world and would soon be born. She told him to fetch some more water from the stream, and while he was at the stream, he heard a cry. When he returned to her, he found she had delivered the child and was bundling it up in a small blanket pouch.

"Here is your son," she said, handing the child to him. Buffalo Horn looked down into a small screwed-up face and realised this bundle of human flesh was his own son. He had never considered having a son of his own before and found many emotions flooding into him: wonder, delight, grandeur, and amazement.

This little woman had given him the most precious gift a man could want: a son. He had no words to say but placed a soft kiss on Storm's cheek as she lay in peaceful slumber. Sometime later, she awoke and took the child to her breast. She was full of milk, and it seeped out of her. The boy child was small but fully formed and healthy, with a lusty appetite, feeding frequently. The next few days were a round of eating and sleeping while the outside world went by. Buffalo Horn spent his days in hunting, to make sure they had plenty to eat, so Storm had plenty of nourishment to make the baby's milk. Buffalo Horn found autumn hoards of nuts and berries and began seeing other forest delicacies he had not noticed before. He now understood why his mother and sisters were always pleased with White Feather when he brought back such things from his hunting trips.

Buffalo Horn's focus had shifted from being exclusive to Storm to now living for both her and his son, whom he would call Mountain Shadow. Storm said she had been instructed by the Sky Spirits to start back to the village of Buffalo Horn's parents as soon as spring brought warmer weather. It would take them some time to travel the distance, as their pace would be slow, but they would arrive before the year was up. When Mountain Shadow was a few months old, they started their journey back to Buffalo Horn's village. By this time, Storm was back to normal and invited Buffalo Horn to lie with her. He felt she was still fragile and did not want to hurt her, so he hardly dared to touch her in the way she wanted him to.

Once again, Storm exerted her will and began to control her husband's actions. She looked into his eyes and bedazzled him with love and desire, and he soon became aroused and felt things he thought he had forgotten. They entered into their own world once more and began the life-making process all over again, savouring each other's touch in a more mature and evocative way.

Each night, after the baby was fed, Buffalo Horn was enticed to feed upon the spoils left by the competition from his own son. He lavished every moment and enjoyed this time even more, as now another dimension had been added to his life. By the time they eventually reached Buffalo Horn's village, Storm was expecting a second child. She was blooming in health, and with the fullness of her figure still evident from the birth, she looked even more peculiar, as she was becoming a rounded ball in her body. Her breasts were still enlarged because of mothering, as was her belly, as it once again began to swell. Buffalo Horn did not worry if she looked different from other women, as she held a woman's secret, and her secret was safe with him.

She needed her daily sexual attention, as this was her way of controlling her man and making sure of his undying loyalty. He knew she controlled him with her wiles but did not care. He loved this woman, who had given him everything and more, so he was quite content to devote his life to her and his growing family.

Morning Flower and Black Buffalo were pleasantly surprised to receive their natural son back into their village and were surprised at the change in his personality and attitude. He was a changed man. They never imagined that Buffalo Horn would have a family and were glad that he had chosen to return home. The little boy, Mountain Shadow, looked like he would grow to resemble his grandfather, Black Buffalo. Life was looking better these days as Buffalo Horn's sisters were also due to give birth anytime now.

Bright Eyes smiled as he caught the eyes of Morning Flower as if to say, "I told you so. All would be well," and so it was.

CHAPTER 21

WHITE FEATHER AND GOLDEN DAWN, ALIAS JAMES AND ELAINA ADAMS

To James's surprise, Elaina gave birth to twins: a boy first, followed by a smaller but perfectly formed little girl. The girl was half the size of her brother but was so finely formed that it was hard to believe she had been hiding behind him; against all the odds, she had survived the ordeal of birth. Elaina was exhausted, even though the birth had been made much easier with the help of James and her father. The glow of surprise and love emanating from James was something to see, as it was not often he was bemused. He could not believe his good fortune in that his woman had given him a double present in the children she had just birthed. The little girl reminded James of his mother, and he named her Jasmine Elizabeth, with Jasmine Flower being her native name. His son would be called John Edward Adams, as these two names were reflective of his white ancestral heritage, and his native name of White Buffalo was reflective of his Indian heritage.

A few weeks went by, and the babies grew in health and size, with little Jasmine catching up in body weight once feeding times were regulated. She showed herself to be a determined character. Baby John was relaxed and glowed in the love of his parents, smiling and cooing at every opportunity. He developed blond hair and, with his light skin, would most likely take after James's white heritage, as all signs indicated his relaxed attitude to life was very much like his grandfather, Jonathan Westwood. He had inherited James's eye colour, which was amber, and he tanned nicely when caught by the sun. Jasmine's hair was dark, and there were no signs of it becoming any lighter. Her skin tone was a light golden, but she had inherited her mother's bright blue eyes, which were like deep pools of water reflecting a lifetime of knowledge. She too soaked up the sunshine and became easily tanned. Her personality was more energetic, and curiosity played a large part in her activities.

Both Lena and Lois arrived at the mission, ready to have their babies, and Joe and Pedro were expected to arrive any day now, to be present when their respective children were born. Another development had occurred which at first seemed to be rather embarrassing. Jonathan Westwood made the announcement that his wife, Camille, was pregnant, and the baby would be due in six months. This was why Camille had been feeling somewhat unwell of late and had to rest. Once the news had sunk in, everyone thought it was a great joke and congratulated the couple at being older parents, pointing out they could look forward to a future of sleepless nights. Jonathan was highly delighted at the turn of events, as this was highly unexpected. This child would be younger than his two grandchildren by six months. He had never thought about being a father again and realised it must have happened when he had visited Lois and Lena in Mexico, where they had been surrounded by the array of expected new life.

Elaina's quick recovery enabled her to take up part-time duties, helping James in the mission clinic. With her father and Camille also working part-time, they were able to cover the volume of patients arriving for medical attention. This was in addition to all the well-wishers wanting to come and take a look at the new babies. More baby activity occurred when Lois went into labour just hours after Joe and Pedro arrived with a wagon load of produce from the Mexican plantation. The two men were able to bring in such a large load on the pretext of taking it to market in El Paso, so they did not have any problems crossing the border. The children were looked after by Lena, Pedro, and Camille when Lois indicated her labour pains were coming on a regular basis. Elaina prepared a bed and took her through the preparatory stages of relaxation and breathing. By the time it became late evening, Lois asked if her husband, Joe, could come and hold her hand, so he was called and was pleased to be by his wife's side.

James had Lois follow the same procedure he had used fourteen months previously, when little Eve was born. Within another two hours, Lois was delivered of a son, and Joe was ecstatic. He had become a father, and now had his own son. They named the new baby Strong Arrow, after his dead grandfather, who was also James's grandfather, and gave him the American name of Hank, as it was as short like Joe and easily remembered.

Lena had to wait another week before it was her birthing time, but sure enough, the moment came when her child decide it was time to enter this world. Just after the four families enjoyed a grand communal meal outside in the courtyard, Lena doubled over as her waters broke. Elaina and Camille worked together to get the clinic ready for yet another birth, and the two doctors made sure everything they needed was to hand. Lena was the first person James had tried his birthing technique on, so he knew she was a good subject.

Lena had experienced a few minor problems in this pregnancy, so everyone thought she would be delivered of a girl, as her first child had caused no trouble at all. For some reason, Lena was not as calm as she should be, and it was found her blood pressure was rather high. James decided to give her a sedative to calm her down; this would also be good for her baby.

Lena's first birth was straightforward and very quick, but this labour took a little longer. She was impatient, and this was why she was more agitated than normal. James came to the rescue, and once Lena took the medicine to calm her down and it began to take effect, she was able to focus on James and his words and be carried into the birth process, which resulted in the smooth delivery of her daughter. She was a large baby and yelled heartily. Obviously, young Lisa would become another Lena, as both had strong wills and were able to express them vocally. Father and mother were content with having a daughter, and this meant that each of the three friends now had one son and one daughter each, so making them all even and rounded as families.

Lena and Pedro were scheduled to spend a couple of weeks at Lena's parents' farmhouse, situated on the higher ground near the forest treeline. Fernando and Consuela were frequent visitors to the mission, as Fernando continued to sell them quality produce from his own farmlands. Joe and James decided to take a trip back to their respective Indian villages to show their children to their elders. Joe had taken two months leave from the Cortez plantation, as Pedro would be returning after a month, so he could resume cover and give time for Joe and Lois to make the visit to Joe's family village, which he knew was important for the acceptance of his son, the new Strong Arrow.

Joe knew that little Eve would be accepted as his adoptive daughter, because her mother's family had once been part of their village community. Joe also wanted to make sure that if anything ever happened to him, Lois and his children would be welcomed back by his village family. His family had an old heritage, which was important, and while present friends could compensate for the absence of these people, it was good to keep the connections to original sources of family, if at all possible. Joe's elder brother, Grey Arrow, was now the chief, while his mother was the senior chief wise woman; she held centre stage in the ceremonial meetings when the Ancestors were contacted and consulted. If James and family travelled with Joe's family, they could both pay tribute to their relatives in Grey Arrow's village, and then James could journey on to Black Buffalo's village farther north. Both James and Joe would have been away from their home villages for nearly two years, and what adventures they now could relate.

The three friends all had a tale to tell and a family to show others. They remembered that the first child of Lone Eagle (Emile) would be born soon. All three friends were so pleased at how the Great Sky Spirit had orchestrated their lives. James was looking forward to talking again to Bright Star and introducing his yellow-haired wife and son, together with his adorable daughter, who looked so much like his mother, Yellow Blossom. Although James could not remember his own mother, he knew his daughter must look like her, as Morning Blossom, his aunt, who became his actual mother, had the same looks, and he recognised the similar features within the face of his daughter (the only exception being the colour of her blue eyes).

And so it was that the three families parted to go their separate ways. Pedro and Lena remained at Fernando's farmhouse, while James and Joe and their respective wives and children began the journey north, following the trail amongst the high hills. This would be a slow journey, as the land would not take a wagon, and so a travois was erected to enable the children to travel along with the blankets, tents, and other baggage they carried. By the time the two families reached Grey Arrow's village, they were weary of journeying and were glad of a place to rest.

Grey Arrow and his family were so pleased to receive this visit from Grey Fox (Joe) and amazed to see he had a ready-made family to introduce to their mother. She had been kept active and young by looking after her great-grandchildren and in particular the two-year-old boy Strong Bow, who was born just before Joe had left the village. When she was introduced to her new grandson and told his name was Strong Arrow, the same as her late husband, she beamed a wide smile with this knowledge, as the Great Spirit Ancestors had told her only recently of her husband's spirit again being born upon this earth and within the family. She hadn't believed this information, as no one in the family was expecting at this time. Spring Blossom had forgotten her youngest son, who had journeyed away from home, and didn't know he had married or had any children.

James and Joe with Lois and Elaina witnessed the ceremony where young Hank, the new Strong Arrow, was lifted up high in his grandmother's arms and shown to the Ancestors to receive their blessing for his life and future. The sun shone brightly, and the breeze was cool. Spring Blossom did the same ceremony again for James's children only an hour later. She was particularly interested in Jasmine, for as she held this small child in her hands and lifted her up high, the clouds drew together in a peculiar way; the skies seemed to react to this blessing, which was a special and significant event. Spring Blossom stared into the blue eyes of her great-granddaughter and could see into her soul. She saw an event-filled life and wonderful fulfilment in personal and everyday events; this child was indeed blessed by the Sky Spirits and would be well loved.

When she did the ceremony for John Edward, thunder boomed in the sky, even though it was warm and sunny, and there was no sign of rain. She looked into the Indian eyes of this white child and saw the leadership of nations fulfilled. Spring Blossom knew that the life of this child would be meaningful to the American country and all its peoples, regardless of colour or race. This was a child of two nations who would spend his life trying to achieve unity of peoples. He would rise to prominence in government and influence, so he would be responsible for historic changes that would be felt throughout the land. Spring Blossom looked at James, her grandson, and told him he had greatness to look after. She saluted Elaina for being the mother of such greatness as seen in her children and assured her she would always be welcomed in their village, as her husband held a special place within the hearts of all the families, and so they would like to receive further visits when possible, to maintain contact.

James had retrieved his bow and arrow when last at Fernando's farm after remembering he had left some things hidden in the small cave under the waterfall. James had also been given the knife that Grey Arrow had given to Fernando, and this time, Fernando was returning the knife as a way of recognition, to thank his friend for remembering him. When time allowed, the adults gathered together and related their experiences to Spring Blossom and Grey Arrow. It was explained to them that James had inherited some wealth from his white heritage that was sufficient to provide anything the village may need. This meant that if there was any large need that the village members could not gain themselves, word could be sent to the mission for assistance; whatever the occasion or circumstances, the mission would always be able to contact James if the need arose.

Elaina found the Indians quite civilised in their family groupings and passionate towards their children. She didn't understand the language fully, as the dialect was slightly different from the more southern Indian tribes she knew. She could understand some common words which sounded like Spanish, but with local idioms, she was at a loss. Lois was surprised she remembered more than she thought and was soon talking with some people who had known her family many years ago.

James and Elaina felt they could not visit for long, as they had to make the journey further north to James's own village. This would take three days, as the journey could only be taken slowly with young children to attend to. Elaina was still feeding the children and augmenting their feeds with goat's milk. They had brought four goats with them and were leaving two behind with Joe and Lois. It was arranged that James and Elaina would return to Grey Arrow's village on their return trip in approximately two weeks. James and Elaina made their way north with John and Jasmine. They did not hurry but enjoyed the time on their own, just being with their children. It gave James a chance to revert to his Indian ways and catch wild fowl and small mammals to roast over an open fire. He found he enjoyed providing for his family and using the skills he had grown up with.

James realised that Elaina, although not complaining, sometimes found it difficult to manage two small children and all the chores required for outdoor living. She had not been brought up for this type of life; in fact, it was surprising how well she was managing. Eventually, they came to the outskirts of the village, and a lookout raised the alarm that strangers were approaching. It was quite a surprise to see everyone in the village turn out to welcome James home, as the moment he was recognised, the word spread throughout the village like wildfire, and everyone came to have a look.

Morning Flower, his aunt and adoptive mother, was crying in delight, with Black Buffalo beaming with pleasure. Surprisingly, he was standing next to Buffalo Horn, who was holding a small child in his arms. This was a surprise, as Buffalo Horn had never shown much interest in young children. Well, there were more surprises to come, once everyone calmed down, and James and family had been given a tepee to use as their accommodation.

Morning Flower was full of information regarding her two elder daughters, who had married and had new babies. The greatest surprise was Buffalo Horn, who was now a father of two and showing a changed personality, which had surprised not only his parents but everyone who knew him from before he met this peculiar-looking woman and married her. No one could understand what his wife had that was so special, but Storm had singly been the instrument for his total change of character and personality, all for the good. The two eldest daughters of Morning Flower were now married to Lone Eagle's half-brothers, and they each had a child.

The youngest daughter, Summer Rose, was the only one yet unmarried, but she was only fourteen summers old and was still living in the home tepee with her parents. It was Summer Rose who was most interested in the twins, Jasmine and John; they seemed to like her company and particularly her singing voice. Her chanting was melodic and sent the babies to sleep.

In the next few days, the families were all introduced to the new arrivals, and many stories were related between the groups. James introduced some of his herbal remedies for general use, and Bright Star was most enthusiastic and supporting in all that James had to say. With the death of Rainbow Man, Bright Star was now the spiritual and medical authority within the village. He had grown in stature and was a fine-looking brave. His parents were now very elderly but they still looked after him and treated him as they always had, as a very special person they had been given to nurture and respect. Bright Star was considering marriage himself and had his eye on a great-niece called Night Star. She was a slender young woman with mystical tendencies of her own, and being from a large family, she was used to looking after elderly relatives. She could move into the tepee he shared with his parents without any real upheaval. They would be well suited, as their temperaments were very similar, and they could work together with the herbal remedies, as she was a healer and understood the beneficial effects of herbs and plants.

James met Night Star and agreed she would be an excellent helper to Bright Star. She understood immediately the beneficial effects of the different herbal remedies and asked many pertinent questions. James had no qualms in leaving some medical supplies for Night Star to administer as needs arose. While James was discussing remedies for common ailments, he suggested they try out the skin creams he concocted to eliminate rashes and infections. The creams also assisted in clearing the effects of skin blemishes and scars, which both native men and women could appreciate. At first, volunteers were sought, then when those who had tried out some of the creams learned how soothing they were, the word spread, and everyone wanted to try some remedy out, so they could give their verdict. There was even great interest in the horse remedies, as the animals were lifelines for travel and were very important to each family.

When evening came, Bright Star and James were able to talk privately. Bright Star was pleased James had brought his yellow-haired wife to visit, and he commented on what beautiful children she had produced. He recognised the healer within Elaina and told James she would always be his anchor and connection between the two different worlds. He also told James that in his future life, he would build a home on new land, and that he would leave the mission complex in the next year to go to the land that was his. Bright Star said he would have more children who would all be talented in different ways; one would become a practicing doctor and medic versed in both traditional and modern medical disciplines.

Bright Star was thoughtful for a moment and then stated that if James's sister asked to join him and his wife in their life far away, they should consider this as a blessing, as Summer Rose would make a wonderful nurse and helper to any clinic, as well as a wife to an Indian brave from another tribe from the south, which he could see occurring. This connection would be beneficial to James, as it would establish peace upon his land of plenty, so two tribes of peoples could live in accord, side by side. James didn't really follow all of what Bright Star was telling him, but he respected him and knew that the Star Ancestors were always right in their predictions, even though understanding eluded him at the present. James tucked this information into the back of his mind, as he believed that time would reveal all, as events predicted came true.

Elaina was resting to regain her strength. Many relatives saw to her children, who were happy to be the centre of attention. Elaina viewed the village occupants with a healer's eye and made her rounds to see if anyone needed medical help of any kind. She found she could make herself understood by combining Hispanic words with sign language. This proved very effective, and Elaina soon found out that the womenfolk wanted to have a female medic they could consult with about female problems, and so it came about that Night Star became the designated village medical woman in charge of herbal remedies suitable for women. The women who used the skin creams were willing to gather local plants and vegetation to be used for remedial potions and medicines. Stomach upsets were often common when eating some foods and drinking the fermented corn juice. In springtime, the mountain water was high in salts, and this could affect the balance of digestion in the elderly.

Elaina had a gift of understanding native women, and they responded to her likewise. They did not treat her as a hostile white woman, as she had approached them in the native way, with respect, and showed she was one of them and was willing to work beside them. James was always astounded at the talents his wife showed, as she could switch from one culture to another without much difficulty. There was no artifice or snobbery about Elaina, just the willingness to make friends and to understand another's point of view. James glowed in appreciation of his woman, and Bright Star smiled knowingly. The time flew by, just being immersed in village life, the one highlight being the birth of a new baby, native style, without any aids or special equipment. James and Elaina were invited to watch the birthing by two mature native ladies who specialised in this work.

James volunteered to aid in the pain relief and began his chanting and massage of body pressure points to assist the natural birth. The birthing women were most impressed with James's method and were soon making signs for Elaina to join in and do her bit, so they both stepped back to see how she and James performed. It was a straightforward birth of a second child to a young mother. She had a daughter of a year old and now was delivered of a son. Elaina handed her son to her so she could hold him in her arms, while she dealt with the afterbirth and cleaned her up from the birthing process.

The new baby boy was then placed in a baby bag and laid beside his mother while she dozed. The birthing women thanked James and Elaina for their assistance, and everyone was pleased with the outcome. Later, some young boys were treated for swellings and abrasions after injuring themselves while playing. James's cold creams worked wonders and impressed even the most sceptical. The village members wanted Elaina and James to stay for longer, but they knew they could not. Summer Rose asked Morning Flower and Black Buffalo if she could go with James and his wife to look after their children; that would enable her to learn more about herbal remedies, as she wanted to become a medic and nurse to help people. This stirred up some conflicting feelings, as Morning Flower did not want to lose her youngest daughter.

Morning Flower consulted Bright Star, who made her realise that the opportunities in life were greater where James and Elaina came from and were going to. So on the strict insistence that Summer Rose would return in two years to visit her parents, it was reluctantly agreed that she could accompany James and Elaina on their travels back to the mission. Packing resumed and farewells were made, and with certain regrets, the family plus one extra young woman made their way back to Grey Arrow's village. Summer Rose and Elaina soon struck up a close friendship, which was a combination of mother and sister. With another pair of hands to look after the twins, Elaina felt more confident in her role as mother and found she had more energy for all her activities. By the time the group reached Grey Arrow's village, they were renewed with added strength and entered the village smiling at those who had come out to welcome them. Joe and Lois were pleased to see James and Elaina again, and surprised to see Summer Rose so grown up. Spring Blossom was pleased also for she recognised in her granddaughter a zest for learning and knew that the association with James and his family would be beneficial to her in her life.

Summer Rose had already proved helpful with the children and was also keeping her eyes open for certain plants James could use in his healing remedies. The two families and Summer Rose made their way slowly back to the mission complex. For Summer Rose, this was a journey of discovery, for she had never made such a long and interesting trip into the high hills before. Coming to Fernando's farmhouse was a delight when he and Consuelo welcomed the travelling party with a good hot meal and plenty of cool drinks. By nightfall, the party of nine was comfortably settled within the mission, with children safely asleep. The adults gathered in the open courtyard for a cool drink before turning in for the night and were joined by Jonathan Westwood and Camille. It was all agreed that discussions could wait for the morning, with Jonathan having a quick world with James to ascertain if he was available for the morning clinic.

James, still an early riser, was the first one to enter the clinic the following day. He noticed that it had been redecorated and painted and made fresh looking by colourful matching bed covers and some small flowers on the table. This was Camille's handiwork, as only a woman would go to such trouble. She had made a point of making the place more homely and less clinical than before. James was pleased to find that Jonathan had been using some of his herbal remedies, and when he looked in at the pharmacy, he noticed new creams made with a lovely jasmine perfume. Jonathan joined James and started the day with his cup of tea. James was willing to try this brew but found he preferred it more when cooler rather than when it was very hot.

While these two men busied themselves with morning patients, the women looked after the children and sat in the shade within the courtyard, talking to all who passed by. Joe was the only man who was not involved in the medical field, so he went off to see the horses and discovered he was needed to sort out their welfare, as some were showing signs of droop, because they had been left out in the sun too long and not given sufficient water and feed. It seemed the man in charge was off sick, and no one had been appointed to coordinate the horses' care. The field labourers needed to be told what to do and when to do it, so Joe stepped in and became quite busy sorting out all the horses and field hands into their respective working teams. Once each team had been given a leader and instruction for the day's tasks, they were happy to start work, knowing there was someone back at the mission who was in control of things.

One of the monks, Father Sebastian, came to help Joe, and together, they devised a plan of action to cover the sick period of the estate field manager, José, a small man who knew all about working horses and farming. He had a fever, someone said, and lived in one of the estate workers' huts, which were saved for the important workers of the mission. Jonathan and James were alerted, and after the morning clinic, they went to visit José. Sure enough, he was sick and had a fever which his wife Rosa said had broken that night. He was sleeping now, which was the best thing for him to regain his strength.

Rosa said her husband had been bitten while out in the fields; she didn't know whether it was a bee sting or something else, but he had something like an allergic reaction. James and Jonathan said they would send some medicine over and some creams which should help the situation and thanked Rosa for the good job of nursing her husband. After a week at the mission, a trip to Mexico was scheduled. Joe and Lois with their family, decided to accompany the Mission Group as they would provide an escort all the way back to the Cortez plantation, as this Group of Monks would pass by this estate on their way to Mexico City.

Goodbyes were once again said between the friends, with promises to meet up again by next year. James assured his uncle Joe that he would always have a home with him, if he decided in the future to journey to his ranch lands in south-east Texas. James had decided to visit his land and possibly make his new home there if it proved suitable. The area could certainly benefit from a clinic, and James was contemplating fulfilling this very need.

CHAPTER 22

ENDINGS

A few weeks went by after Joe and Lois had left the mission when the subject of visiting the land James owned surfaced for discussion. Jonathan Westwood, Father Carlos, and James sat round a table to look at the options available and determine what James had in mind for his immediate future. From what was already known about the inherited Adams land, it contained a sizable ranch house. Although it was of a wooden construction and built some time ago, the home was said to be strong and in good condition, as a number of ranch managers over the years had lived in the place as they managed the southern pastures of the Adams holdings.

At the moment, James's half-sister Julianne was caretaking this land by allowing her herds of cattle to roam freely. After marrying Antonio, she had doubled her landholdings, as her new husband's family owned the ranch next door, and he was the son and heir. Antonio's father had let it be known that he wanted to retire and take his wife on a long trip back to Europe. This left Antonio in charge of the family ranch as his only sister was at present away in the East attending a teachers' training college.

While Tony had to wait until his father died to inherit this land, his father wanted him to join it with his wife's and make it one big ranchero, for all practical purposes. This would bring economies of scale, and when grandchildren came along, there would be plenty of space for them to grow into adults and plenty of scope if the two properties and estates needed to be split again, if any of the next generation wanted to farm independently.

From recent information, Julianne was already expecting her first child; she and Tony had moved into the Adams Ranch permanently, and he had been fully accepted by the ranch hands. They already knew him well as their neighbour and knew he would be a good influence for the Adams Ranch as well as a good husband for Julianne.

The problem area or unknown aspect that had not been explored was the fact there were a group of Indians living in a camp on the most southern areas of the acreage now owned by James. This area was near to the sea, and by all accounts, fishing was the natives' general pastime. The odd steer went missing occasionally, and it was known that these Indians liked to eat beef once in a while. The small tribe were very self-contained; one or two of its younger males had come to the Adams Ranch and been hired to take care of the horses.

The Indians seemed to have a way with horses, which even the ranch owners could recognise and appreciate. Arrangements were put in place for more travelling, so that James's family and Summer Rose, his sister, could all travel in some comfort. It was decided a wagon was the most suitable vehicle for transport, for goods as well as people. The distance to be travelled was amongst dry arid country, unless you travelled to the coast and followed its boundary to enter the Adam lands from its most southern regions. Father Carlos and Jonathan were concerned for the young children, who were only months old.

However, both Elaina and James were not unduly concerned, as with Summer Rose providing an extra pair of hands, all that was needed to be done was accomplished in good time to enable both Elaina and Summer Rose to help James with other things. Summer Rose was proving to be a godsend. She was good humoured and willing to turn her hands to most things of a practical nature, showing very little effort as she accomplished her tasks with ease. She liked to try new things and showed a zest for living; she had a thirst for new life experiences which could not be quenched.

Summer Rose could help James with hunting and fishing, as well as looking after the babies. She was quick to pick out medicinal herbs and plants that James was interested in and to her surprise she found that different plants in different areas could have similar properties and applications. What this meant was that in each location, there was the prospect of a garden of medicinal cures, if you had eyes to see and an interest to seek and find. Summer Rose was learning she too had an eye for such finds. From the cactus and succulent plants of the arid regions to the lush vegetation of the coast, with its more tropical climate, the array of plant life was wide in southern Texas, and the terrain varied considerably, providing a continual carpet for exploration.

Such was the scenery that confronted James on the journey from the mission to the south-east of Austen, where his landholdings lay. Julianne had been given advance notice of their arrival, and so she and Tony were at the old homestead when the family party arrived. It was midday, and the shaded veranda surrounding the wooden homestead was a welcomed and pleasant place to sit and unwind. Cool lemonade was distributed while Julianne showed Elaina around. The home was well equipped with all the basic needs. Tony was kept amused by the twins, and he welcomed the chance to have a private word with James.

He told James that one of his best horsemen was an Indian, the son of the tribe leader, who governed the native group situated on the most southern pasture near the coast. Nando (full name Night Hawk) was in his late teens but was already showing signs of becoming a great horseman.

He was accomplished in his dealings with horses, and they responded to him like he was one of them. Nando also proved he was trustworthy and said he was willing to update James on the tribe's current status and composition; he would also act as an interpreter and guide, if he decided to visit. James was most impressed, for he did want to visit these Indians and see if he could help them in any way.

The women came outside again, emerging from the cool shadows into the glaring sunshine. After looking around the house, Elaina picked up John, while Summer Rose held Jasmine. They walked into the garden, a short distance from the ranch house, with Julianne a few paces behind, and suddenly, when James looked back towards the house, he registered the view of his vision, when he saw Elaina standing with their blond-haired son and in the background was Julianne, his sister, and behind her was a mechanical contraption. He now knew that this mechanical contraption was an oil pump for an oil well, which continually provided a rhythmic hum as it moved back and forth. This was the main source of his wealth; there were at least three oil wells he knew of, and possibly a couple more behind the hills. A few cattle could be seen grazing upon the grasslands which stretched all around the homestead. The hills were about half a mile away and made a ridge, which cut off the view towards the southern pastures and coast.

Tony and Julianne took their leave, riding back to their own ranch in a buggy, as Julianne had given up horse riding due to her pregnancy. Her first baby was due in about three months, so she was glad that James would be around when her time of birthing came. Julianne had found the heat and the sun of Texas particularly trying in recent weeks; her energy levels were lower than she was used to, so this trip to greet her half-brother and her cousin was enough exertion for the day. Tony told James he would send Nando over to speak with him as soon as he was able to and would loan him for a few days, so he could attend to any matters arising. Nando could also take this time to count what stock was grazing on the lands nearby, so records could be updated. The next few hours were spent in unloading the wagon of all they carried and becoming acquainted with the homestead.

There was a freshwater pump outside the kitchen door, and once all the household items were unloaded and stored away, beds were made up for the children and for Summer Rose. The homestead had four bedrooms all along one side of the ranch building, which opened to the hills.

Each room's door opened onto the veranda, so you could move beds outside if preferred. The homestead was plainly appointed but contained the essentials of a good dining table and six chairs, a dresser, a washing tub, and a fire stove. The living quarters were large and airy, and they faced the open landscape, showing the farthest views. This room was cool in the summer; it was large and spacious, with canvas chairs and a daybed. A large open fireplace was the centre point of the inner wall, for the temperature could drop remarkably low after sunset. Cool winds blew in from the coast at certain times of the year, so the provision of an open fire indoors was considered a luxury. Summer Rose was enchanted to find herself amongst such finery with a room all to herself. This felt a bit strange, so she positioned her bed in the same room as the children's, as she felt more comfortable keeping them in sight.

James and Elaina's room was on the other side of the children's. Soon all the doors to the bedrooms were opened to the veranda to allow the evening breeze to enter into the homestead and give it an airing. Just as the sun was lowering in the horizon, Nando arrived with three horses attached to a buggy; he introduced himself to James and Elaina. He was tall for an Indian, being just a fraction shorter than James. He was slim but muscular from his physical work with the horses and cattle. He spoke American with a slight Hispanic accent, and when James began speaking to him in his native tongue, it became apparent that the natural language of the southern native was a mixture of Indian and Hispanic, very much like James's own. Only odd words were different, which related to locality and the strong association with Americans.

Elaina and Summer Rose soon joined in the conversation, alternating and drawing from three languages. Nando told them that the native group located near the coast consisted of around eighty Indians, being the product of three main families. Nando's grandfather was chief, although his elderly great-grandfather was still alive. Both his grandmothers were also alive as well; his grandmother, Clear Skies, was the group's wise woman and had prophesied the coming of a native healer. "He who comes will represent the two cultures and will arrive from outside of the tribe, and through him the native peoples of the area will unite into a larger group and will have a voice of their own," Nando said, repeating the prophecy verbatim.

It transpired that there were three other groups dotted around the coastal region, which migrated within the coastal lands, according to the seasons and availability of food and work. During these visiting times, a steer would be caught to provide a feast for relatives and friends. Farther along the coast were farms and orchards growing vegetables and fruit. Where the hills joined the coast was where the produce farms were found, and that was where the natives worked in the seasons of planting and harvest. At other times, they fished and sold their excess produce to local ranches and the mission complexes, where they were able to gain a decent price for what they caught and sold.

Some of the natives had settled permanently and had set up their own ranches, mainly to breed horses. This was how Nando had learned about horses, as his father, Jet, was one who had set up a permanent homestead. All was on a much smaller scale compared to the large rancheros of the Americans. Nando admitted he had come to work for the American lady because it was known she treated natives fairly and offered the opportunity to learn all about becoming a stockman and running a large outfit. Never to miss an opportunity, James arranged with Nando to visit this tribe next day, and he suggested Summer Rose should accompany them.

Elaina would welcome the time to settle into her new home and have John and Jessica to herself for a few days. Julianne would visit her to find out if there was anything she needed which they may have overlooked. Julianne and Elaina, being cousins, needed time to catch up on family matters and memories, and they could do this while setting up the clinic, which Elaina had suggested they do, using the spare room. This room was located next to the main front entrance, so it could be altered to have its own entrance door. When visitors attended, this entrance would be independent to the living quarters of the house. The nice thing was that the veranda provided a wonderful area where people could sit while waiting their turn for medical attention.

The views were stunning, and you could see all who were coming and going, far into the distance. Next day James, Nando, and Summer Rose set off, travelling south. They took two horses and a buggy, which Nando drove, with Summer Rose sitting beside him. James rode a horse Nando had brought with him, as Julianne had anticipated the need for fresh horses. The three passed through the hills which divided the coastal region from the inner pastures and plains. Once through the pass, the land stretched out and sloped downwards. James was surprised to see antelope, and deer at the edge of wooded areas. Nando told him there were plenty of native animals within the woods such as bobcats, raccoons, and also coyotes. James felt very much at home with such a familiar landscape around him and now understood why there was a minimum of cattle theft, as this area was actually teeming with wildlife.

The winds from the Gulf of Mexico could become strong at times, and the effects of such winds continually changed the coastal area's contours. It was a place of much variety, as there were freshwater lakes, rivers, and swamplands of brackish water, which attracted a variety of birds from far-off lands. The seafood caught and eaten were mainly large- and small-mouth bass from freshwater lakes and sea bass from the coastal shores, as well as clams found around the Mexico bend.

By the day's end, the three had travelled some distance and were nearing Nando's parents' homestead. There was a small rise beside a wooded area, and beyond this, the homestead came into view. The hacienda had whitewashed walls Spanish/Mexican style, with bright flowers decorating the archways which led into a well-seasoned wooded entrance and continued with beams amongst whitewashed walls and ceilings. Nando's mother came to greet him with opened arms, followed by two youngsters, who turned out to be his sister's children.

After everyone had been introduced to each other, Nando's father arrived, followed by his parents, who had been outside in the stables, so more introductions followed. A table was set up on the terrace outside, and everyone enjoyed bowls of fish stew, which was freshly caught that day. Lovely bread with goat's butter and cheese was sliced so everyone could have a little of what was available. Jet turned out to be a Christian convert, as he had been brought up and schooled by the local mission before it had been badly damaged by the hostilities of the Civil War. It was still occupied by Spanish missionaries, but their impact on the local population had been greatly reduced.

Those who remained housed within the mission grounds were like everyone else, trying to eke out a living as best they could. Their speciality was beekeeping; they made honey and wine from the local fruit which often ripened too quickly in the warmer climate or became damaged by high winds (cyclones were common in summer). James found this surprising, as the climate his side of the hills was much dryer and less volatile. Winds whipped up the dirt, bringing dust storms to the prairies, with very little water content to show for such activity.

Rain was frequently deposited on the coastal plains, and that gave the region its more tropical climate, in contrast to the dry, hot weather in the inner regions. This explained why James's land was greener than that of Julianne's, which stretched farther to the north and was not in the path of the coastal storms, winds, and rains. The hill barrier seemed to also be an ecological barrier, separating two distinct regions.

James found out much about the life here and was satisfied that the standard of living was in fact quite good, as natives had plenty of food and comfortable shelter. Jet was obviously Americanised more so than most, because of his mission education and association with the Spaniards. James noticed Nando's interest in Summer Rose as he showed her around. The young people seemed to be getting on very well. James enquired about what medical help was needed in the area, and Nando's father was very interested in getting care for women who were expecting.

This was not considered a medical necessity, but there was a shortage of qualified women who could assist in the natural birthing process. Hence, many babies died because of a lack of knowledge and help. Broken bones were always a problem because if the healing produced disfigurements, then a person's working life was affected, and they became a cripple, at the mercy of other people's charity. Fevers were another area of concern, as the climate brought in many foreign elements, including insects which carried disease. Those who worked in the cotton fields of the large Southern plantations could become infected by the cotton bug, and others could suffer from the bayou malaise brought about from the rotting vegetation, which produced spores. James listened intently as Jet described the experiences of his people and vowed to stock up on suitable medicinal plants that could dissipate many of the symptoms described.

James and Nando spent the night sleeping in the barn, while Summer Rose had the luxury of sleeping indoors. She automatically took an interest in Nando's niece and nephew, who looked upon her as an instant friend. On the following day, after an early meal of bread and cheese, the two men went to look at the horses grazing in the corral. James was interested in finding another horse for himself, as everywhere he went, his horse was left behind. He missed White Blaze and wondered if he would ever have such a horse again. James was pleased with what he found, as two horses caught his eye. One was a black beauty, sleek in structure and form; he wondered if he would be as swift as he looked. The other, a light chestnut, was a more rounded horse with pleasing lines of rippling muscles and a solid stance, which appealed to the rider who wanted to have a reliable companion and steadfast steed.

Nando's father had told James of a nearby family that were desperate to birth a living child. The woman had lost three babies already, and this was her fourth attempt to give her husband a child. Jet came running up to the corral to tell James that Marylou had gone into labour and would welcome any assistance he could give her. James grabbed his medical bag and followed Nando's father to where saddled horses were tethered. Nando and his father each took a horse and beckoned for James to do the same. Jet led the way, and just over the next incline, several wooden homes were seen positioned in a semi-circle. They stopped outside the first one and tied their horses to a tethering rail. James entered the small abode with Jet, while Nando stayed outside with the horses.

Marylou's husband ushered James into the bedroom, where his wife was lying in quite a bit of discomfort. James introduced himself as a natural healer, conversant with the birthing procedure. He examined Marylou and found she was very tense and anxious indeed. She was experiencing pains at regular intervals, and it was apparent the baby would come sometime soon. James sat himself beside Marylou and began talking to her in a matter-of-fact way, so she would understand the procedure she was about to follow. He asked her to concentrate on his voice and his words, so she would know how to react to his commands.

It didn't seem possible for her to relax because she was so consumed with fear, but somehow, after he talked to her for ten minutes, she began to relax and become drowsy. Once James touched her on the head, she fell into a light sleep. This gave him time to ask the husband about the other births. The first had been premature; the second had been a stillbirth. The third had been born alive but was sickly and weak, and had died within twenty-four hours.

There was no logical reason why Marylou should not give birth to a healthy child, as she was a born mother and made for having children. She was a wonderful person and very much loved by her husband and the local community. She had been unlucky, her friends had said, so she had kept on trying for another baby, in the hope that she would one day have a healthy child. She had wondered if there was something wrong with her, but everyone said it was the Lord's way of testing her faith. Clear Skies had predicted the arrival of a natural healer, and she hoped he would help her when her birthing time came. Here he was just arrived, and Marylou was in need of all the help she could get. James set to work chanting the birth call and talking to the child within about to be born.

James knew it was a boy, and boys had to be strong to survive, so he was asking the Sky Spirits to guide him in this new land to bring forth life in all its glory. Once the birth channel was fully open, James touched Marylou's head, and she once again opened her eyes.

He caught her focus and told her to push on his command to bring her son into the world. He then said she was to relax, as birthing her son would be easy; it was a natural event which all mothers went through. James reassured Marylou that the Sky Spirits had decreed that she was to become a mother, and the time was now. Marylou now concentrated on the physical reality at hand, and on James's command, she managed to push her son into the world. There was a hearty cry from the newborn boy and smiles all round when James put the baby into his mother's arms.

The baby was as healthy as it could be, and there was no reason why he should not grow to adulthood. James was able to give him some herbal medicine which would clear out its digestive tract so it would be ready to receive his mother's milk and nourishment. Marylou's husband was overjoyed and wanted to know what James wanted as payment for his services.

James mentioned he was looking for a horse, so Jet said he could take his pick from the corral. It was early afternoon when they returned to Jet's homestead. They found Summer Rose playing with the young children and Nando's mother looking pleased and contented with her grandchildren around her. Her daughter and her husband had gone to market for their monthly provisions, so that was why the young ones were with their grandmother. James, Summer Rose, and Nando said goodbye to Nando's family, promising they would visit again soon.

Joining the returning group were two horses from the corral, as James could not make up his mind to choose between the two, and Jet said, "Take them both."

They travelled all day, and by the time they reached the old Adams Homestead, it was late at night. Nando saw to the horses and bedded down in the stable. He told James he would like to stay and work around the old homestead and help out his family in any way he could. It had been his father who had put this idea into his head, as he wanted to make sure that James would return to his people, and Nando would be strategically placed to arrange his visits.

James and Summer Rose entered the homestead. A low light shone in the hallway, and they made their way to their respective bedrooms. Elaina was fast asleep and so were the children, sleeping next door where Summer Rose had her bed. The next day, Elaina showed James and Summer Rose the new clinic room, which had previously been a spare bedroom; it opened onto the surrounding veranda. Some workers had built cupboards and other storage facilities at Elaina's request, so the new clinic could function at quickly as possible. There were some jars of James's creams and lotions as well as a medicine cabinet.

Jars of herbs and plant parts were similarly stacked. Once James had related all the events he and Summer Rose had experienced in the last three days, it was time to attend to daily needs. The children were cleaned and fed and handed over into the care of Summer Rose. Elaina and James entered the clinic room just when a patient arrived with severe cuts and bruises. It was Manuel, who had been thrown from a horse and had been badly trodden on.

His bruises were extensive, and he was barely able to walk. It would be some days before he could be released into the workforce again, so once his cuts were attended to, he was placed on a makeshift bed on the veranda. Elaina spread soothing lotion onto his limbs and torso, which would help bring the bruises out and relieve the uncomfortable pressure they were causing. He would be tender for a few days and stiff for a week, so Manuel was told to enjoy this time of inactivity, as he wouldn't be going anywhere.

James and Elaina's first patient turned out to be a mine of information, for he was one of Tony's men and had come across to Julianna's ranch only recently. Manuel was of Mexican origin and had been working with horses and cattle for over twenty years. It was the first time he had experienced an accident of this sort and was rather embarrassed, as he had lost concentration when something had made him sneeze at a most inappropriate moment.

Manuel knew everyone on both ranches, together with all the wives, children, and girlfriends. He also knew the land and gave James some ideas on how he could use it more productively, as the southern pastures were more fertile and experienced a higher rainfall from the spill-off coming from the coastal regions. James knew he would love this land and the people on it and around it. It had so much potential to give people a good living, which would provide a home and sufficient income to sustain a family.

The immediate future looked good, and James smiled at his good fortune. He could now sit back and grow roots into his own land. He thanked the Sky Spirits for bringing him this far and sent out thoughts to his friends in Mexico and to Elaina's father, Jonathan Westwood.

James knew that his uncle Joe, Lois, and the children would eventually join him on this ranch in Texas. They could start their own tribe and look forward to seeing more babies born to populate this vast country. This would become a new group of multiple races, cohabiting as one big family. James wondered if Elaina's father would come to live with them also, now he was to become a father again.

With that thought in mind, James walked outside into the sunshine and gloried at the beginning of this new life in this new land. The Sky Spirits had brought people he loved together, and his greatest loves were now around him. If all he sensed and knew came true, James could look forward to having more family members around, and with plenty of children to produce laughter in this land of prosperity and sunshine, the life ahead looked good.

James looked up at the sky and thanked the Sky Spirits for being with him on this journey of discovery, which had brought him to experience his heart's desire and provided him with all he could possibly need and want.

The End.